2255

E.S. DAWSON

PROLOGUE

umans. The place smelled of humans.

The first rains had barely touched the earth before it stopped, but the leaves and shrubs that it moved over still retained some moisture on them. As it slid through the foliage, it inched closer towards the place where these humans were. There was only one thought on its mind: "Food."

Heather

2258

She walked briskly in front of the other scouts, wondering what this place had in store for them. There were just four of them now, but she was certain there were other groups out there, moving through the ruins, scavenging for ruins of the recently destroyed human civilization.

The air smelled of dampness and the early morning mist obstructed their vision. Heather sighed. She had been given the most ill-prepared team of all, but she would make something of them, yes she will. *Mira could use her powers to dispel this mist, but that girl is waiting for me to tell her!*

She turned back to look at the group. Mira was not even watching where she was going. Her eyes were on the structure of a building that could be considered as belonging in the past civilization, a building of stone walls, with weed growing all over it. The entries were open as most of the wooden doors had rotted on the ground where they had fallen. Some of the weed slithered across the empty windows, gliding over their sills the way a snake would glide over a surface. They were not moving, but they had that likeness for Heather. They reminded her of snakes and costly mistakes.

"Mira!" She yelled.

The whole group came to a sudden halt. Mira turned towards Heather, smiling sheepishly. She was supposed to be the most promising of the three, but her wide-eyed wonderings never let her stay focused on anything. She floated, as a feather would, in the sky, while she walked or worked, neither here nor there. Maybe, she was a wanderer in her past life, just like Heather. Heather had gone to Africa to get a tan or to get away from her father, she did not know which to present to herself. It was what she always did, while her father threatened and tried to make her see reason. He wanted her to take over from him as the manager of his company, a company that was in affiliation with the stupid technology that had wiped out almost all the humans.

Inwardly, Heather chuckled—it was funny. His father was always telling her how she would get herself killed because of her endless wanderings, the parties she was always going to, the booze, the drugs, the friends she kept, pretty much everything in her life. Her mother wanted her to repent or perish. "Give your life to Christ," the woman would always say. They were dead. She was here. Maybe she should have given her life to Christ. Maybe this was the great tribulation.

"Heather?" Carl called.

Heather came to herself. She turned to look at Carl. He was almost 7 feet tall and huge. The strongest among them. He had fists that would bang the sense out of anything. Perhaps, he was the best trained. Heather turned away from him and faced Mira, trying to gather her thoughts.

"You, what exactly do you do apart from staring at ruins?" Heather asked.

"Thought that was, kind of, our thing," Mira replied wittily. She had a snow-white cover all tightly fitted to her body so that all the outlines of her body showed. In fact, they were all dressed in the same thing. The only difference was the color of their suits. The badges and the designs were the same. They were scouts, and they belonged to the same group. Here, the suspicions and distrust people of their kind harbored towards each other were completely quenched. Well, mostly... *humans would always be humans.*

"The mist can hardly let us see the way," Heather continued, ignoring the girl's witty retort. "What if there is danger close by?"

Mira waved her hand at this and the mist before them cleared. She looked at Heather with a raised eyebrow, and the latter wished that more had been said about disciplining teammates. Maybe, she could send her back.

She turned around and saw that the mist was being made into a giant snowball. Levi! She groaned. When she glared at the last member of her group, the rain came crashing down to the ground. Levi quickly turned away from her gaze. Perhaps, Levi was the most useless. He was young and beautiful with fins running down the sides of his neck. He was what could be truly called starry-eyed with his big eyes. He stared more than Mira, and wanted to touch everything, which was dangerous. Heather felt responsible for him in ways she could not explain.

"We don't know this place," she said gravely. "Anything could be out there waiting for us. Guess how it would find us; unprepared... playing around."

There was something heavier than seriousness in her voice, something that made the air thicker and more difficult to breathe in.

"Something is coming," Carl said suddenly. He bent down slowly and touched the ground. With his eyes shut, he held his hand to the ground. "This is fast, faster than anything we have yet encountered and gliding... a snake."

"A snake?" Mira asked. There was fear in her voice.

"It is big," Carl said, then he quickly stood up. "From there." He pointed towards the north.

"Formation!" Heather shouted. They formed a semi-circle, with Heather and Carl facing the threat directly while Mira and Levi faced the other sides.

"It is slowing down," Carl said.

"We are going to die!" Mira screamed.

"Silence!" Heather commanded.

There was a shuffling of leaves, then the creature came into view. Its width was at least two feet bigger than Carl's height. Its length was something that the team could not ascertain because most of it went on and on into the foliage past where their eyes could reach. The creature had a gaping maw with sharp teeth of human height lined along the insides.

Fire started glowing in Heather's hands as she watched the creature. The fire was reflected in her eyes, and her face was grim.

The creature lunged.

Carl was the first to react. He rolled out of the formation, and quickly sprang to the left, so the creature's mouth missed him, and tried to strike the snake with his fist.

It was a mistake... the snake waved its head quickly towards him. The hit took Carl towards the trees, slamming his body against it and leaving him out of breath. It wanted to go after Carl.

"Hey!" Heather called.

She could hear the other two teammates behind her whimpering. They were practically useless in the face of real danger. *All of that training never quite prepared one for situations like this.*

Heather shut her eyes.

"We are going to die!" Mira screamed again.

Pitiful... if these two are to become anything, then I will have to do better.

Time slowed down. Heather could hear five hearts beating at close range. She could make out the heat each body was giving off. There were others, but they were too far away for her to pick up anything meaningful.

One of the bodies was too cold and big. Heather took a deep breath. She had never tried anything like this, not of this magnitude, but she had to. Their lives depended on it. The snake was moving towards Carl.

Slowly, she concentrated and started channeling energy through the body of the snake. It was like defrosting ice with her mind. It was part of the training she had undergone to become a scout. She held the heat in her mind, forcing it through the body of the snake, and started hitting it up.

The first long hiss told her that something was working. She opened her eyes and found that the big snake had stopped moving towards Carl. It turned towards her, red eyes filled with anger and pain. Heather was burning up the beast's internal organs.

The snake slid across the ground towards her, but she held her ground.

"Run!" Levi screamed. Heather heard their footsteps as they abandoned her, but she continued standing there.

The snake was having difficulty moving now as it came towards her, but she was not sure the fire would finish burning up its cold heart before it would attack.

The snake lunged at her. It was too fast. She had too much faith in her ability to heat bodies up quickly that she did not jump out of the way. Instead, she saw something slam into the snake's side and the monstrous head missed her by whiskers. Heater moved past her. She felt it and knew that the battle had been won.

Beside her, Carl stood, looking at his fist as the rock hardness rescinded back into his bones. The snake started burning up from the inside and thrashing all over the place.

"Are you okay?" Carl asked as they ran for cover.

The snake would be dead in no time, burnt to crisp and ashes, another lesson in human resolve for survival.

CHAPTER 1

Jan. 2255

Roland

The car drove towards home. The night was dark and in the skies, the moon was hidden. Streaks of lightning flashed through the dark clouds heralding an oncoming downpour. Roland would love to be home with his girlfriend before the rain starts.

He stared out through the window and heaved a sigh of relief. Their work was almost at an end. Finally, they had been at it for the better part of the last two years, a crazy vision driven by Doctor Barry Stivers was finally about to become a reality.

The buildings outside were dark, which made Roland uncomfortable. *"People sleep too early in this city."* He was not comfortable with that. Before coming to this town with Mira, he had lived in the big city of

New York. Something was always on and about. All night long, one could see people, if one went out. In this countryside, it was not the same.

Of course, there were many people behind closed doors. The last census showed that at least a family in America had ten people and that population was getting out of hand. Roland felt it was more. He could make out the shapes of homeless people lying by the roadside, and nothing scared him as much as being apprehended by any of these people late at night. They could kill him here, and nobody would open his door to look.

"Approaching your destination," the bot controlling the car said.

Roland sighed, the closer he got to his home, the better he could breathe. There was a reason he did not trust cabs that were manned by people, although most of those cabs were not really in business anymore, some people still preferred them, especially in the countryside and other places where the populace was highly opposed to the recent technological development. They believed the technological advancements were for a sinister purpose. Roland did not.

The cab pulled up in front of the house he had rented and he sat there, looking around first. He had to be sure that he was not followed. This car, at this time, was one of the best assets America had, and he was not prepared to risk it.

"We have arrived at your destination," the bot said. The door was unlocked.

Finally convinced that there was no one else about it, he got out of the car and hurried towards the front door. Mira would probably be sleeping by now, but that was okay. The busiest days were past. Soon, he would stop working entirely when his vision of expanding the human colonies had come to pass. Then, the earth would be free of some of its burden and heal.

He let himself in with a swipe of his thumb on the sensor. Once inside, he pushed the door shut and hurried through the hallway.

At the landing... leading to the room he shared with Mira upstairs, he paused. He noticed that the vase was out of place. It was usually sent on the table in the middle of the living room, but it was on the ground now, shattered to pieces. He wondered why he had not seen it earlier. *Shit.*

Since he started on this project, he had always been paranoid. His permutations were the key to the success of the project. Granted, the idea was not his, far from it. It was the idea of the genius mastermind, Doctor Barry, under whom he worked, but he was an indispensable player in the project. He knew people would want him—the extremists. The ones who felt that a dangerous approach should be reached for making the earth whole again. These people hated the government passionately and Roland worked for this government.

"Mira?" He called. It was a whisper. He wanted to know where she was, and at the same time, he knew he was making a mistake alerting the intruders of his presence if they were still here, but he had to know.

He climbed up the stairs slowly, hoping he would not find what he expected to find. *Palms, blood maps on the wall. Fuck! Jesus. Mira be safe!*

He dashed up the rest of the stairs. Upstairs, the little hallway was lighted, which was usually not the case whenever he came back late from work. Something was definitely amiss. On the ground, he saw a blood trail. It was not much, but it was enough to bury his heart in his stomach.

"Mira!" He shouted as he barged into their room.

There was one man there, on the floor, bleeding from a gaping hole in his head. The bedroom tiles were stained with crimson. Even the bed sheet had blood on it.

At the far side of the room, Mira hugged the wall. She looked like she wanted to go through the wall to somewhere else.

"Mira," Roland called again.

He walked towards her, his arms were outstretched towards her. She was shivering and trembling with fear. Her lips were the most unsteady things he had ever seen.

"...tried to kill me... murderer... through the door."

"It's okay now, Mira... it's okay," Roland gathered her in his arms and pulled her close to him. She was still shivering.

The bedroom was in a state of disarray like there had been a struggle here. On the ground, a bloody life lay, the liquid essence of another human's life... the only thing telling a story about what had happened here. The bedsheets were rumpled, and the pillows were thrown to the ground. The flower vase that usually sat by the bed was on the ground, shattered in a similar fashion like the one he had seen in the living room.

Quickly, Roland pulled his phone from his pocket and dialed 911.

Carl

Inside the car, he felt like sinking through the seat. His partner, Eva, was not even looking his way. What was wrong with her anyway? Just last night, they had been all cuddly and loving, pouring into each other's hollows. He had not believed she could scream that much or love that much. She had always been cold, but last night was a revelation. So was the ring in his pocket, but he could now not find the courage to go on his knees. He stared at her again.

"What is it, Carl?" She asked.

They were both cops, and their positions were already at odds with what Carl wanted to do. Who gets married to his partner? The superintendent would not want to catch wind of that. He did not need to.

"Uh, nothing," Carl replied.

"If this is about last night, then stop. Whatever you are planning would not go through. It was a one-time thing, okay? Both of us were high-strung last night. We needed comfort. That does not make us more than what we are now."

It was the longest stretch he had heard her speak today, and the more she went on, the more he felt needles piercing his heart. He was already getting hooked on her that he felt like a drug addict being warned of his drugs.

"Okay," he replied.

"I think this is wasteful, sitting out here all day, waiting for a transaction that would never happen based on your hunch, detective."

It was one thing to turn him down even before he had asked. It was another to talk him down. But then, Eva had always been cold. It was as if she thought if she hurt people first, then she would never get hurt—it was crazy.

Carl did not say a word. He simply slipped his hand out of his pocket where he had been touching the box, thinking of the right words with which to propose to her. He realized he had been sitting at the edge of his seat. So, he slid back and let his head feel the headrest. He tried breathing in deep.

"Let it go, Carl. Let it go."

When he looked up again, he realized a man was walking through the crowd. The man seemed different from the people walking along the street. He seemed to have a purpose whereas people here walked about aimlessly.

"There," Carl said, pointing. That was his man. If he had not looked up when he did, he would not have recognized him. He took his dark, computerized glasses from the dash where it sat and checked the man out.

Gary Winfield, extremist/terrorist PTE.

"That is him alright," Carl said, pulling the car door open.

He thought it was a bit of an irony that a group who called themselves PTE—Protect The Earth—would be bombing up places on earth just so they could achieve their mission. Their end justified the means, and the means were nasty.

Eva climbed out of the car and whispered to it, "Shadow us."

As they went after the man, walking through the street and trying to blend in, Carl wondered if the car's automated system would manage to find a way to shadow them. The traffic might become too congested at a point. Whatever, he tried to pull his head out of the thoughts that were beclouding it and focused on the prize right in front of him. It was hard keeping him in sight, but Carl was tall, 6'4", and the glasses helped. Beside her, Eva walked, cold as ice.

The man in front of them suddenly wheeled into an alleyway and disappeared. The two detectives hurried to the corner and peeped in to make sure no one was lying in wait for them. They were there in time to see him open a door and slip through it. Quickly, they dashed into the alleyway, walking briskly towards the door. There was a dumpster nearby. They walked around the container and were almost at the door when they heard it.

The sound of a drone stopped their movement. The drone was flying overhead from somewhere farther down the alleyway, coming towards them.

Weapons activated, the glasses informed Carl.

"Shit!" He cursed, then pushed back against Eva at the same time the drone started firing bullets at them.

Together, they dove into the dumpster, rolling over packaged garbage. At least, it provided cover even if it reeked to the high Heavens, especially as one of the bags got torn.

Carl pulled out his gun and waited, hiding behind the side of the dumpster, biding his time and waiting for the drone to get close. He was sure it was manned by an amateur. An expert would have wasted them before they could even make it to the dumpster.

Bullets slammed into the sides of their hideout, and Carl got infuriated the more. Being trapped among a heap of dirt by an amateur extremist was not the way he had imagined that his day would go. He wondered briefly at the irony of the development when human life was fragile. There were so many things to get used to in the world, so many technological advancements, yet bulls could end one's life. The bulletproof vest did not provide as much protection as the people thought it did. What about their heads? Neck?

He sprang up and aimed at the drone. Two quick bullets did the work, piercing through the drone and sending it out of control. The rotors must have been damaged by one of the bullets. The drone was still firing blindly as it went down. The detectives heard the crash on the ground and quickly jumped out.

Somewhere farther up the alley, they heard running footsteps. The door close by swung in. It had been left open by whoever was hiding there. The idiot was probably the one who had been controlling the drone.

They raced after him.

CHAPTER 2

Levi

ental blinkers," the coach said. "Focus."

"MLevi was running as fast as he could. He had taken the lead immediately after the race started, but now, he could feel the other runners creeping up on him. The faster he moved his legs, the slower it seemed he moved.

"Mental blinkers," the coach shouted again.

The coach's words were carried away by the wind sailing past his ears. He could not even concentrate on his own heartbeat, let alone the race. Everything was happening so fast, and his legs were beginning to feel like lead.

The first person zoomed past him, and no matter how hard he tried, he could not match the other runner's pace. *Just give it up. Your heart is almost bursting.* With that thought, Levi slowed down. Another runner zoomed past him. The finish line was getting blurry; his eyes were getting heavy. After the third runner moved past him, he made it to the finish line, tired and out of breath—he was panting hard.

"What was that?" The coach shouted. "What the hell were you doing?"

Levi could not speak, not yet. He took more deep breaths and tried to get the thumping in his chest back to normal.

The bathroom walls mocked him when he went to take his bath. He could hear the four walls jeering him. It was claustrophobic, the walls bearing down on him. He could hear the coach screaming in the background: *What the hell were you doing?*

He took his bath quickly and got out of the bathroom. Outside, he found Jeremy sitting on the curb, watching the tracks. Jeremy turned on his approach and smiled at him. There were none of the pitiful stares he had been getting lately.

"Nice run, soldier," Jeremy said.

"Hey, stop patronizing me," Levi replied.

"I ain't patronizing shit. You should see the way you shot off like a bullet."

"And I still came 4th."

"Stamina. Stamina, my man."

"I cannot win the 400 meters if I keep falling short just towards the end."

"Maybe, you should not get to the end. Maybe you should not win it."

Jeremy had that faraway look in his eyes that appears when he comes upon some great discovery.

"What are you saying, man?"

"Have you ever thought of going for the 100 meters?"

"No, no, no... my elder brother ran this race and I want to..."

"...keep up the family legacy? Pull your head out of the sand, my man. Get in the game."

"You don't understand."

"You must not do what your elder brother did. Both of you are different, and hey, you will set up another legacy. I am sure no one can beat you in a 100-meter race."

"It's too easy."

"You think that was why your brother did not go for it? It was hard for him. Now, go talk to the coach."

Levi found himself walking towards the coach. He could not explain the force that was propelling him towards the coach, but he knew that his friend, Jeremy, was right.

Heather

She was lying inside her house, waiting for the night to come. In the morning, she had gone through three wraps of the sweet-scenting leaves by herself and subsequently fallen into hallucinations. Her visions were of her sister who was lost in a plane crash while she was going to her new school to further her education. She was the one that was left, the black sheep of the family.

She turned around in bed and sighed. The time was moving at a slow pace. She could see the digits on her luminous watch—it was six-fifteen. In the dimly lit room, it seemed time was just crawling by.

She rolled away from the watch and buried her face in the pillow. Somewhere, in the house, music started blasting through a speakerphone. Although her shut door served as a soundproof, she could still hear the blast... the boom. It would not let her sleep.

She pressed her pillows tightly to her ears and held on, trying to drown the sound from her ears. It sounded to her like an explosion... would have been that her sister was taken from life too early. She was not there. She had heard about it over the phone with her parents. She still remembered.

Her phone had rung long that night. When she checked the caller ID, she discovered it was her mom. The woman never called her. Dr. Laura had other things to do, things that were far more important than calling her first child, especially as the first child had chosen to follow her own path and not the path that she had set out for her.

Heather ignored the call. She was not in the mood to get some berating about her career choice. There was none. She had none. She just wanted to do what they did not want. She was not to absolve herself of the blames. She was to be blamed for most of it but having parents who wanted her to do exactly what they wanted did not help matters. She was tired of the conflicts and the pain that came afterward, the realization that in the process of rejecting the path that her parents had set out for her, she had lost her way. She was now drifting on the air, aimlessly, directionless.

The phone rang again. Again, Heather ignored it. She was not interested. Her parents were no longer in her life anyway. Her stubbornness made them withdraw from supporting her and she found herself working odd jobs to stay alive. The population was brimming over, so getting a reasonable job was out of the question. Besides, she dropped out of school. She did not know why exactly. Maybe, it was an act of defiance. She wanted to be in control of her life, and not have it in the hands of some couple.

The phone rang nonstop till she was forced to pick it.

"Yes?" She said.

She was prepared to end the connection once the woman started berating her, but the woman did not. Instead, there was grave silence on the other side. It seemed the woman was thinking about the best way to start her talk. Heather had been known to hang up the call on her parents.

"I need you to come home," Doctor Laura finally said.

Heather chuckled. The woman—it was strange how she had begun to think of her mother as a woman—and Doctor Johannes thought she was not good enough to stay in their house. They had threatened to throw her out. When she moved, they called her on phone and ordered her not to come home until she does exactly what they wanted. Finding her mother over the phone asking her in the calmest of voice to come home was the most surprising thing she had ever experienced.

"No," she said.

"What?"

"I am not coming home."

"You don't understand, you have to."

"You can't make me... I told you two, you and your husband that I am not my sister. You can't bend me. You can't shape me. It is for me alone to do."

"It is about her."

"Who?"

"Marie."

"Marie is in school."

"No."

"What?"

That was the first time Heather felt something, the first time she felt at one with her parents. She could sense something in her mother's voice. There was no strength there. There was a void, a void that smelled of sadness. She was tempted to ask what was wrong, then she was gripped with fear that something had happened to her sister, but she could still not bring herself to ask.

"You have to come home," Doctor Laura said again. She could have as well been begging. Still, Heather did not want to go.

Sure enough, she was afraid of the worst. She feared that Marie was gravely sick where she was pursuing the path these two had set out for her. She knew how sick she had gotten trying to follow their path. Her head had become a pressure cooker where the only thing she ever thought of was being the best. After high school, she snapped out of it, went to college, and became the rebel they did not want to see.

"What is at home? You two?"

There was a sigh from the other end. Doctor Laura was tired of speaking.

"Your sister..."

"Is she sick? Have you finally stretched her to her limits?"

"She's dead."

That was the bomb that the woman had been trying to keep away from her. Heather could feel the grief from her side of the phone seeping through her handset. She was rooted in her seat, staring at the wall.

"Are you there?" The woman asked.

The world stopped moving then. Nothing made sense, not even her sense of freedom, of being in charge of her life; not her feud with her parents. Life suddenly seemed too meaningless for anybody to try to make meaning from it, to try to get angry with something someone else had said.

"I will make arrangements for you to come home," Doctor Laura said. It seemed like she was trying not to cry. "To pay your last respects."

CHAPTER 3

Mira

S he had not been herself since their house was broken into. The countryside was not safe anymore, not the way the city was safe. But at least, robot policemen who were enforcing the law. If a house was being broken into at the dead of the night, they would be there immediately. The crime rate was not high in the city. Most of the people living in the countryside were fighting against technological advancements, using its harmful effect on the environment as their backbone.

She had managed to kill the intruder, and she feared that her life was in danger. It was probably because of Roland's work. She had been shaken by the incident. She was still shaken and the smile on her face was not genuine. Only when she got out of this neighborhood would she feel safe and start to smile genuinely again.

Until then, she had to pretend that she did not allow that their next-door neighbor could belong to one extremist group or the other, people who wanted to save the earth by destroying the earth and its inhabitants. Things were slowly running out of hand, and she was not sure if the government could handle it... if there was an uprising. One thing she did know for sure was that she had to get out of this place and get out fast. She wished Roland would follow her, but there was no use trying. She had already begged him to in the house, but he was afraid her father would conclude that he was right, and term him a worthless bag of shit.

Mira sat in the car and waited for her fiancée to come outside. He would come with her bags, as carrying those bags might ruin her nails. She would wait for him in the city till he was done with this project of his, then they would get married.

After a little while, she saw him walking towards the car. He let some of the bags down before he pulled open the back door of his Tesla Model electric car. The bags were settled into the backseat.

"Are you sure you would not want to stay in our house?" Roland asked, coming around to the front of the car.

"No, I have to stay with people. You know I easily get bored," Mira said. She knew some people referred to her as a spoiled princess and daddy's girl, but she had no problem with it. She was beautiful, extremely so, and did not think she was supposed to be working, not when her husband-to-be is an important man in one of America's foremost innovative companies. She should not be working. Besides, what should she be doing? In her father's house, there were servant robots who did everything for her. She has one that kept her company when Roland stayed away too long.

"Your friend then, Kenya would be a good one to stay with," Roland opined.

"God, she has precious little robots, and she would expect me to do some things by myself. I will stay with my parents," she said.

Roland's face fell. He walked away from her window side and around to the driver side of the car, got in, and engaged the auto-pilot system.

The car pulled away from their house and was soon on the road, flying towards the airport. Roland's face remained clouded over, and he remained silent. After two or three furtive glances his way, Mira was forced to speak.

"Hey, it is not like my parents can make me not to marry you," she said.

"You know how they are."

"Come on, they cannot make me change my mind."

"They would invite every man that they want you to marry, everyone that they think is better, and I would be away here, working. I won't even get a chance to defend myself."

"You don't need to... you know that I never listen to them."

"Anything can happen, Mira."

"Anything, but I will never stop loving you."

"Will you still marry me?"

"I would be stupid not to. Of course, I will still marry you."

Feeling reassured by Mira's words, Roland engaged the engine, set it on autopilot, and sat to enjoy the last moments he would spend with his fiancée before she got on the plane.

Carl

They were hot on the rebel's heels, turning into the alleyways, they had not realized were in existence. Homeless people were lying by the side. The place was filled with the stench of sweat. The farther they ran into the network of alleyways, the more Carl realized that they were making a big mistake. They were not supposed to come down here. This territory was for the Botforce, and even then, it was still risky as the most extreme of these fanatics could take apart a robot. There had been news of the extremists taking apart a robot, the very first one. Since then, the government was planning a coordinated attack behind closed doors, one that would take the rebels down.

"Stop," he said, and pulled to a halt. Behind him, Eva stopped too.

"He is getting away, damn it!" She cursed.

"We have to go back."

"You little coward..."

"This place is dangerous... we have to leave."

But it was too late. From all corners of the alleyway, the extremists started coming out of their hiding. Even the people they had considered beggars and homeless people lying by the side of the street, all got up to their feet.

Carl counted. There were at least twenty people in the alleyway, and the numbers kept increasing. Someone was telling the others that there was meant to be hunted. Like blind birds, they had flown into a gate and the door was about to be shut on them.

Eva slowly turned around, taking in the crowd of people that were surrounding them now. Carl could see the fear behind the mean demeanor that she tried to portray. He knew that the both of them were as good as gone. Carl's GPS was still functioning, but he knew that if he tried to radio this in, it would agitate the crowd that was slowly closing in on them.

"Before you all get too excited, I would like to remind you of the crime you are about to commit," Carl said. His voice was firm and bold, bolder than he felt.

Eva looked at him quickly, and at that point, he saw something other than the coldness he was always seeing in her eyes. There was admiration there too. There was also fear. He nodded reassuringly at her.

"You are about to attack two top officers of the police. I know you know what the Botforce would do to you if that happens. We are going back. Now, get out of our way."

The last words were said with so much force that the crowd actually moved out of their way. It was like magic, like Moses stretching forth his hand towards the red sea. There was a pathway for them to walk through, a pathway of angry and intimidated faces belonging to men, women, boys, and girls.

Carl made a show of looking around at all the extremists, eyeball to eyeball. He was bent on showing them that he was not afraid of them. His heart was beating the whole time. Finally, he turned and started to walk through the pathway that had been cleared for them. While he walked, he pressed the button to summon their car.

"You don't go out of here without leaving something behind," one of the people suddenly said, coming to stand in front of them.

"Get out of my way," Carl said. His voice was deadly and menacing, but the fundamentalist did not budge. Carl had been afraid this would happen. One small thing could trigger the crowd of fanatics into attacking them. While he could hold them off for some time, he was not sure the time would be enough for backup to arrive at this hidden location. The police force was stretched taut fighting cases of extremism all over the places. There were men, women, boys, and even girls sneaking into places and murdering important people all because they have been convinced that these people were harming the earth.

"You leave the lady behind," the fellow standing in front of Carl said. There were screams of approval from the crowd when he spoke, and Carl had to swallow his saliva. This was getting more heated than he had planned.

The man standing before him was homeless. He had tattered clothes and was bare-footed. His beard was long and dirty, probably one of the tenets of becoming a fundamentalist. He was shorter than Carl too, but his eyes blazed with defiance when he stared back at Carl. He knew that if the officer touched him, the crowd would come to his rescue.

"You don't understand," Carl said, slowly. "This is not a negotiation. Get out of my way."

More people were coming to stand behind the man, and the others who were not standing were daring the two officers to take action. There were probably about thirty of them now, Carl was not sure.

Eva acted first. Carl could see that she was tired of the talk. This was her way, action. She shot the man straight at the head with her laser beam, making a hole in his head. The man fell to the ground, lifeless.

"Does anyone still want 'the lady'?" Eva asked.

Carl was still staring around carefully without moving his eyes. He could feel the people's hunger, their thirst for their blood. He could feel the bluffing leash he had tied around their neck loosening.

The first person was from the back. He sent a projectile of a bottle aimed at Carl. Carl's reflexes were sharp. He swirled around, saw the bottle, and held up his head to deflect it and protect his head. It was like the gates of hell had been opened. The crowd descended on them. The guns were useless. Carl slipped out a knife. Someone slammed his fist into the back of his head. It was painful, but he managed to keep standing, swinging his hand backwards to bury his little knife in the person's chest, then he twisted and turned and pulled it out. He did all of this fast, and was just in time to see a fist coming his way. He dodged smoothly and smacked his knee into the attacker's groin.

This is not the job that I love. I want to protect lives to maintain law and order. But Carl found himself killing the extremists without feelings. A part of him thought that they deserved it. They bombed public places even with people inside; they select sections of the country to be rid of people, even thought that their plans had been kept at bay by the elevated security provided by the government.

As Carl sliced through them, he suddenly experienced a moment of panic when he remembered that Eva was here with him, fighting through this mess. For a moment, he lost concentration, and that was when one of the men struck him across the head with a club.

He staggered to the ground. The club was strong and thick. It was enough to knock out an able-bodied man, but Carl struggled to remain conscious. He was on his knees now. Everything passed by in slow motion, and he noticed that he could hardly see. He knew they would be on him in no time.

"Get up!" Eva yelled, coming over to where he was kneeling. She was still using her gun, and he could still hear the cries of agony coming from the crowd.

He got to his feet quickly and continued swinging with his knife. His movements were becoming slower and he knew that he was getting weaker. But he held up steady beside Eva. More than anything, he was afraid of what would happen to Eva if they both were overpowered by the crowd. He knew that they would kill him off as fast as possible. Right from time, the male gender of every species hated competition. But for Eva, he was afraid that they would pass her around, have their turns with her before they killed her.

Someone rushed headlong at him. He stepped to her side and buried his knife in the person's throat, twisting and dragging it out together with the assailant's throat, then he pushed the assailant back into his people. But that did not stop the people. More and more people were coming after them. Men, children, women, transsexuals. He could no longer count.

Just when he thought they were about to be overrun by the crowd, he heard the sound of a car horn beeping. It sounded like salvation.

"Down," he screamed and dragged Eva to the ground with him.

When the bullets came, there was no other noise, just the steady sound of machines of death pumping bullets into a crowd of people who had no response to it, but screams of pain. The bullets could shoot through walls and many armors, and were coming from guns fitted into their car. The shooting gave the extremists no chance.

By the time, the bullets stopped pouring into the alleyway, there was not one outlaw left standing. Slowly, Carl stood up, helping Eva to her feet. He surveyed the carnage that they had done, holes tore into walls and people, brains were splattered against the wall, and their guts were strewn all over the place. In their eyes, he could see the fear of death and the suddenness with which the grim reaper comes. It sickened him.

"Come on," Eva said, pulling him towards the car.

The Bot force was arriving now, accessing the situation and still ending hostiles that looked like they could attack.

"Stop it," Carl said inaudibly.

"What?" Eva asked. She worried that her partner was behaving strangely, but wanted them to get to the safety of the car first.

"Stop that!" Carl screamed at one of the robots. It looked like a human apart from the tag on its forehead: *alpha*. It was one of the best robots in the force, the leader robot, designated its place in the chain of command.

The robot accessed Carl and turned away to shoot at another hostile. Carl lunged at it, striking it with all the force at his disposal and slamming its body to the ground. The alpha pushed Carl away before he could start fighting him, got up again, and accessed Carl. Eva rushed and pulled Carl away, towards the car.

"Come on," she kept saying as she dragged the big man to the car. When they got to the car, she pushed him into the passenger seat and slammed the door shut.

"What is wrong with you?!" She screamed after she had gotten into the driver's side of the car.

Carl did not respond. Instead, he stared into space. He had no idea what was wrong with him, but he felt something had been broken, something that could not be repaired.

CHAPTER 4

Heather

"Our only consolation is that we all shall meet on the last day, and we will have a lot to say," the reverend was saying. "It is the promise we have in the Lord."

Of course, Heather only heard what he was saying because there was no one she could wrap up her ears and keep them closed. They sound like poison to her. It was annoying, the kind of things they said when they understood nothing—these charlatans.

At the periphery of their gathering, she could make out drones at a distance. These drones, were the things that gave her parents the confidence they moved with, knowing that in the event of an attack, the drones would see it before it happened. But the drone had not saved their daughter's life, and she had come too late to ask how she died. She was not sure she wanted to know, but her mind would never let her rest until she finds out.

All that perfection, all that struggle to become something, all the inventions, and we still have death. An irony, she thought. It was as if they were all bound by fate to come to an end, some faster than others. Heather had often joked that if her parents and the mad, famous scientist could find a cure for death, she would come back to stay with them and do whatever they wanted. She would apply herself to making their names and keeping their legacy, or whatever nonsense it was that people did these days to pretend humanity was important. They were not; none of them were.

She watched the coffin. Marie was there, white as a light paper with a slight smile on her lips. If not for the whiteness, Heather would have believed that she was still alive and was only resting. But she was unnaturally white. She was dead and so peaceful and quiet, offering no resistance. She was allowing these people to carry her to her grave when it was not yet her time.

As they started lowering her kid sister into the earth, Heather turned and walked away. She was tired of all of these. Mentally, she was at zero. Her landlord was threatening to push her out of the house. Getting the odd jobs was getting more difficult by the day. Robots were taking over, and only highly skilled people were still retained. Her parents still found it difficult to believe that she was their daughter.

Tired, she turned and walked away from the funeral. The cemetery was one of the places that, even though it was overpopulated, it still had quiet and peace. Apparently, humans were better dead than alive.

She got under a tree and sat down there. Maybe she should not have returned. She did not even get to say goodbye. What was the use of seeing Marie's dead body when she was long gone? Marie would not know that she came back for her. Marie had always wanted her around, so this death hurt her the most. It felt like she abandoned her kid sister in her search for freedom, and the girl had no other choice than to follow the path that her parents had carved out for her. The path had now led her to an untimely death. Who knew what stupid meeting she was flying to before the tragedy struck?

"It was the rebels," a voice said.

Heather was so shocked that she jumped up from where she was sitting. She thought she was alone and had not expected to see anyone here. As it was, she could see no one… but the voice, the damn voice.

She looked up into the tree just as someone was getting down from it.

"Hello," the man said as he slid down. "Sorry for startling you. My name is Andre."

"What are you doing up there?"

"I could not come for the funeral."

"Why would you…"

Andre. Isn't that...?

Heather remembered now. Her sister had only mentioned Andre once in their chats that seldom happened. She did not say much about Andre except what Andre thought. That was all. Heather had been immersed too deep in her own world to care about Andre so she had not asked. She did not even know where Andre was from, his status, where he worked.

"Do you want a drag?" Andre asked, picking one from his pocket.

Heather shook her head, still observing the man. He was of average height, had a full beard and hair locks. He looked like he should not be here. Maybe, that was exactly why he was hiding in the trees. But the drones should have spotted him by now. Knowing her parents, they would input the name of every guest that would be present at the funeral, so no one they do not want comes here.

"Who are you to my...to Marie?"

There was no need to reveal herself now.

"Your sister, you mean," Andre said as he lit the paper. He inhales deeply. When he exhaled, the smoke was thick. "She told me a lot about you. She admired you, you know? Admired your will and resolve to say go to hell to your parents and match right off to your own destiny. She did not have that much strength."

"Who are you?"

"Her boyfriend," Andre said and sighed. "We planned to run away, but then, this mission came up, so we decided after she was back and the security was lax. We would go to the other cities. She would send a message to your parents, telling them to leave her alone. We would find you..."

Here, Andre stopped. He was almost sobbing, so he was trying to gather his emotions and put them in a bag. He looked like that kind of person, one that would be smiling when he was dying.

"You knew her?" Heather asked.

She returned to sit back against the tree. She did not feel threatened by the man anymore. He was on her side.

Fuck! If only I knew. I would have helped her.

Andre sat besides her, still smoking.

"You are not supposed to be here," Heather said.

"I know... neither are you."

Heather turned upon him with wild eyes breathing fire.

"What is that supposed to mean?"

"You are a bird, just like me, just like your sister. The only difference is you and I, we have flown before. Your sister hasn't. I could not teach her. Or should I say, I taught her late?"

"I am to be blamed."

"Sometimes I want to believe that, then I think of your parents. They knew about the dangers of going to

England. The terrorists are getting a stronghold there. Still, they sent her. They were too busy to go."

"Typical of Doctor Laura and Doctor Johannes. They can sacrifice anybody for their savior-complex."

"So, maybe it is not your fault."

"It is... I knew I should have taken her with me the night I walked away, or at least talked to her. I guess I was angry. She was always doing what my parents wanted."

Andre sighed and took yet another drag. Heather watched him. There was an economy in his movement and the way he sucked on the pipe. He knew exactly what he was doing. It was like art.

"How did she die?" Heather suddenly asked.

Andre looked away. When he turned back to her, he was trying to smile with gloomy eyes.

"An explosion in the sky. There was a video of it that kept being replayed before the government censored it."

"An explosion?"

"Yes, an explosion that was supposed to ensure that there was no part of her to bury, but Marie had always been a smart one. She had locked herself up in a cargo compartment in the plan when it was sure they were going to crash. But even then, death followed her."

"How?"

"A rod, a particle, speared through her chest. They covered it up."

"How do you know all these?"

"I'm always snooping around."

"You are a hacker," Heather said, and it was not a question.

Hackers were endangered. It was either they were locked up to work for the government or they were eliminated. Despite the improvements in technology, there were still numerous backdoors that could not be closed. Hackers could access governments' top secret files. They could, potentially, start a world war. It was funny though that hackers would be accused of this when, in essence, it was the governments that had these problems around them in the first place. If there were no secrets to cause wars, hackers would see nothing.

"Is that how you got in here?" Heather asked, turning to look at him.

"See you around, Heather," Andre said, getting up from where he was sitting. He dusted his trousers and started walking away. Then he stopped and turned. "That is if you decided to stay."

Levi

"There's no way I'm doing that, Levi. We already have someone running the 100 meters for us," the coach said.

He was moving away from the dressing room, but Levi followed him.

"Well, I'm not any good in the 400 meters," Levi said. "And you have seen how fast I am at the beginning of the race every time."

"Doesn't guarantee that you will be the best in 100 meters."

"How about a test, coach?"

"That would mean I'm listening to you, which I'm not."

"I don't get you, coach. Does the school want trophies or not?"

"You don't understand, Levi. Let it be. Practice harder."

As Levi walked beside the coach, things started getting clearer to him. He respected the coach so much that when the rumors broke out that Ethan was only in the team and doing 100 meters because that was what the boy's father wanted, he did not believe it. He felt the coach knew what he was doing. Ethan was fast, quite alright, but he had no competition. The coach made sure of that. While other athletes had people that could fill in for them when they were not around, or people that could actually beat them and take their spots away, Ethan was the only one being groomed for the 100 meters.

Mr. Willis had made so much donations to the school that he practically owned the school. The principal hushed at his arrival. The teachers giggled and twittered, and the sports coach, well, even though he was not one to show these ass-licking traits, he was doing something that Levi had not expected of him.

"It is because of Ethan's father, isn't it?"

"What the hell are you saying?"

"Mr. Willis, he practically owns this school, so you do whatever he wants."

"Shut up, boy. One more word and I will suspend you from the team."

"I always thought you were better than all of them. I always thought you were your own man. Guess what?"

"You are crossing the line now, boy... watch what you say."

"I was wrong."

"Okay, that's it."

The coach stopped, turned, and glared at Levi.

"You are off the team. Next time, you watch what you say."

"You don't mean that."

"Do not come to training tomorrow. In fact, do not come to training at all."

"The scholarship I got is tied to the games."

"Well, find another game, Levi. I have seen you swim once. Go there and become a nuisance."

The coach walked away, leaving Levi standing there.

What could they have offered him? His job?

There were so many things going through Levi's head that he did not realize that the orange bulb at the horizon was the sun sinking for the day. The night would soon be upon this place and he had to get home.

Well, thank you, Jeremy. You have fucked me up again.

Slowly, he started walking towards the exit. Jeremy would be there waiting for him so they could go home together.

When he got outside, he saw Jeremy smiling and wanted to punch that smile off his face. What was so funny? What was he smiling about? Jeremy with his big head and lanky body. The boy looked like a scarecrow that escaped some old farm and ran up to the countryside.

As he approached, the smile faded from Jeremy's face. Yeah, the idiot could read the room. What was he seeing? His misery? The misery he had caused him.

"Why did I ever listen to you, Jeremy?" Levi lamented.

"Uh... you know I'm right."

"Well, you are stupid being right just got me kicked off the team."

"What?"

What was all the faux pretense about? Like the idiot did not know the coach could take someone off his team? Everyone though except Ethan. Probably Ethan

50

could yank the coach off his job. It was fucked up down here.

"I knew this was going to happen," Levi cried.

"Still, you went ahead to tell him?"

"You asked me to tell him, you numb kill."

"Well, I could be wrong."

For the love of everything sensible, why can't I break Jeremy's head?

"I should have your head broken open and checked."

"You want to blame me for this now?"

"Look around, Jeremy... who should I blame?"

"Well, you knew all about your coach's madness and you still took my advice. Maybe, you are not happy running."

"Fuck you!"

Levi went to unchain his bike. He got on top of it and cycled off towards home. In his mind, he made a mental note to get rid of Jeremy in any way he could. The idiot was a family friend and a childhood friend who would not just let him be. Whatever he did, Jeremy would always be there with his own stupid opinions. His opinions messed things up for him.

"Come on, wait up, Levi. You can't tell me you are that angry," Jeremy called, ambling beside him.

The use of private cars had been limited for obvious reasons. The planet was overflowing with humans who could hardly find a space to live in. Only top government officials had cars. Others used bikes or public transport. Self-driven cars. Of course, in some places, people still had cars and were opposing the law. They were the rebels. They wanted cars and felt the government was subjugating its citizens, so they would have everyone under control.

As Levi weaved between the cars and other bikes on the way, his mind was not really drawn to the affairs of the day, the threat of the production of a weapon that takes out the whole world. There had been debates and debates on it via the TV. While a group argued that it would make for sustainable growth, other groups who wanted the environment to heal, said it was one of the poisons of humanity.

Levi got home and rolled his bike in. It was a tenement building, divided into sections. With the population surging every day, this was how most people lived, even people who were thought rich.

"Levi!" Jeremy called from the road.

"Stay the fuck away from me!" Levi screamed back.

CHAPTER 5

Roland

"P romise me that you will be fine," Mira said, turning to look at Roland.

Roland was taken aback. He loved Mira, greatly, but he had also come to terms with the fact that Mira was selfish. She was mostly thinking about her makeup, or her gym, or her clothes, or her jewelry. He was always the one doing the loving, pampering her, worshiping her. So, it came as a bit of a shock to him that she was actually interested in his well-being for the time she would be away in her father's house.

"I will be," he said. "Just one more week and I will leave this place and get to the city."

"You will have to pick me up from home."

"The wedding is very close, is it not?"

"It is."

She reached out and planted a deep, wet kiss on his lips. He responded and they stayed in that way for a long time.

The jet was there, put on the runway, waiting for her. All Mira had to do whenever she wanted to travel was to call her parents and she would have a pilot waiting for her. Sometimes, it irked Roland, but he hardly said anything about it. After all, when her family finally accepts him as one of their own, he would be entitled to all the perks she gets as an only child.

Still, he could not help but wonder sometimes, how unfair the world was. There were many homeless people sleeping in the street, but one girl had a private jet at her beck and call, and she did nothing all day except ride on the achievements of her parents whom he had a great dislike for.

"What are you thinking about?" Mira said, pulling away from him.

"Me? What? Nothing."

"Your mind faltered in our kiss. What were you thinking about, babe? Do you want to cheat on me?"

"Why would I want that?"

"Well, I'm leaving and the house is going to be empty. You may get lonely within a week. There are beautiful ladies in this little town. It is like a concentration of beautiful, shapely ladies with backsides bigger than mine, and I know..."

"Stop... just stop. What the hell are you on to, Mira? I would never cheat on you. I'm sad that you are leaving and this might be the last kiss I will get from you."

"Last kiss? Are you planning to die?"

"No."

When Roland did not speak again, Mira stared closely at him.

"Oh, not again. There is no way I'm leaving you, Row. I love you."

"Your parents are very persuasive. I have seen them talk."

"Well, they do not speak for me. I live to make them know that."

"I dunno... I really don't like this."

"Listen, bear. I will call you on video chat once I get there. It will be the first thing that I will do. And every other day till you are done with this project, I will keep calling you."

That sounded reassuring. Row had this fierce determination on her face. He had learned never to underestimate it. For all the times that he did, he lived to regret it. For the time being, it washed his doubts and fears away.

The door opened and he watched Mira walk through the airstrip. Someone was coming to meet her. He sat there to be sure she was expecting the man.

He was still there when the jet ran through the runway before leaping into the sky. Then, he started the car and headed back towards his place. He hoped nothing would come between him and the woman he loved, but he was afraid. It was as if he could already see the end, and it was not nice.

Barry

He walked through the lab, looking at some of the workers. There were scientists there working for him, brilliant minds in their own right. As he returned their greeting, he was struck with a bout of self-doubt. Certainly, most of these men were better than he was. He was just lucky, lucky to have found a book and a solution to the world's problem.

He got into his office and shut the door, taking a deep breath. Staying outside to explain 'his' work always has him jittering. He was afraid of being seen as a fraud, and he knew that was exactly what he was. How could he tell anyone that his late brother had started this from the start, and he was just coming in at the tail end to claim all the glory?

He sat down on his swiveling seat and surveyed his office. It was not much, certainly not what he was used to in the big city. But they had to hide now, and there was nowhere better to hide than in the countryside where it was easy to fish out the extremists and deal decisively with them.

Barry Stivers was tired of all the stories about extremists trying to depopulate the earth. Perhaps, that was why he was still battling on with the feeling that he was a thief when he could just leave everything and move away. He wanted a better earth, just like any right-thinking human. He wanted an earth that was free from the pollution that they had gotten used to. But if that earth was only achievable by killing some people, then he wanted no part of it.

His phone was ringing. He stared at it, afraid of picking the call. Most calls frightened him these days. The top, they always wanted something. He was scared. The series of experiments, the inventions, all of them seemed to be geared towards one thing, and he still could not make sense of it. He wanted something else, but it seemed the people that were financing the invention wanted something else.

He picked the call and waited. The number was an unknown one, but the caller had to be one that was at the top of the chain because it was a secret line.

"Hello," he said into the phone.

"Hello, Doctor," an emotionless voice came from the other end.

Barry Stivers shivered even though this fellow talking to him was not here. He felt like he was being watched. Quickly, he stood up and hurried to the window. While he was there, he stared this way and that, furtively, as if he was expecting someone to be hiding somewhere farther up the road. There was nobody in sight.

"Who's this?"

"You know who, doctor. What you are doing is the devil's work."

The doctor quickly ended the call. He was not in a mood to listen to threats. They kept assuring him that he was protected, yet he kept getting these threats from numbers that could not be traced.

I have to get out of this place. In the city, I'm pretty sure the drones would be with me.

He knew that the presence of the drones here would arouse suspicion and the do-good journalists would be snooping about all over the place, looking for their stupid information.

He dialed a number quickly. When the call was answered, he spoke rapidly.

"Hello, sir," Barry said. "I would like to let you know that the muon-catalyzed fusion is in its final stages. We will be doing a demonstration tomorrow morning."

"Good work, Barry. Good work."

There was silence. The man at the other end of the call did not end the call. It was almost as if he knew there was something he wanted to say. Barry swallowed.

"I got the call again," Barry finally said.

"What call?"

"You know. You promised me this would not keep happening, yet here it is."

"Barry, my good friend. The work is almost done."

"I don't feel safe."

"Nobody is safe anyway. You know this."

"That is not what I mean. I can be assassinated here, at any time. I can't even stay in my house. How will I find the presence of mind to finish this?"

"You are protected, Barry. You will always be."

"The drones are not here. "

"We have been over this already."

"I don't think it matters what anyone would think."

"We have to keep this a secret."

"Why? If it is for the good of the world, why should we horde it?"

"What has come over you, Barry? We can't be doing this all the time."

There was silence from Barry's end as he thought about it. He could go on to complain to the senator, but he was miles away. He would never understand the fear of having someone that could take a bomb into the midst of people and bomb those people together with himself.

"You are right. We can't."

He ended the call and walked to the window again. He was terrified about the night, but he was also feeling claustrophobic, feeling the room closing in on him. At the window, his eyes went to the Café down the street. Coffee would help clear his mind.

He left the office and walked towards the stairs. Outside, it was already getting dark as the day was put out like a feeble-lighted candle. His cap was on his head, helping him hide his identity as he walked towards the Café.

When he got in, he noticed there were few people scattered around the Café and went to his favorite table by the corner. He loved it there. It helped him stay away from public eyes. He became the eyes, observing everything happening around him. Like now, a woman had walked into the Café. She was tall, around 5'11". That was his height. With high-heeled shoes, she would definitely be taller than he was. He watched her sit at an empty table, then he looked away. He was not tempted, no, he was not.

Days of being secluded in this godforsaken countryside would make any sane man go crazy. Barry was not one that went after every woman he saw, but he understood that a man's body had needs, and sometimes, it so happened that a woman's body had needs too. They complemented each other. When was the last time he had felt a woman's touch? Damn, this was becoming embarrassing.

"Hello, do you mind if I join you?"

Speak of the devil! Barry looked up to see the woman looking down at him. There was a slight smile at both ends of full lips, and her eyes were grayish-green. They reminded Barry so much about the snake while raising in him an insatiable curiosity.

"Yes... I mean no, you can sit down," Barry said. He wondered about the universe bringing dreams to reality, making wishes come through. Maybe there was something that they were missing, something about the interconnectedness of the universe and the mind.

"I don't see you here often," the woman said.

"I don't come here often," Barry replied.

Now that the woman was here with him, he was finding it difficult to talk. His tongue was stuck to the root of his mouth, and there was some heaviness in his Jaws.

"I see, but you have to confess they do have the best coffee. Have you tried their hot chocolate?"

"I have a feeling you did not come to my table to talk about drinks," Barry said. It was typical of him to see the end before looking at anything else.

**

She kissed him hard and he marveled at how her lips could be that soft. It had been a while since he had been touched by a woman, and she seemed to just know what to do. Her hands pulled his clothes off very quickly, and before he knew what was happening, they were naked.

They had gone to her house after communicating with their eyes. The doctor wanted one thing badly, and it seemed the woman wanted the same thing too because she read him beautifully. She was not talking. It was only her moans that filled the room, setting off the beastly man in him. But she pushed him down to the bed and got astride him immediately, continuing the kissing there. Her hand moved down into his briefs and started massaging him down there. The more her hand moved, the more he gasped and groaned. He was spiraling out of control before she slipped him into her.

She knew how to move. Doctor Barry Stivers had never had anyone like this. And he did not even know her name.

It took 5 minutes before he was done. She seemed disappointed as she slid off him. Barry was concerned. Something terrible had happened. It was as if she wanted to be pregnant. That was the second of his worries. The first was that the lady did not look satisfied.

"I am not usually like this," Barry said. "It's been a while."

"No need to talk about it," the woman said. "I would like to sleep now."

"Will I see you again?"

"I'm not so sure."

"Come on. I really need to see you again."

"What you really need to do is to start going."

"You can't possibly mean that."

"You don't know me, Barry."

"Barry? You know my name?"

She got up from the bed where she was sitting with her back to him and pulled on her pantie. There was a robe hanging by the wardrobe, silky white. She put that on and tied it around her waist. Her waist was so tiny that the doctor wanted to hold her again. He had not really done much this night, but he felt some satisfaction. It made him ashamed of his masculinity. 5 minutes? What is 5 minutes? He could go on and on for at least 15 minutes, but he did not have the strength and control these days. Besides, why did she take over everything and relegate him to the background? Why did she make him lose control? All the fault lies at her doorstep anyway.

The woman went to the door and pulled it open, holding it for him. God! He was still naked. He had not even put on his briefs. What was wrong with this woman? The more he agonized over the woman's behavior, the more he wanted to know more about her. Surely, he had to. She knew his name. She had to return the favor.

"Can't I, at least, know your name?" He asked.

"Dora," she said. "Dora Martinez."

CHAPTER 6

Roland

He sat in his car, holding his head with both hands, and thinking about Mira. Mira, the beautiful Mira, the sexy Mira, the lovely Mira, his everything. He had no idea that he and Mira would end up as husband and wife when they first met. His first impression of her was as a spoilt child to a rich scientist, till he found out that one part of her that was her saving grace. He did not want to let her go, ever.

Still, he could not help but see an end that looked inevitable. He sighed. The jet was in the sky by now, and Mira was on her way to her annoying parents. Of two parents, not one of them liked him, not even one. Crazy motherfuckers. Pompous asshole that walked about like the world was stuck somewhere between the cracks of their butts. They were both working on another man's invention, but because they felt it could save the world, they were now the darlings of the government. Other governments were coming to them for solutions. As far as Roland knew, the new invention was volatile and most of the countries that had made any headway at all in it did not want other countries to know anything about what they were doing. Sometimes, Roland felt like he was working for the secret service. Everything was done in such a secretive manner that he felt his very existence was a sin, and he had to stay hidden till the government called the project to an end.

Roland pushed his door open and stepped out. It was time to go up to the house and languish in loneliness and maybe a little misery mixed with Nostalgia. Ah, Mira.

He had met Mira at a ball where he was presenting his own theory, the theory that brought him in contact with Doctor Barry Stivers. Mira's parents, Doctors Phil and Melinda, were present there. They were even among those who stood up to clap for him after he had made the presentation till they realized their daughter was interested in him. Someone that was without a doctorate or even a Masters could not marry their daughter.

Once Roland was done with his presentation, he walked outside and found the girl, Mira, standing by the door. A simple hello was all he had the time to say.

"Follow me," she said.

That was it. The confidence with which it was said. Even before saying it, she believed he would follow her.

"Pardon?" He said.

"I said, follow me. Come talk to me."

Again the command came. Roland made the biggest mistake of his life, a mistake that would have cost him a great opportunity. He ignored her and walked away. But she never left him alone. She was always on him, incurring the wrath of her parents, making them feel disgusted by him.

Maybe it was her obsession with him that made her parents hate him the way they did. They felt he was too little for her to be falling all over him. These days, it made him a little afraid and insecure. What if Mira suddenly loses her obsession with him? What if she gets tired of him? The father had once told him he was one of the men that Mira would normally bring home, have a fling with, and cast away. Well, it had been 2 years now and the girl did not seem to be losing interest in him.

Roland unlocked the door and stood there, worried. The house felt empty, and at the same time, he could not help feeling that someone was there. It was a feeling and nothing else. But it was too strong, strong enough to make him pick up the bat by the door as he moved into the house.

"Anyone here?" He asked.

It was a stupid thing to do. If there was an invader in his house, the person certainly would not come out to announce himself no matter how nicely he asked. So, he decided to take another approach. He had heard that violent people like the one he felt was in his house only responded to violence.

"I have a gun," he said, menacingly, "and I will not hesitate to use it."

Again, he wondered if it was not all in his head. There was no one here. He had not seen any sign of his house being broken into. He had heard nothing. It was just the feeling that would not unclasp its hand from his head. He sneaked in deeper, wondering what Mira would say if she saw him sneaking about the house like that. She would probably have a good laugh and then torture him with this memory for months on end. No, no, that was before. That was before she was attacked in his own house even though they had been promised security by the government. He missed the drones. He had a high government clearance and the drones saw him as one of their major concerns. Being stuck here at the edge of the world where nothing happened except homeless people and beggars lining up the street and reminding one of how compacted the world had become, was not good for his peace of mind at all.

He walked up to his room and looked around it. Mira, as spoiled as she was, was the bravest woman that he had ever seen. He was not sure what he would do if he was faced with an assassin that was actually out to kill him. He knew he was deceiving himself with this bat. He did not even know how to swing it. He was a nerd, spectacles-wearing nerd, who wanted nothing more than for his work to be written down in history as that which had saved humanity.

The bedroom was empty, but the feeling persisted. He decided that he could not sleep there that night. Maybe he could see Rudy. Rudy would be sleeping alone as well. Rudy should be glad to have his company.

He walked away from the room, went down the stairs, and walked out the front door. Outside, he turned to put his apartment under lock and key.

Rudy's house was farther up the road. A 2 minutes' walk would bring him right up to Rudy's doorsteps. He smiled. They were among the elite, chosen to live in different apartments all by themselves while their lesser had to struggle with little rooms allocated to them. All of these, Roland had achieved without a doctorate. He had his Masters now, but he was not sure he was willing to be called a doctor. He hated the sound of the name and the pomposity that came with it. Doctors that could not save lives had no business being called doctors. What was the idea behind all of that bullshit anyway?

He started up the road, realizing that it had gotten later than he bargained for. It was after 10, and around here, people retired to bed as early as they could. That meant that by 10, there was hardly anyone on the streets, except people running to keep fit. He saw one now and looked away.

The locals were weird. They worked out at night when they could do the same in the morning; they hardly spoke to foreigners even if the foreigners patronized them. They were a reserved lot, preferring instead to stay on their own instead of mixing in with anybody.

The runner came closer, and it appeared to Roland like he had had a Déjà vu. He had seen this moment before, but he had not realized exactly how it ended. He knew, however, that it ended in a bad way. But all he could do was look as the runner got closer. His eyes widened with surprise and dread.

The runner ran past him and he stood there standing for some time. Anyone watching from the window would see him as a man lost in thought. But as the footsteps of the runner faded, Roland first got on his knees. It was strange. The night was cold and chilling. Then, Roland fell face forward and landed on the road without fear of striking his head against the concrete.

There was no car coming from either direction. The runner was already long gone. The houses all around had sounds coming from there, happy voices, sad voices, young voices, old voices, all from behind the protection of their locked doors and the 911 that was just a phone call away.

The night got colder as if it had just learned a secret and witnessed something it was not going to tell anyone. In front of Rudy's house, on the road, Roland lay lifeless, a hole in the middle of his head pouring out blood. The crimson was slowly flowing towards the gutter, while Roland's sightless gaze followed it.

Heather

Since the visit from Andre at the burial ground, Heather had been going to the burial ground, looking into the trees, at the flowers, on the gravestones for any signs of a yellow-complexioned fellow with hair locks. She did not see. Her parents left her alone. There was nothing they could say now that would bring her sister back, and she wanted them to know clearly that she was not going to become one of their puppets.

Doctor Johannes had barely talked to her since she returned home. As for Doctor Laura, she claimed she understood what a loss meant, but would always put her glasses on and go on to read a stupid theory. She was tired of both of them.

The graveyard was where she found peace. It made her think of the memories she made with her sister before she left, little, beautiful, nostalgic, priceless memories. That was all she had of Marie. She wished she had more, but she did not. She had left home after all, and she was angry with her little sister for being the good child while she was always lauded as the bad child.

She got to the root of a tree and sat down there, under the canopy of the tree branches and leaves. She stared up as well, half-expecting to see the boy up in the tree watching her. But there was nobody there.

"Well, fuck me," she said. She was close to her sister's grave, staring at it. Marie. She missed that girl a lot and wished there was a way she could talk to her.

After she had sat down for a while, she stood up and walked towards the headstone. *Marie, 1931—1955.* She read the inscription sadly and a tear slipped from her eyes.

"Marie," she began. "I am really sorry that I was not there when you needed me."

She was staring directly at the tombstone, wondering if Marie could hear her or if she was beginning to act like a madwoman. Maybe all of that suffering and catering for herself had finally made her lose her mind. But she knew she had to keep talking. It was the only way she could let out the grief that was stuck in her throat, the grief that was making it impossible for her to breathe.

"I should have been there for you. I should have protected you from them. All they want is their legacy, their accomplishments. Doctors."

She sniffed. She was going on too much about her disgust for their parents, and she knew that Marie would not like that, so she pulled back a little. There was no use going there. She could talk to her parents when she got back home. This moment was for her and her little sister.

"Marie, I'm sorry for neglecting you. I didn't... I didn't..."

She broke into a sob that she could not control. The tears flowed freely now.

"You don't have to apologize," a familiar voice said.

Heather's whirled around to see Andre standing there. He had a wrap and he was smoking from it. There was a smile on one side of his face.

"Andre," Heather said, breathless. She had been startled, but she had not been scared. Somehow, she knew Andre would mean her no harm even though he was the picture of everything that her parents agreed was the cause of the deteriorating health of the society.

"You come here often," Andre said. "Why?"

"She's my sister, lying there... dead."

"You did not know that when she was alive?"

"Don't fucking start."

"You never come with any flowers."

"I don't need a flower to open my heart to her. She knows exactly how I feel about her."

"I'm not very sure about that. You did not show her all the time."

"Well, I was not at home all the time. I had my own battles to fight."

"That's life," Andre said sympathetically. There was something with the way he spoke. He was neither here nor there. Even when he was attacking her, she still was confused about where his stand was. "We don't know when the people we love will go."

"Why are you here?" She asked.

"She is my girlfriend."

"Anyone could have said that. You have stalked me for a while and you found out who I was. Who are you really? What do you want?"

"Nothing... I'm missing her."

"You have to give me something more than that. I could let my father know that someone has messed with their control panel."

"I would be long gone by the time you return."

"You would miss out on what you have been snooping around here for."

"Here," he said and handed Heather a flash drive. "That belonged to your sister. She let me watch some of it. You really should see it."

Heather looked closely. On the body of the flash, there was an inscription: *M. J.* It was most definitely her sister's. She wondered what was so important that the sister wanted her to see even after her death.

"Thank you," she said, still looking at the inscription.

"You are right, I have been stalking you. Your sister wanted me to make sure you are still the same person you were years ago when you left your house."

"Why? Why would she want to know that?"

"You will see when you look through that."

"What is in it?"

"I can't tell you... I'm taking a risk talking to you as it is."

"Why?"

"Look through what I gave you. Do that when you are alone."

Again, Andre started walking away. This time, Heather followed her. She was confused about what was in the flash, as well as apprehensive.

"You have to tell me what is in this flash," she said.

"I can't do that."

Andre started running and Heather went after him, but she could not keep up. All her years of trudging around the planet did not prepare her to run after a nimble-footed stranger. She let him go when she was out of breath and stared down at the flash again. She was afraid of what she would find.

CHAPTER 7

Carl

C arl sat in his office, but the only thing he could think about was all the dead bodies. They nauseated him. They accused him. He could still hear their cries as they were being gunned down. The saddest thing about it was that he had summoned the car himself. At the time, all he wanted and cared about was getting away from the murderous horde. But as the murderous horde turned into dead meat, the guilt was eating him up.

He still remembered Eva trying to talk to him inside the car, but he was not listening. He was long gone. All he was thinking about was the faces of women and children riddled with bullet holes and bloody. It made him ashamed. If they were only men, he would have killed them and returned to the station without feeling any remorse about it.

The weight of guilt hung heavy on his head, and his hands flailed around for something to hold onto to stop the fall, he remembered that Eva had shot one of the men first. He had everything under control, well, sort of. In as much as his mind was trying to absolve him of every guilt, he could not help seeing things from her point of view. A stupid partner could hand her over to those men for his own life, and Eva was not the trusting type. Eva did not trust him, not even after the night of intimacy they shared. In fact, after that night, she seemed to move farther away from him. Maybe if she had trusted him, if she had known that he would always have her back, this would not have happened.

It was funny, Carl realized. The blame had gone full cycle, and somehow found a way to come back to him. It was his fault that he could not make her trust him. She was just recently transferred after all, and all he could think about was bedding her and getting all mushy with her.

Someone knocked at the door of the office and without waiting for him to say a word, slid right in. It was Eva.

"Hey," she said. "How are you holding up?"

He shrugged. He truly did not know. He did not know if he wanted to kill himself as an atonement for what he had done. He was not sure he would ever lift a finger to fight a rebellious group anymore. Much had been said about how these extremists groups were looking for a way to wipe off half of the world's population, how evil they were, but maybe the government was the problem instead. America masquerades under the pretense of democracy. He had been seeing the shift as the research for sustainable energy for life intensified. Buildings were seized and they were all in service to the government. Many things were happening that were over his head, but he felt the government's clampdown on its citizens was the most visible and the worst. It was almost as if a few individuals were trying to control the majority. That would mean there would be no elections anymore if it happened.

"The result just came back," Eva said, settling into the seat in front of him.

"The result was ready half an hour ago," Carl said. He knew. He had delivered this type of news before. It was always nasty. There was always no way to put it.

Eva sighed. She has gotten softer.

"Before I tell you anything," she said. "I have to let you know that I appreciate what you did for me back there."

Carl chuckled. There was nothing as far away from heartfelt as Carl's chuckle. His eyes were dead and expressionless. It was only his lips that moved, but nevertheless, he chuckled and looked Eva straight in the eyes.

"At first," he said.

"I owe you," she continued.

"You owe me nothing."

"I really didn't see us coming out of there alive. You..."

"Just read the damn result!"

Eva swallowed. In her eyes, Carl saw something new. Respect. But it was too late for all of that now. He was not going to be with her anymore, and even if she wanted him now, he would reject her. Something had changed. Something snapped when he went to fight their bot, something inside of him. Something he had no idea if it existed.

"The report says you are to be suspended," Eva finally said. "Indefinitely."

There was silence in the room when the news came. Carl had been expecting it, so he was not really surprised. He had been the boss of this precinct for close to 2 years now, and nothing had happened, no misconduct. The Botforce machines had never malfunctioned for once because he was always making sure they were maintained. Now, he was getting suspended indefinitely. He might as well quit. There was nothing for him to do here. He was afraid that he would start fighting against his own people the longer he stayed.

"Of course," he said, standing slowly from behind the desk. Eva would be in charge now, and they would send her one human that would run the place with her. Every other personnel was Botforce. They were quicker, stronger, and more efficient than humans. The humans were only there because they had emotions, and that was where the latest robots were failing at. "I was going to resign after all."

"What happened?" Eva asked, standing up quickly to block Carl's way as he walked around the desk.

"What do you mean?"

"What happened back there? Why were you fighting our own?"

"They were wasting time."

"I'm pretty sure that was not why you wanted to tear the robot to shreds."

"None of my business what you think, Eva. Get out of my way."

"I'm really concerned about you. They say you might become a threat."

"Who told you that?"

"The drones, they have accessed the situation, and they see you turning for the other side."

"I see."

"So what happened?"

"It is easier for you to form an alliance with robots than humans. Why can't you just request to be made into one?"

"This is not the time, Carl."

"You are right. This is not the time. Now, get the fuck out of my way!"

As Carl walked through the station precinct doors, leaving his badge on the table, he knew the dangers would start pretty soon. The government was clear on what they wanted: absolute submission. He could very well be an enemy now.

Detective Shaun

It was drizzling, and it was ice cold. As a child, Shaun would always run out whenever it was raining, and there would be hundreds of kids from the neighboring houses all around who wanted to play in the rain. They would dance and fight and just run around doing nothing except enjoy the coolness of the rain as it fell on their cracked, childish skins.

These days, Shaun hated the rain whenever he was not inside, watching people run from it. He hated the cold it brought and the medication that came afterward if he spent too much time in the rain.

He traipsed through the wet ground and hurried into the shed that had been erected over the crime scene.

"What do we have here?" He asked, pleased to see that there was a human here amidst all the robots. He was getting sick and tired of the humanoids. There was always something about them that set him off.

The one that walked up to him together with the human had gray eyes. Gray eyes meant they were the alpha and had stupid egos, which the real investigators had to contend with. Shaun had not believed yet that these robots were more efficient than humans. They were created, after all, by humans.

"A scientist. Shot dead in the late hours of the night in front of his friend's house," the man said. "Name's Lucas."

"Shaun," Shaun said.

"Were you the first responder?"

"We are," Lucas said, indicating the robot and himself.

Shaun frowned. He did not like what he was seeing here. Lucas and the robot seemed to have built a camaraderie, one that Shaun was uncomfortable with. Shaun had this fear that the robots would rise against humans one day. He tried everything that he could to learn about them, their weaknesses, and stuff. The only thing he was afraid of were the drones. There was no record of those ones anywhere.

"I'm Lobo," the robot said. "The victim was shot with a point 22 magnum bullet, probably a silencer, straight to the head and up close."

Shaun tried not to cringe. Lobo and his whining voice. Who names a robot Lobo? What sort of name was that? Why make them talk? Many would refer to Shaun as old-fashioned, but he did not care. He did not move around with robots and had one of the most embarrassing moments of his career when he had to call in drones to help him fend off an attack.

"Before you continue, Detective, this one is off the books. You have to report to us only," Lobo said.

"Are you out of your mind?" Shaun asked. He could not imagine reporting to a robot. "Do you even have a mind at all? Who's in charge here?"

Shaun noticed that Lucas was not going to step forward. He was moving back instead, and he set his eyes on the man.

"Are you not supposed to be in charge here?" Shaun queried further.

"Actually," Lucas said. "He is."

He indicated the robot and Shaun got angry. A robot? How the hell was he to coordinate with a robot? What does a robot know?

This shit is getting the fuck out of hand!

He walked away from the robot and the stupid *simp* of a human and pulled his phone out of his pocket. He still preferred having his phone in his hand, although he had been told that that might soon be a thing of the past. He dialed Aaron. Aaron was the man he answered to, the coordinator of detectives. He would know what to do.

"Hey, Shaun, how is it going down there?"

"It is fucked up. Why did you not tell me I would run into a robot here?"

"Listen, Shaun, I know you don't like it..."

"The stupid robot thinks I have to answer to it!"

There was silence on the line. With each minute that passed, Shaun got more infuriated. Aaron was probably thinking the same thing that the robot thought.

"That is a newly improved alpha robot with an intelligence quotient of..."

"I don't give a fuck what the IQ is. I am not answering to no damn robot. I would sooner get the fuck out of this place than to answer to any damn robot."

"You don't understand. Lobo is doing you a favor."

"What the fuck did you just say?"

"He is giving you a chance to work under him."

"This must be some stupid joke."

"I'm not joking, Shaun. We need to show what we are capable of in order not to be replaced by a robot."

"What are you saying?"

"Work for him. Show your skills. I'm sure he would keep you."

"Are you out of your mind?"

"I am talking to you as a friend that I would love to keep seeing."

Keep seeing. What the hell was that? Is there something that Aaron is trying to say?

The government was shrouded in secrecy. The government also hated opposition. His wife had warned him about getting in line, but he was too old to start changing his principles. By 55, he was no longer young. He did not care about robots and machines. The only machines he cared about were his cold, stainless steel and his brains.

"Aaron?"

The line went dead.

"Well?" It was the annoying whiny voice of Lobo. At this point, Shaun hated the whiny voice more than ever. He wanted nothing more than to turn around and throw a punch into the face of the mindless robot.

He did not. The premonition in Aaron's voice was still settling in his mind. The look on the robot's face was another thing. There was a smile on his face. The smile of a maniac.

Shaun was a smart man, and sometimes, he knew that pride had to go. He knew that his ego would not always keep him alive. He smiled at the bot.

"I guess we can do it your way, eh?"

Heather

Heather walked into the house, as usual, her parents were making a pretense of staying away from work to mourn. In the living room, Johannes sat with a newspaper. Heather was not sure he was reading it. She could see in him this uncontrollable desire to get back to what he was doing before this little incident occurred. It was the kind of mild irritation one got when he kept swathing a fly that would not just go away.

She walked past the living room without saying a word to him and was about to climb up the stairs when he spoke.

"You know you cannot keep acting like you don't know us," Johannes said, looking up from the newspaper. He had big, round glasses covering his eyes, and Heather could make out gray hairs at the fringe of his hair. He did not look remorseful. He looked... resigned.

"You know you can get me out of your house whenever you want?" She asked.

"Don't be silly, you are my daughter."

"You seem to remember that only when it is convenient for you."

"We remember a lot of things when we are well-rested and in our right mind."

"I don't have time for this."

Heather started back up the stairs.

"What do you have time for? You have been in your room all day. Then you go to the cemetery. You do nothing. What could be taking up your time?"

At the head of the stairs, Heather paused and looked down at her father.

"Grief," she said. "Grief for a life you threw away because of your stupid, selfish reason."

With that, she walked into her room and banged the door shut. It was a statement showing she did not want anyone knocking at her door. Not a Botservant, not her parents. She wanted to forget them all.

Inside, she discovered she left the TV on when she went downstairs. The screen was part of the glass wall. As she settled on the bed, she heard the news being reeled out by the reporter.

Anonymous reports tell us that a scientist by the name of Roland Gilmore was shot dead in front of a friend's house. He had gone to the countryside for a little vacation...

Heather turned off the TV. She was not ready to hear more bad news about the country or even the world at large because that was all everything seemed to be giving her. Where she was, it seemed the end was near too. There were too many people than the earth could accommodate, but these people spent the last moments of their lives living out their fantasies. They felt if humans had to die, then everybody had to go.

It was unselfish and she liked it. Scientists these days would map out the group of people that should die to give the earth a breather. Their names and their family members' name would not be there of course.

Heather's mind went back to Andre. So secretive, and at the same time, so open. It seemed the Andre guy was trying to tell her something, something about the place she left. It could only be about her parents or the people they work for.

She pulled out the flash from her pocket and set it down on the table. Before she pressed play for the hologram to play out of the flash, her eyes went to the door to make sure it was locked. Andre had been adamant about her watching it alone. She wanted to see what her sister thought of her, and afterward, she would decide if she wanted someone else to see.

The door was locked. She swallowed and tapped on the flash. Holograms sprang out of it. The action was already underway. She saw a room full of alpha bots, getting ready to be fitted into the environment. Someone had a camera. Another person was whispering inaudibly. Then suddenly, she saw herself.

Shocked, she almost fell back into the bed before she realized it was a robot. It was not yet completed, but it looked so eerily like her that she was disturbed.

I don't know what this is about, Marie's voice came from the hologram. I can almost swear my parents want to replace their child.

The video skipped, and another scene presented itself. In this scene, someone was somewhere, hiding, recording her parents.

"Maybe we should not do it," Johannes said.

"*Why shouldn't we? We will have our daughter back,*" Laura replied.

"*To get her consciousness into this robot, we would have to lure her home. We would have to do it against her wish. It does not sound nice.*"

"*It has to be done. Think of the new generation of humans. She would be on the front lines, and most importantly, under our control. Press a button and she would be out cold.*"

"*She will hate us for this,*" Johannes said.

"*We don't have a choice.*"

Heather was frozen where she sat. She was frozen and confused, but she could not bring herself to turn off the flash. She continued watching, getting more frightened at what she would discover.

CHAPTER 8

Mira.

Mira saw the news, and for hours, she could not do anything except to keep staring at the TV screen. It was surreal, unbelievable. She had just left Roland days ago and could still remember how worried he looked when she said she was going to stay with her parents. The concern on his face, the jealousy. She knew Roland did not like her parent's one bit, and she also knew that between them, there was no love lost. But she could not bring herself to choosing one and leaving the other. They were all her family and she loved them.

Someone quickly turned off the TV, but Mira's eyes did not leave the screen. She continued staring at it like she had lost her mind.

"Mira," her mother called. Mrs. Melinda looked worried for her child. For all their disagreements, Mira meant the world to her, and she could not imagine losing her, not even to the impostor scientist, Roland, but she feared that the worst had happened.

Mira did not respond even as Melinda shook her. She continued staring vacantly at the space.

"Mira, come on, let's get you to bed."

Mira looked at her mother like she was just seeing her for the first time.

"What did I just see?" She asked. Her voice came out a whimper that she could hardly hear her own self.

"It's nothing. Come on. Athens, take her to bed."

The robot called Athens moved forward. It was a humanoid, even mirroring concern on its face as it moved towards Mira.

"It's nothing!" Mira burst out. "It is nothing!" She screamed again.

She got to her feet, eyes blazing. Melinda was taken aback. Athens paused as well, and they both exchanged glances like they were both humans.

"I have to go back," Mira said.

"Go back? No, baby, you can't."

"I must... I have to see for myself. Maybe, it is all a trick. Maybe he's been abducted and declared dead. Maybe he is still alive. I will find him."

"Listen to me, Mira! He is gone. He is dead. You will find nothing."

"Then, I have to confirm. I have to be sure."

Mira stood up and dashed towards her room.

Melinda held her palms to her head as Mira dashed up the stairs.

In her room, Mira picked the few things that she thought she would need in this journey towards finding what had really happened to her fiancé. She convinced herself that the report she had just seen was a lie and that Roland was somewhere safe.

Still breathing hard, she swiped the phone built into her hand and dialed Roland's number. She hoped she would hear his voice at the other end telling her that he was alive and everything was just a ploy to distract the enemy, the extremists who would not stop breaking into his house.

Extremists! The bloody hypocrites and cowards! She remembered how they broke into the house and almost ended her. That was when she had needed Roland the most, and he was not there. Now, she feared that when Roland needed her the most, she was here in her parents' house just because she wanted to be pampered and have robots attending to each and her every need.

The phone rang and rang, and nobody picked the call. She dialed again and waited. There was the same result. She kept dialing, afraid that she would keep calling the phone till the next day as it was already evening. Still, no one picked.

She was making the last call, after which she decided she would head down to the countryside.

"Hello, Detective Shaun here," a voice said at the other end of the call.

Mira froze, what was a detective doing with Roland's phone? Had he run into trouble? What was he doing with the police? From the sound of his voice, Mira was certain it was a human behind the phone and not a robot.

"What are you doing with Roland's phone?" She asked before the cop had had a chance to say anything.

"If you want to find out about Roland, you can get down to Waterloo," the detective said and ended the call.

For a minute or more, Mira kept staring at the phone, perplexed... what was that? Then, another thought came into her mind. The detective did not say that Roland was dead. That meant something. That meant that he was alive and he was being kept somewhere. The news of his death was a specious endeavor to mislead the tenacious group of terrorists that were springing up all over the country to 'protect the earth'. Stupid groups, all of them. She had to go. She had to see where Roland was being kept.

She tried the number a couple more times before she realized the phone had been turned off.

Quickly, she threw some clothes into a bag and headed downstairs. She was going to see her lover and nothing would stop her. It was stupid what she did, leaving him to come back here when she knew that the place was dangerous. Roland was a nerd who could hardly defend himself.

Downstairs, she noticed that the bots were blocking the entrance. There was Athens, Micah, and Livah. Three of them... before now, they were dedicated to making her comfortable, but they were now hindering her movement.

Melinda sat on the sofa looking at her with pity.

"You can't leave, baby. It is not safe out there," Melinda said.

"What is this?" Mira asked like she did not hear her mom.

She walked towards the door but Micah and Livah dragged her back to the sofa, kicking, and deposited her on the seat.

"This is stupid. Let me go!"

"What if something happens to you out there?" Melinda asked. "I would never forgive myself."

"Roland is out there."

"He is already dead."

"He is not dead... I called him!"

Carl

Immediately he left the station, he knew he was in trouble. No, it was not the kind of trouble that involved rebels surrounding him while he called in the robot to come to save him. This type of trouble had no savior. Or maybe the solution to the troubles were those he had already alienated.

He got into his car, disabled every autopilot mode, and drove into the street with it. He was concerned about going to his house while he was no longer working for the government. But he knew that it did not matter. Wherever he went, this new kind of trouble that he had just incurred would follow him around. The drones, they were always in the sky, always present, watching one even when he thought he was not being watched.

As the car sped through the traffic, he wondered why the drone did not fly down at once to help the two human officers get out of trouble. The drones were the closest thing to God, and they were working independently, accessing dangers and situations. The only control that the makers had over them was the kill switch—this ended everything.

The day was just only disappearing for the dust to take its shift, and Carl did not like that one bit. He was thinking fast, but nothing was coming to his mind. Could it be that his people set him up? The drones.

Like about 30 percent of the population, he lived in fear of computers malfunctioning or getting a life of their own. If the drones ever got independent, and the kill-switch is disabled, there is no imagining what the drones could do. They would spiral out of control, and humanity would have only themselves to blame.

After driving for a while, he pulled over by the roadside and took out a cigarette pack from his glove compartment. It had always been there, doing nothing. Maybe he had put it there because of days like this, when he would lose his mind and need a smoke. What he really needed, however, was too high. The cigarette was like a preamble, something to occupy his mind for the meantime. He knew the den of thieves and low-lives who lack of evidence kept out of prison. He could go to these people and get what he wanted from them, any type of drugs at all.

Someone knocked on his window, and his hand quickly went to his gun. He knew that some privileges would be taken away from him, but he did not know it was going to be this fast. When he looked closer though, he realized that the man by the side of his car did not look like he was sent by the government. With his hand still on the gun, he pressed the remote for the window to wind down, then he positions the barrel of the gun to be pointed at the man while out of the man's view.

"What?" He asked.

"I seem to have missed my way, and I was wondering if you could give me a lift," the man said.

Carl shook his head. He was not in the mood to give anybody a ride or talk to anybody.

"No, no rides," he said and wound the glass up again.

When Carl heard the first bang on his car, he quickly looked behind him. The fellow he had refused a ride was by the side of his car, hitting hard at it with a stick. As he looked behind, he saw two other men with the fellow. They had stones with them. A quick throw shattered the window of the car. Carl was incensed, but he knew he was not going to do anything to them. Quickly, he started the car, stepped on the gas pedal, and sped off.

Behind him, the incensed fellows were growing into a little crowd, screaming about preferential treatments and the government's biases. Carl was already aware of this. It was now that he was getting away from the set establishment that he was beginning to see things he should have seen before.

He drove straight to his house and parked the car in the garage, then he walked into his house. He had tendered his resignation, and before long, this house would be taken from him and given to his replacement. Again, now he was going to be among the crowd, he realized how uncomfortable they must have found it living in a tenement building, jam-packed spaces, and terrible ventilation system.

He walked into his room and sat on the bed. He had made sure he locked the door downstairs in case any of the men who had attacked him on the way followed him to this place. They would have to breach the perimeter and an alarm would set off, preparing him for them. He sighed. He was not going to fight them. He had already done enough harm.

He shifted his bed from the center of the room to the side and pulled the rug off the floor. There was a door down there, but it looked just like the marbled floor. He had to feel around before he was able to insert his thumb in the lock. His thumbprint was read and the ground slowly opened.

There was a series of steps that led into the ground. Without wasting time, Carl proceeded down it. He walked quickly. Once he was in, he closed the latch and hurried down the stairs in the darkness, groping and feeling his way about.

On the ground floor, there was light in a single room, which was where the stairs stopped. He walked into the room, and it was like walking into an armory. Years ago, Carl was one of those that had been charged with disposing of the old weapons, which were now considered obsolete. He kept a few for himself for reasons he did not even understand. He took down the guns now, a pistol, and slipped just one bullet into it.

"You have fucked up, Carl," he whispered and knelt on the ground. "May God find something in your soul worth saving."

He rolled the gun chamber and cocked the weapon, then put it against his head. Finally, he would be at peace with himself. The guilt that had pressed against his mind these past few days were still hanging around, trying to drown him. If he was not existing anymore, the grief would not have anywhere to stay. He would finally be free.

He shut his eyes and pulled the trigger.

CHAPTER 9

Barry

H e stood at the window, looking at the Café. He was thinking about the woman again. She was way different from the women he had had. A lot of people thought people like him were nerds who did not have enough time to go out there and socialize with people, but he was the opposite. Whenever a theory failed to make sense, Doctor Barry Stivers would walk out of the laboratory, move down to a clubhouse, and party all night till he found someone to fuck. Working for the government meant he had more money and privilege than most men. Apart from that, he was also handsome, with thick lashes covering his eyes. He was the dream of many ladies, and he got them without even letting them know who he worked for.

Those ladies were sexy and made him have a good time, but none of them was as energetic as Dora Martinez. None of them were as mysterious. She made him want to know her more, and he was left wondering if it was deliberate, if that was what she really wanted to achieve, or if she did not want to see him anymore. He could still remember her face when she dismissed him. There was no atom of expression on her face. To her, she was probably just one of the men she had a thing with. She painted a picture of a predator, going around hunting for men to sleep with. Other predators hunted for money and information. Barry was suddenly alarmed.

What if what she wanted was information about the work he was on? That would explain the way she came straight to his table.

No, it would not, you knucklehead. You were the only male in the place at the time.

The thought burst the doctor's ego. Could it be that she simply settled for him to satisfy her sexual hunger? He felt used, but he could see the irony and appreciate it. He too wanted to use somebody. Why then was he concerned about being used?

He spared a glance at the Café one more time before he walked away from the window and went towards the fridge. He got a beer from the fridge and shut it, then he returned to the window. Yesterday, he stayed here all day after the presentation, wondering if he was going to see the woman walk into the Café. But it seemed the woman had lost whatever interest it was that pulled her to the place—so much for satisfying a need.

The doctor went back into the room and sat at his laptop. The screen was projected on a glass wall and the glass table had a keypad. Quickly, he typed out the name of the woman in full, and her picture appeared. There were many other Dora Martinezes but her picture set her apart. She still looked like she looked before.

Daughter to a high school teacher who died during a flood. There was precious little on the lady that, once again, Barry had an alarm somewhere set off in his head. He chuckled and pushed it away to somewhere at the back of his mind. He was not ready to deal with any of that now. Besides, he had been assured that he was sufficiently protected.

There was no known residence for the surviving Martinez. Both parents had been killed by the flood, and Dora subsequently disappeared. Barry chuckled. They would have a lot to discuss if he saw her again. It seemed inappropriate, considering the kind of project he was undertaking. It was an unnecessary risk, but it made him feel alive. Yesterday, he had replied greetings like a man who had recently won a lottery, so much that everyone he worked with was pleasantly surprised.

Barry to the window again and stared out at the Café. Maybe Dora was somewhere watching the Café too, waiting for him to make his move first. If he did not get into the Café, then the woman would not come. Again, it seemed suspicious. Why would she be monitoring him? But he wanted to see things to an end, so he pulled his overcoat from the chair where he had hung it and was about to find his way downstairs when his phone rang.

He paused, staring at the screen of the little phone that he carried. He was supposed to have a phone built into his hand, but he did not entirely trust the system. Sometimes, he worried about the government spying on him even though they were both on the same bed.

"Hello," he said, picking the call.

"Good work, yesterday, Doctor Barry."

Barry could not believe it. The President had taken it upon himself to call Barry instead of calling through his contact, Ned, the man who kept promising him that he was protected. Well, guess what? He did not believe it.

"Mr. President," Barry gushed. "I er... I was not expecting your call."

"A lot of people are not expecting my call, Barry, but you should have though. You have saved our planet entirely by your own doing."

"Thank you, sir."

Barry wondered if this was the right time to come out with the truth and tell everyone that his idea belonged to his late brother, and that his calculations were mostly not his own. When he saw the implications of what his brother was doing, he was awed, even though he knew he should not have read his late brother's diary.

"I hope you can start production immediately. We need this energy to stabilize our environment and keep hope alive."

"I'm aware of that, sir but..."

The line went dead. Barry took the phone from his ears and stood looking at it for some time. He wanted to tell the President that the product was not stable yet. It was invented to provide sustainable energy and save the earth, yet any little mistake could cause an explosion of atomic proportions. He was afraid for the countryside, but to have this produced everywhere. It would be a tragedy, one that would forever haunt him.

Levi

Home did not smell like home. It smelled like a disappointment. He did not know how he would tell his parents he had been thrown out of the school team. His little brother was looking up to him, waiting for when he would make history, so he could follow in his footsteps. His older brother was late, probably looking down at him from wherever he was with great disappointment. Levi sighed.

He knocked on the door, and his younger brother, Joe, pulled the door open.

"Mom, it's Levi!" Joe screamed, running inside and leaving Levi standing there.

Levi followed the boy in and shut the door quickly before the neighbors would hear that he was home. Already, Joe thought of him as some kind of hero. He did not blame the boy. When he was 7, the same age his brother was, he had the same thought of his elder brother until that one died.

The tenement had apartments that were too close together in the quest to conserve space and provide dwellings for the population of humans who were ballooning out of proportion. He would often hear Ashley, the girl next door, shouting at her brother.

"You are back," his mom said as he walked into the living room. There were just two rooms with a toilet and bathroom, and it was enough for them. His mother was in the kitchen connected to the living room, staring at him proudly.

"Yes, ma."

"How did it go today?"

I was kicked out of the team, mother. The coach said I was not good enough. He would not let me run the 100 meters. Everything is biased for the rich, people that have connections in the government.

"It went well... I came first today."

"Wow. That is beautiful," his mom exclaimed. "Joe and I were thinking about making you talk to the coach. I think you are fast and you should go for 100 meters instead. But since you are already coming first in 400 meters, maybe you should stay there."

"I told him," Levi said.

"What?"

"I told the coach."

"You did?"

It did not go well. He kicked me out of the team because of it.

"Yes, he said I should stay where I was."

"I think so too, I'm making your favorite."

Levi walked into the room where he stayed alone and fell on the bed. His mother was doing everything she could so he would become a celebrated champion in the sports world and represent the country. That was the only way one could be anything in this country apart from having too much wealth.

On the bed, he wondered if his lies were too much. He did not want anything that would break her heart or destroy his people's faith in him.

Tired of staying alone in the room, getting sad over the whole of his life-shattering to fragments before his eyes, he got up from the bed and walked to the door. He opened the door just as Joe was about pushing it open, and the younger boy staggered into his room. Joe almost fell to the ground as Levi stepped out of the way.

"What do you want?" Levi asked, his voice colder and harsher than he meant for it to be.

"Mom said food is ready," Joe replied as he regained his balance.

"I'm not eating now. I'm going for a walk."

Levi walked out of his room and walked down the stairs, intent on getting to the door before his mom would realize he was on his way out.

"Mom! Levi said he is going for a walk!" Joe announced, running down the stairs behind his elder brother.

Joe could be such a nuisance when he really was fond of a person. He would snoop around the person and never give him a break, even a little. Before now, Levi would laugh it off as the big, elder brother who was going to be a star and still remain family. But now, it infuriated him.

"Shut up, Joe!" He yelled, and pulled the front door open.

"Where are you going?" His mother asked, sticking her head out from the kitchen window.

"Outside, for a walk," Levi said. "Don't wait up for me."

"Your food will get cold..."

The door banged shut before the woman could finish what she was saying and Levi found himself in the street.

It was already dark. The road was filled with people from all walks of life taking the sidewalks. The main road was reserved for government vehicles and the vehicles of the capitalist geniuses who had wormed their way into the hearts of the government. Bicycles stayed on the other side of the road specifically created for them.

Kevin walked with his hands in his pockets, worried about the division that he had been too blind to see because he was the coach's darling. It was glaring now that the world did not belong to poor people. Rather it belonged to the rich and the government helped make it stay that way.

Further ahead, he saw Ashley through the crowd of people. She was standing by a statue of a family. The statue symbolized the policies that governments were making to help control overpopulation: a family of only one child.

It was either two parents, two children, or one child. Recently, the one-child policy had been enforced, and families who broke it had their children put to sleep and saved for a future no one knew if it was coming.

He walked up to Ashley and stopped by the statue. He wanted to talk to her, but the only thing that came from his mouth was 'hi'.

"Hey," Ashley said and looked away. She looked like she was waiting for someone, and Levi wondered if he should just let her be and walk away.

He turned to look at the crowd, wondering if anyone was seeing him and his awkward act. The crowd of people walking by was not at all interested in him or the girl, and the darkness provided enough cover.

"Hey, you are the big next door," Ashley said, calling his attention.

He turned back to Ashley. She was smiling now. He noticed that her eyes were green rimmed with golden specs. She had a straight, delicate nose, and had a ring at the end of it. Levi had always known that Ashley was beautiful with her remarkable eyes and pink, soft-looking lips, but with her smiling at him, he lost his senses.

"Ye...yes," he managed to say.

"Going somewhere?" She asked.

"Well, not really. I just came out to take a walk," Levi swallowed. His voice was finally returning to him. He cleared his throat and hoped Ashley would not know that his palms were sweating.

"So, you can walk with me then?" She asked.

"Sure."

"Come on, there is a friend of mine I have been waiting for. Looks like he is not coming out today."

Ashley took his hand to his surprise and joined the traffic of people walking down the street. He walked along with her like a zombie without any idea of where she was going to.

From time to time, she would look at him as they walked along the street.

"I heard you are an athlete," she said, almost hopping along the road now.

Levi wished she would stop hopping like someone that was over-excited. She was almost reminding him of his brother, Joe.

"I run," he said modestly.

"You run," she mimicked. "Such a modest reply."

"Well, I do."

"How fast can you run?"

"I don't know."

Levi did not want anyone bringing up running to him again. It was annoying him, besides he felt like shit after what he told his family. Why did he listen to Jeremy? If he had not, he would still be on the team. He would learn how to run the 400 meters, conserve his energy at the beginning, and then burst forward towards the end. But he had to listen to the raving lunatic that thought himself to be his friend. The fool was no longer his friend.

"I got kicked out of the team," he said before he realized what he was saying.

"What?"

"The coach and politics. I got kicked out of the team because the coach would not let me replace another athlete who I was clearly better than."

"Damn, that sucks."

She laid him into another street, a quieter street, this time. They walked till they got to an abandoned building and got inside.

"This person you want to replace knows the coach?"

"The father donates to the school."

"Fuck... that's messed up."

"I know, I don't even know what to do or why I'm telling you this."

"You love my smile... You trust my eyes."

The doors of the building were broken down. The windows were open. Inside had sofas with torn cushions. Levi paused at the door. He had not seen Ashley as someone that would come to this type of place. She moved into the first room.

"You and I, we are particularly vulnerable this night. If not, how can I explain bringing you to this place?"

"What is this place?"

"In a world filled with the madness that we have today, I supposed everyone needs to retreat once in a while from everything... with people you select."

Levi was humored to think that Ashley selected him.

"I really don't know why I brought you here," she continued, walking up to him.

She stared him down. He was taller, but that was exactly how he felt. She was probably used to being praised for her beauty, and she had in abundance, plus a physique that went right to his head. She was made of an hourglass, tiny at the waist, thick at the hips and thighs. She knew the aura of sensuousness that she exuded.

She turned away from him and went to sit on one of the torn cushions. As Levi watched, she pulled out a wrap from her pocket, slipped it between her lips, and lit it with a golden-colored lighter. She inhaled deeply.

"I'm full of surprises, ain't I?"

Levi thought of walking away from the place. He was a runner and had been warned about inhaling these things and how it was bad for his health. But then again, he remembered that he had been kicked out of the team and might lose his scholarship just because his coach was a coward. He walked into the room and sat down.

"Many people leave me sitting here and walk away," she said, chuckling. "It's crazy how humans want to leave longer once they hear humanity is in danger of dying off."

"You are not afraid of not existing?" Levi asked.

"No, are you?"

"Not anymore."

He stretched out his hand for a drag and Ashley let him have the stick. He inhaled deeply, held it, and handed the stick back to Ashley. He started coughing.

"Easy," Ashley said, laughing and rubbing his back.

After almost a minute of coughing, Levi finally recovered his breathing space from the Marijuana. Ashley was laughing at him.

"You have never had this before," she said.

Levi shook his head. Footsteps sounded outside the door. The two new friends stopped talking and listened.

Someone stopped in front of the door, his shadow elongated by the street lamp further up the road and falling on the two.

In the semi-darkness, Levi thought he was waiting till his eyes got used to the dimly lit place. When the strangers' eyes eventually did. They moved past his face to Ashley's, then back to his face again.

"Who's this, Ashley?" The fellow asked, indicating Levi.

"Levi, this is Rami, the friend I was waiting for. Rami, this is Levi, my new friend, an athlete."

Rami grunted.

Heather

She wanted to go out of her room and confront the people that had been masquerading as her parents ever since she was born, but she held back herself. She did not know the extent to which this had carried, and she was not prepared to take it head-on. She was certain it was her sister in the video that she had just watched. The girl had not been on her parents' side all the while she was there with them. She had been pretending, merely. Her parents were mad. Science had created lunatics out of them, and she could no longer recognize them.

She sat on the bed, wondering about what she had just seen. Towards the end of the video, Marie had said: I'm not sure father is father.

It scared Heather and infuriated her at the same time. The importance of what those words mean. It would make their mother a monster.

Someone started knocking on the door. Heather ignored it. Her spine was literally shaking. Could it be the reason that she was lured back here? Laura hardly ever spoke with her. Did she now want obedient children too badly that she would replace them with machines?

The knocking stopped.

"Heather, it's your mom, open the door. We need to talk."

Again, Heather maintained a stoic silence. Her eyes went to the door and she almost screamed in fear. The door was locked with her biometrics but the doctor could have easily added her own when she was away. She dashed up from the bed and hurried towards the door. Quickly, she engaged the good, old-fashioned bolts that they had been so gracious to include in the house's security system and stood in front of the door, waiting for her mom's next action.

"Heather? What is wrong with you?"

"You are everything wrong, Laura. You and your stupid government projects."

"Can I just come in?"

"I don't want to see your face."

"What would your sister say about this behavior?"

"Since you have killed her, we will never know."

"Take that back!"

"You killed her. Did you ever ask her what she wanted to be?" Heather kept talking. She wanted to push the discussion away from a direct accusation. She was not certain of it. Also, if Laura knew that she knew, she would be in a big soup.

"Stop this!" Laura cried. Her voice was infused with passion and pain, so much that Heather was almost tempted to pull open the door. But she controlled her hands. If what she watched was real, then the woman outside was a good actor. She knew what she had to do. The man she met in the burial ground. She had to see him again. There was just too much going on that she knew nothing about. She was like a child that had been thrust into the whirlwind.

She heard rescinding footsteps and realized that the woman was tired of calling her. She heaved a sigh of relief and went to sit in the bed. Memories flooded her mind.

As a child, she was reminded that her father was playful. He worked hard and sometimes would not come home. But when he did, he was always playful. It was easy to see that he missed them. Then, she became a teenager and the man would barely show any emotion. Maybe, it was not him. Maybe, it was something else. In other things, like reading newspapers and drinking early morning coffee, he remained the same person, but that emotion that Heather knew him for was gone. He was the one she could run to when Laura forced her to learn what she did not like. She wanted to sing and play instruments, but Laura said the times did not demand for such nonsense. The world foul end very soon, they said, and knowing how to string a guitar would not get her far in the next if she survived humanity. They thought her to shoot, and fight since she was slow in science, or deliberately just did not want to learn. *Do you realize this would make you a servant to your younger sister?* Her mom had asked one day. She did not care. Then, she ran away.

She stood from the bed and walked to the window. There was too much space at the back of their garden. Heather wondered why few people should have so many while others had few spaces. It was sick.

She remembered Andre again and wondered where he had come from. There were few people like him around. In the midst of a few, humanity was struggling with each other for the few remaining. Most people were trying to gather as much as they could, but Andre was out there, monitoring her.

The time was already 11 pm, and she could not make it out of the house that night. She dreads sleeping here, listening to the footsteps of people walking up and down the stairs, wondering when her door would be broken down and her mind stolen. Her parents were even worse than the government. They wanted to control everything, down to their children.

She walked to the bed and sat back down on it. She did not need any clothes. First thing, in the morning, if she survived the night, she would be out of here. She hoped she would be able to find Andre. There was still a lot he had not told him.

CHAPTER 10

Carl

T he gun was still in his hand, and there was no hole in his head. He still knelt there, breathing hard. He was close to death. He could swear he had seen the people he had sent to the beyond, people demanding who were accountability from the government. He should be there with them. He should be gone, dead, in the other dimension of life, and not existing.

He put the gun back on the desk where he had taken it from. There were other guns there, even the outdated AK-47 that no one used these days. The laser gun would make a toy gun of this weapon of death. But he did not care. He loved the old-fashioned weapons. He loved the old-fashioned ways. Maybe that was why he kept feeling for the people they were meant to take down. Eva behaved like the cold Botforce soldiers, annoying, dead, and without any form of life in her.

He got out of the room and headed towards the stairs. At the top, he climbed out and shut the whole back. Then, he smoothed it over before placing the table on it.

His external camera came on, and a monitor showed people at his door. It was Eva with two Botforce officers behind her. She pressed the bell and waited.

Carl went to the mic.

"Tell those things to back off," Carl said. "You are the only one coming inside."

It was easy to identify Botforce officers. No matter how humanoid they made them, they still had their tags and the awkward movement that followed them. These awkward movements, however, disappeared in fights. Besides, not all of them were humanoids. Only one of the robots at the door was a humanoid.

"We have come for the properties of the police force," Eva said. Her voice was cold, unemotional like she did not know him anymore, but it was to be expected. The police force was like a cult these days, once a person got out of it, he was ostracized. He would be blamed for making the force tinier and stretched in the face of the rising insecurity.

"You could not wait," Carl said.

Eva looked at the humanoid bot and turned back to the camera.

"Open the door," she said.

"Are you deaf? Tell those motherfucking things to back off!"

Eva stood still like she had heard nothing he said, then she turned to the humanoid and began whispering with him. Carl could not make out what they were saying even though he tried hard to. They were speaking way too fast... wait, what the fuck! They were speaking in codes. Computer fucking codes! What was the world turning into? No, Eva could not be a humanoid! No, no, no. He fucking slept with this woman. Who was she? What was going on?

"The other officer can remain at the door, but I am coming in with him," Eva said, turning to the camera and indicating the humanoid.

"Are you a robot?" Carl asked, flabbergasted.

"Not exactly," Eva replied. "Now, open the door."

"No, you remain right there and I will have everything sent out to you."

"You don't understand," Eva said. "We have a warrant."

"A warrant? For what?"

"To search your house and take what is ours."

Carl had forgotten the protection the police force offered. He could literally be dealing in heroine and no one would bat an eyelid, but once he got out of the force, it seemed like everything would be geared towards arresting and putting him in prison. Carl knew he could not let them into the house, and at the same time, he did not know how he was going to keep them away from it.

"I can't let you into my house. Machines are monsters, and you are just one of them. I would prefer a human conducts the search."

"We are not asking for your permission... open the door!"

Carl thought fast. He had to. Many things in his house could get him out of the way for a long time. The police were always after their own, once they try to get away. He had heard stories and dismissed them because he was on the side of the law and felt the cops could do no wrong. Now, he was idly wondering about visiting the extremists, learning their cause, and maybe standing with them. The scales had fallen from his eyes.

"I'm still an officer, and you are not getting into my house," he finally said.

"But you resigned," Eva said.

"Something I said in the heat of the moment. I will serve my suspension and return to work for my country."

Eva turned to the humanoid again, and they conversed with their silly codes again. Carl watched them intently. He hoped his bluff would hold.

Finally, Eva turned to look back at the camera.

"You should come to take your badge at the office then," she said. "You left it there... we could give you a ride."

The time was 11:16 at night, and there was no way in hell Carl was going on a ride with three robots at night. They could kill him and dump his body by the roadside. A lot of people were dying these days as if the government is taking terrible measures to reduce the population. He did not want to be among the statistics.

"I will come for it tomorrow. It is night already, and I'm not on duty," he said.

"Very well then, chief," Eva said. "See you after your indefinite suspension."

She stressed the 'indefinite', and Carl got the feeling that she did not want him to return, nor was she expecting him to. It hurt a sensitive part of him that their intimacy meant nothing to her. Then, he cursed himself for not noticing anything odd about her, like her coldness. Humans who were enhanced usually lacked emotions.

He sighed when they got into the car and drove off. Then, he returned to the hole in the middle of his living room. He had to pack out the guns before tomorrow. In fact, he had to leave the place this night.

As he packed the guns into the bags, he made a mental note to start leaving in the early hours of the morning when he was sure the cops were not snooping around. He knew the drill, knew they would watch him for a while to see if he would sneak out.

He walked to the window and watched scanned the periphery for signs of any cop around.

Barry

When Barry finally convinced himself to go to the Café, it was morning, the next day. He walked down the street like a man lost in thought. While he was thinking about Dora and the mystery he was yet to discover, there was this ill-feeling at the back of his mind that he was going to destroy the world. But he countered that with the thought that the world was already half-gone. The number of terrorist organizations that were springing up all over the town was enough testament to the fact. They could not be controlled and had almost thrown the country into a downward spiral. A semblance of sanity had been brought by the drones. He called it the singular most important invention of mankind. The drones eliminated threats without the red-tapism of investigations.

The cage was empty when he got there with only the robot attendant being the one in charge. It did not bother him much. He had always known that these shops would be taken over by robots anyway, while their owners stayed at home lazing around. That was where humanity was headed: hardworking robots and lazy humans.

He sat down at the table and the robot wheeled itself towards him.

"What can we get for you, sir?" The robot asked.

Ungainly creatures, these robots. He would prefer a humanoid, but they were too creepy. What he wanted was an invention that would save the world, and that was exactly what he had gotten, but the feeling of being an impostor still would not let him be.

"Coffee," he said.

The creature wheeled away to prefer his coffee, and he was left alone with his own thoughts. He wondered if the lady would come today. He could not wait to talk with her again.

As he waited, he looked around. The Café was still eerily silent. Slowly, the hairs on his nape rose. There was something going on that he was not aware of. He stood up and walked towards the back of the Café. The robot was no longer there.

The door to the Café suddenly opened and a figure rushed inside. At first, Barry was terrified and stunned. He was rooted to the spot, till he realized that it was the face of the woman that he had been after, staring at him.

"Dora," he said, surprised. "I didn't know I was going to..."

"Get down!"

Before Barry could do anything, she already pushed him down. The glasses shattered next, followed by a burst of gunfire. The guns were the old, obsolete guns, but one that would still be able to end a human life.

"What is happening?" Barry asked, petrified.

"There are people here to kill you. Do exactly as I say and you will be fine."

Dora spoke with a resounding calmness and looked like she knew exactly what she was doing. She slipped out a knife and started crawling on the floor towards the back door.

"Follow me," she said.

Barry had no option than to follow her. Sometimes, he wondered about the use of living when everything was going to shit, but this was not one of such times. When faced with death, it was almost always clear that humans would choose life.

At the door, Dora got up at the same time someone burst through the door.

"They..." the fellow began. Whatever else he wanted to say stayed buried in his throat together with the knife that Dora planted there. She pulled the knife out of his neck savagely and helped him to the ground. He had a pistol, one of the old typed. Without wasting time, Dora picked the pistol up and continued on her way. She did not look back for once to see if the doctor was following her. Instead, she slipped out of the building through the backdoor and headed for the car park. It was only then that she turned back to see if the doctor was following her.

Barry ran up behind her panting and struggling to steady the beating of his heart. Life-threatening messages were one thing. He had been getting those most of his life. Working for the government meant many people in the population were not happy with him. But to actually have an attack on his life, was an entirely different thing.

"Where is your car?" Dora asked.

"Car?" The doctor's mind was freezing up. He could not think. The only thing he could do was follow the woman in front of him.

"You did not come out with a car?" She asked, flabbergasted.

At the same time, one of the assailants turned around the corner and she shot the guy in the head.

"I stay around here," Barry finally said, fear freeing his tongue for a while.

"You can't stay here. It's not safe," she said.

She was off again, crouching low and staying out of sight. Barry followed her until they got to a motorcycle. She worked fast. Barry was too busy looking around to see what she was doing.

The motorcycle came on, drawing the attention of the assailants and the doctor. Barry saw her on top of the motorcycle already and once again found that his feet were rooted to a spot.

"What are you doing? Get the fuck behind me!" Dora shouted.

It was the way she snapped without acknowledging his status that threw him out of his petrified state. He jumped behind Dora on the backseat of the motorcycle and held on for dear life as she made her way out to the road and down it. Occasional bursts of gunfire followed them, but they had gone too far to be hit. Yet, Barry would not take his hands from around her.

Mira

With the robots blocking her way, there was nothing she could do. She had struggled with them for close to 30 minutes and they still would not budge. They deposited her on the sofa and left her there.

She struggled to get up and saw her mother watching her as if she was a mad woman. She was incensed against her. Inside of her, she was bubbling to the brim with anger and frustration. She could imagine Roland tied up somewhere, helpless, held there by one of the mad groups that claimed they were healing the earth.

"What have I ever done to you?!" She yelled at her mom.

"He's not worth it," Melinda said. She seemed taken aback by Mira's outburst, but she did not stand from her seat. "You don't have to kill yourself because of him."

"That is exactly what I will do. Without him, this life is not worth living."

"Don't say that baby," Melinda said.

Mira glared at the robots again. Athens, Livah, and Micah. She hated all of them now. She hated the stupid inventions that had connived with her mom to keep her locked up in this place. Discouragement weighed her shoulders down when she realized that her father, Phil, would be on their side without batting an eyelid. She got up and walked towards the stairs. There was nothing she could do here.

"Mira," Melinda called. "See."

There was the news on the TV station and it was Roland's face that made up part of the statistics. They referred to him as a doctor that was instrumental in the breakthrough of clean energy conservation.

They spoke like he was some kind of unknown doctor whom they were doing a favor by making popular upon his death.

"He's dead," Melinda echoed the reporter. "We have to be careful."

There were pictures of the Robot-cops pushing people away from the site of the crime.

"No, no, he cannot be dead."

"He is, baby. He is."

Mira ran up the stairs, close to sobbing. She could not believe it. She got into her room and slammed the door, then locked it. She fell on the bed and shut her eyes.

Melinda started knocking on the door shortly.

"Mira, come on. Open up. Talk to me."

"Go away."

"Sweetheart, I want to talk to you."

"I don't want to talk to you. Go away."

Maybe life was not worth living. Maybe she could end her own life as well. Without Roland, there was no distraction from the horror of a life her parent were living.

Levi

He could tell that Rami was not happy to see him there, but he did not care. They were here for the same reason, the same girl.

"You now bring strangers to our hideout?" Rami asked as he walked into the room and let himself down on the sofa.

"He's not a stranger," Ashley said.

"I don't know him," Rami retorted.

"Well, I know him. He's alright."

"If you say so."

Levi knew the thing to say at this time was 'don't worry, I will just go', but he did not. He had no intention to leave them. He wanted to sit a little bit more with Ashley. He could not help but keep staring into her eyes. They were two endless pits that just kept up going and going. Levi knew that the more he stared into her eyes, the more he would get lost, but he could not help himself.

"An athlete, eh?" The boy said. "What exactly is it that you do?"

"I'm a runner," Levi replied, angered that the boy had dragged him out of his reverie, and also destroyed any chance of him spending alone time with Ashley.

"I see, do you think there is really any need for athletes? I mean it seems practically useless to me. Like what are you running for? Are you after something? Is something after you?"

"Rami..." Ashley interjected.

"Allow the boy to speak," Rami said. He came with his own blunt. He lit it and exhaled in Levi's face.

Levi remained still. He wished for nothing more than to make Rami disappear. The question about his game was discomforting as he was not really a runner anymore because he had been kicked from the team.

"You can't talk?" Rami asked.

"I don't want to talk to you," Levi replied, surprised at the calmness of his response.

"I don't like him," Rami said, turning to Ashley. "He's trouble. Mark my words."

"Just because he did not get drawn into your silly argument does not make him dangerous. If anything, it makes him smart."

Rami frowned and looked away.

"Are you fast?" Ashley asked, looking at Levi.

Levi smiled. He wanted to say yes, but he decided he had lied too much already. Maybe telling the truth a bit would help him feel better.

"Not really... I try, but I always fall short at the end," he said.

"Too much detail," Rami said. He took another puff.

"That's... that's remarkably honest," Ashley said.

All Levi could offer was a weak smile. He was still thinking about the family he left back home. He was their only hope, and he still had not found a way to tell them that he had fucked up.

"You two should get a room," Rami said and stood up. He walked towards the door, leaving his bag behind.

"Where are you going?" Ashley asked.

"For fresh air," Rami replied.

No sooner had he made it out of the door than they heard running footsteps, raised voices, and gunshots.

"Get the ones inside!"

CHAPTER 11

Carl

I t was 3 in the morning, and Carl was already out by the back of his house. He got into his old car, the van he had abandoned at the back of the house while he patrolled with the police car that he was given. He could not believe now that he was once proud of the patrol car and the sirens. Now, he was avoiding them.

With the bag of ammunition safely in the trunk of the car, he went around to the front and got in. He knew who he would run to. Graham, the notorious mob boss. He had let Graham go while he made up a report about him falling into the sea after being shot. There was too much work for the cops to do. Looking for the dead body of a terrorist was not one of them. If one of their best said he punched a hole through the criminal with his gun, then he must be telling the truth.

Carl drove around the back, into the alleyway, before he made the streets again. He made sure he left all the lights on in his house like he was still there.

Before they would catch up to him, he would have long disappeared underground.

The road was winding and longer than he remembered it. He had always thought the clubhouse was not far from his house, but he was wrong.

When he finally arrived at the clubhouse he found the parking lot empty. The club was run by someone close to Graham, someone who had enough money to make the government look away while the party-goers popped as many pills as they liked.

Carl stopped the car and stared at the neon light sign that said *Drew's place.* Another sign said *closed.* He sat in the car and slowly looked around. He would not be surprised if he was tracked to this place. The police had the equipment, but the car he was driving was not on the grid. An old-fashioned car gifted to him by his father. One of the first cars to make use of electricity.

Satisfied that there was no one about it, he pushed the door open and stepped out of the car. He got to the door and knocked on it.

At first, there was no response, but he kept on knocking. He knew that his life depended on it. He banged harder on the door this time.

"Who the fuck is that?" A voice shouted from somewhere inside the building.

Carl could see someone coming from the inside through the glass door. He could see the hallway that led to the club hall. The man stopped in front of the door and pointed to the neon sign that said: closed.

"I need to talk to you," Carl said. He was already feeling like an outlaw, but he felt like one with a good cause.

"Can't you read the fucking sign?"

"I need to speak with Graham."

"What the fuck? Are you deaf too, man? We are closed!"

"Tell him Carl is here to see him."

Heather

She finally found a way to sneak out of the house when both parents were out. Apparently, they could not stay a while longer mourning their late daughter.

On her way to the cemetery, Heather had the feeling that she would not be returning to their house again, not after what she had seen in the flash. They were something else, the two people that she called her parents.

She got to the cemetery early in the morning and found a shed under a tree. Being out here, she felt like there were many eyes on her like she was out in the open and her parents could get her whenever they wanted. But she knew she had to be here. Andre would be here any moment from now, and she had to see him.

The wind blew over the trees in the burial ground, and Heather wondered if the trees were trying to talk to her. Maybe, it was the dead trying to tell her to get the hell out of this place. There was a lot that could go wrong while she was here. She could lose her life and have her consciousness transferred into that of a humanoid. The thought of being in a body that she could not control scared her. She knew how her father could be at times. Laura was even worse than Johannes. She could not begin to imagine the limitations on her life that this would mean.

"You are here again," someone said.

Heather quickly looked up into the tree for that was the direction from which the voice came.

"Don't look up. They will see!" Andre cautioned. He was up in the tree, sitting on one of the branches. Heather wondered how he managed to find his way to this place. She looked away, across the plains, through the rows of trees standing guard for the dead.

"They are watching you," Andre said.

"Who?"

"You know who."

"How did you get up there again? How did you know where I would be?"

"Luck, mere luck. I suppose, since we talked under this tree the last time, you would naturally gravitate towards this tree."

"Fair enough."

"Did you see anything?"

"Who gave that flash to you?"

"I told you, your sister."

"You lie, she would have sent it to me."

"Do you want us to stay here and keep arguing or do you want to follow me to where you would learn what the hell is really going on?"

"You could be a kidnapper..."

"Or an organ harvester. Yet, you are still here."

"I'm safe here, drones would track you if you tried to take me against my will."

"How about drugging you?"

"Drugging me?"

She looked up quickly.

"Yes, but I won't drug you. You want to know the truth. That is enough drug already."

Carl

At the mention of Carl's name, the man inside pulled open the door and let him in.

"You are Carl?" He asked.

"I am, where is Graham?"

"Graham is alright. I will go get him."

Just like that?

Carl watched the man walk away from the entrance after locking the door, and wondered if he was supposed to wait here for him.

A minute had barely passed before he noticed that at least four men were walking towards him from the hallway. It did not look good. He turned back to the entrance and realized that the door was locked. They got close to him and were about surrounding him when he realized they were braced for a fight.

"Carl," the first man who has walked off to get Graham said. "There are no drones here. No stupid cop cars."

As Carl's eyes moved over the group currently surrounding him, he realized that he had made a terrible mistake once again, acting without thinking.

"You are not feeling so big now, are you?" The man asked. His men came closer. They were all poised to attack.

Carl flexed his joints. If he was to survive this onslaught, he had to be nimble. Most of the men were taller than him.

"Why are you doing this?" Carl asked.

"You don't remember, do you?" The man asked. "You have killed so many of my people that every death is a dot in your memory."

The first man swung his fist, and Carl moved nimbly out of the way. He was just in time to dodge another blow meant for his face before he kicked the second man in the groin. A third hit him in the back, but did not do as much damage as he would have wanted. Carl swirled around and slammed his fist into the man's face. He bent down quickly to miss another massive right fist headed for him, and thrust his feet into the latter's knees, knocking him off balance.

The last man turned and calmly ran back through the hallway, wisely deciding to sit this one out. Carl waited for the remaining four men to get to their feet so the fight could continue.

"I am not here to fight," he said.

One of them dashed headlong at him, without caution, and paid the price when Carl stepped to the side, connected a fist to his tummy, and smashed his head with his knee as he bent over. The man collapsed immediately.

The first man and the other two men circled Carl. They were cautious now. The fight had taken a direction they were not expecting and they did not know what else the cop had under his sleeves.

"You have a lot of nerves coming to this place, cop, after everything that you have done," Carl's first host sneered.

Carl only watched them carefully. One of the three men still standing had brought out a small, sharp-looking dagger, and the traveler knew this had taken on a serious turn. It was either kill or be killed. He hoped it would not come to that.

"Not looking so proud anymore, eh?" The one with the dagger grinned. His blade glinted, like something that was always polished and prepared for use every morning. Was that all they did around here? Carl thought. He had thought they would be better than the damn cops that he was trying to get away from, but they seemed to be just the same thing.

"We can stop all of this now. I don't want to fight you. I am here to see Graham," Carl said.

"What? You want to add him to the list of men you killed?" The dagger fellow asked before he lunged at Carl.

It was an ill-informed move, one he was not supposed to make after seeing how fast and nimble-footed his opponent was. Before the dagger came close, Carl struck out a leg and kicked the man in his stomach. The dagger clattered to the ground as the man doubled over. A punch to the back of the neck knocked the fellow out. The other man rammed into Carl, driving him backwards with his shoulders. Carl's elbows went to work on the exposed back of his enemy when he saw that his first assailant was running up to keep up with them. Carl was slammed into the wooden wall, just beside a glass panel window. The first man hurried towards him and tried to smash his face with his fist. A quick move of his neck to the right ensured that Carl's face was saved and the huge fist slammed into the wood instead. It was painful. Finally, Carl's elbow did damage to the man pinning him against the wall. As the man lost his grip and found himself bending downwards, Carl's knees connected with his face. He was deposited on the ground.

"Fuck you!" The first man screamed and rushed headlong at Carl. "For my people!"

There was no time for Carl to react as they were so close to each other. He pushed Carl from the wall, against the glass panel, and through the window as the glass shattered.

They both fell on the other side of the shattered wall, rolling on the ground, all the while going at each other with blows, clawing away at each other's faces. When they finally pulled themselves away from each other, their hands moved so fast that they both could not follow each other's movement. The only thing they both saw was the barrels of their guns staring into their faces. Their guns were drawn, and death waited patiently by. Carl noticed that the man was still using the old type of gun and chuckled.

The man was red in the face and breathing hard. Like Carl, he had some bruises on his face. Carl stood so still, like a rock, a smirk on his face.

"Is this some kind of game to you, you maniac?" The man asked heatedly.

Heather

The road Heather took was a pathway through the cemetery. Andre had asked her to take this route if she wanted to know what really happened to her sister. By God's grace, she wanted to know.

She had not covered 20 feet before she felt the presence of Andre by her side. He was still looking around like he was expecting somebody or something to come upon them.

"Are you armed?" He whispered as they walked into a hedge of flowers.

"No," she replied.

Up ahead, the path was empty and a curve beckoned. Following the curve of the single road would take them out to the streets where Andre said he had a car waiting.

As they walked through the pathway, Heather had a premonition of being attacked, but pulled her mind quickly out of it. There was no time to dream about what could happen to them.

Suddenly, from the sides of the path far ahead, some figures walked out onto the pathway. Heather counted about four men.

They started shooting at them at the same time Andre pulled her to the ground. The bullets whisked past them and Andre quickly returned the shots. One of the shots hit one of the men that was standing in front of the others, and he went down in a heap. Andre pushed Heather further into the flower hedge where they hid out of sight. He knew it provided little cover, but at least their enemy would not know where they were.

None of them was hurt, surprisingly, but they were frightened. Three other men were after them. They were outnumbered. He looked over at Heather who was breathing heavily. She had probably not been under this kind of attack before.

"Are you okay?" He asked Heather.

She nodded.

"We have to make it to the tree there," he said, indicating a tree. It would provide a better cover. "You are ready? I will cover you."

Heather nodded. Then, she quickly scrambled up from the ground and dashed towards the tree standing by the side. Gunshots rent the air. He felt bullets slamming into the ground beside her. She was crouching, making herself as small a target as possible till she got to the tree and took cover behind it. A scream behind her informed her that Andre had shot one of the men again. The shooting stopped and voices rose high.

It did not take long before Heather heard the steps of the two men dashing into the forest after her. They must have missed Andre. Heather ran faster, wondering where Andre was as the two men came after her. She wanted to fight back, but she had no weapon. Turning back could amount to dying, and while she did not think much about her life, she very much wanted to know how her sister's ended. She had to be alive to know.

She found an outcropping and quickly dove behind it. From there, she waited. Maybe, if any of the men came her way and she was fast enough, she would take him down before the other noticed. She had to wait for long because it seemed the two men coming after her suddenly realized she could be armed. They stopped running and slowed to a halt. They had stealth and for a while, she became afraid that she would not hear them till one of them crept up behind them to put a bullet in between her ears. But she did not have to worry too much. Their stealth could not suppress the sound of the dried leave breaking that they trod upon. All she needed was speed and surprise.

The hums of insects were louder, this morning. The chirping sounds of crickets broke through the silence of the cemetery, then intertwined themselves with it till they both were one. Hiding there, thinking of what she was about to do, Heather suddenly felt excited. It was as if she was in another body, the one that took her away from her parents when she was younger.

She clenched her teeth and waited till she was sure she could see one of the men moving through the bushes. As she prepared to spring out and surprise the man, the deafening sound of a gunshot shattered the balance that the quiet sounds had created. The peace and serenity were momentarily toppled. Heather heard a body drop and slid down behind the rock and out of view. Bullets grazed the top of the rock. Someone was shooting back at her, but the shots were unfocused. For the life of her, she wondered where Andre was again, and why they were shooting at her instead of him. Now, they would hit off the top of the rock, then they would hit the trees standing six feet to the right. It was clear the shooter did not really know the shooting had come from. Heather smiled from her hiding place.

"You fucking sly," she murmured, thinking about Andre. Her smile, however, dried up and slowly turned to a frown when she realized that Andre was using her as bait. She heard the shooter move through the bush to his fallen comrade. She could imagine what he was doing now, probably checking the pulse.

Slowly, Heather lifted her head over the rock and peered. She could see the shooter squatted beside his partner. Then the shooter quickly turned towards her. She was sure the man saw her because as soon as she slipped down and out of sight, bullets hit the top of the outcropping, biting into the stone. She waited until the man stopped firing.

She heard the man's footsteps coming, at first hesitant, but as the man got closer, his footsteps became bolder. A lone sound of gunfire pierced through the night, and a scream announced that the last shooter had been shot. Heather heard the man fall before she peered around the outcropping.

Chapter 12

Levi

et the ones inside!

The words resonated in his ears while he looked around worriedly. Ashley was the first to get to her feet as if she was used to this kind of onslaught.

"Come!" She called, dragging the astounded Levi by the hand.

Levi did not know when he followed her. Fear and excitement were running through his veins as she led him down the hallway. There was no time to say anything, no time to explain. Running footsteps could already be heard as the men that took Rami bounded into the abandoned house in search of them.

Right from the very beginning of the pursuit, Levi knew that something was wrong. Some of the footsteps sounded like iron clanging against the floor. They made him wonder what kind of footwear the people in pursuit of them might be wearing.

"Come," Ashley whispered.

Instead of running towards the other door, she pulled him with her towards a room. They got in, while she kicked some tin that was lying around in the house farther down the hallway. They hid behind the door.

He found himself drawn close to her, within inches of her breath. It smelled like mint. Her hair had a luscious, overpowering aura. He wanted to sniff it a little but gathered himself together enough to remember that they were still in a big problem.

As expected by Ashley, footsteps ran past the door, heading towards the other open doorway that led out to an abandoned yard. That was where the tin she kicked had rolled to.

Still silent, they waited until all of their pursuers had gone that way. Ashley was about to speak when she heard it. Soft footsteps walking down the hallway. She paused and her breath caught in her chest. Levi was about to say something, but he felt her hand clamped across his lips. It felt oddly romantic, especially in that kind of situation. Levi wondered what was wrong with him.

They were so still as the person walked by. He stopped at their door and sniffed. Up Levi's spine, fear became a spider and ran up it, dread tickling his fancy.

He could see almost see the door open and a flood of men coming in to sweep them away.

More sniff through the broken doorway, they saw a silhouette standing, about to get in. The eyes of the man standing at the door suddenly turned red. The eyes were illuminating in the darkness of the house, except it was digits falling on the floor of the house while they hid beside the door.

He was about to step into the room. If he did and turned his head to the left, he would surely find them, and Levi was sure as hell that this thing was not a human.

As if on cue, voices sounded down the hallway. The pursuers were returning. The fellow at the door pulled back and turned to the approaching men.

"They got away," one of them said.

Levi thought they wore police uniforms. Their torches shone light on them, revealing their identity.

Police, he thought before a hand from the back started drawing him away and towards the window. Over the window, they went, and all the while he was thinking about why the police would raid an abandoned house where some youths went to get away from the stress of existing in a country and a world that was hanging by the edge.

They ran through the thrushes, crouching, heads down until Ashley felt they were far from the house. She turned to look. There was no one in pursuit of them.

It took a little while longer for them to get to the streets. All the while, they would not stop looking back over their shoulder, expecting the man with red eyes to come after them.

Cars were still busy on the road. Cars, which frightened Levi when he stared into them and found no one there. He could not bring himself to ask about Rami. For all they knew, they wanted this to be a nightmare. They wanted to go to bed and wake up, and discover that the world had not taken another stupid twist.

"Rami," Ashley finally said as they walked towards their respective houses.

"Jesus," Levi exclaimed. "What happened? Who are those people?"

"How should I know?"

"They looked like the police."

"The police does not go about kidnapping people."

"I saw their uniforms," Levi insisted. "I saw their robots."

"The man at the door," Ashley said, breathless.

They got to her house, and she clung onto Levi.

"Her, erm... would you stay with me? Just for this night. My parent went out. They would be coming back the next. I'm... I'm afraid...

Gooey eyes did the work of begging for him, and Levi began to consider his priorities. Before now, all he wanted was to go home and fall into bed, stay with his family and pretend that all was well. Perhaps, it would introduce some normalcy into his life. But he was now rethinking it. After all, staying with his family would make him uncomfortable, and saddle him with burdens and the lies that he had been picking through. How would he respond if they kept asking him about the race, not knowing he had been kicked out of the team?

"Hold on," he said, looking at Ashley.

Doesn't look bad at all. She was very beautiful, and he felt she was hiding her feminine figure under the big goodies and tracks that she loved to wear.

Levi sent his mom a message telling her not to wait for her. He could come back home in the morning. He did not mention what he had seen. Then, he turned back to Ashley.

"Okay then... let's get inside."

Inside, the house looked very much like Levi's. His eyes traveled the length and breadth of the house, taking in the little details. At the back of his mind, something snapped and held onto him.

Carl

The fight was over before it even started. He felt that no matter the number of people that kept coming out through that place, he would keep beating and keeping them aside till the person he wanted to see comes out.

The man that was opposite him was sweating and red in the face, plus he had bruises on his face. Clearly, he had been the one taking the bulk of the beating in the fight, but he seemed like he wanted them to keep fighting on and on till one of them dropped from exhaustion. Carl knew he would end the man long before then.

"What's going on here?" A voice screamed.

Carl recognized the voice... Graham. There was no other person with a pitchy voice like that who commanded the amount of respect that he did.

The man in front of Carl immediately stood down. He was no longer poised to fight even if his eyes were still daggers that could not wait to puncture Carl's body. Carl wondered if it would have been better not to come here at all. Maybe, he should have just returned to a life of normalcy, without the police, without having to kill anybody for them. But he knew too well that life would never be normal, not after what he had seen.

Graham looked taller and bigger than the last time he remembered, and he walked with a swagger as if he had the whole world waiting on him. But there was a certain caution in his steps, a certain humility. He still knew that it was because of Carl that he was alive, and his people had just tried to kill his savior.

Carl turned away from his opponent and faced Graham.

"Your men just tried to kill me," Carl said, casually. He said it so casually that he was afraid of his own disposition. Seeing many of Graham's people killed had started a change in him, one where he did not think his life was to be valued that much, one where he did not think that the life of any law enforcement agent was to be valued that much anymore. There were just so many things wrong, and he had been part of a system that had kept it that way.

"You are the enemy, Carl," Graham said.

"Not anymore."

Some men had come out with Graham. Some of them had the crude weapons of old, guns that could hardly punch a hole in the new generation robots.

"What do you mean?"

"I came here to..." Carl wondered why he had come again. "I resigned from the police. I have seen enough, done enough."

"You resigned by yourself?"

"Yes, after the AI car opened fire on your people. I don't have to convince you, Graham."

"I say we kill him here," one of the men shouted.

There were shouts of approval all around the small crowd of men that had formed, but Carl did not feel afraid. After all, this morning, he had pointed a gun to his head and pulled the trigger, and nothing happened. His life was a gamble. If the dices fell on the wrong side, then he would be content with death. He had done enough harm and damage as it was already. He could also see the pain in the eyes of the people surrounding him. In Graham's eyes, he saw cold math. Of course, it was Graham calculating always. He hardly ever let his emotions get the best of him. He raised his hand.

The noise stopped, but the tension still hung in the air, waiting to explode. It was like a living thing, and Carl could feel it breathing on him. His eyes began to go around the crowd as he wondered what professions they had before deciding to fight the government.

"Why?" Graham asked.

Carl's eyes went through the crowd again. There was a lean man. He looked like he was a shop attendant before robots took over his job. Another was fat. Carl wondered what the man did. Still another, muscular, probably a mechanic. The muscles seemed to come from heavy lifting rather than purposeful toning. There was him also, if they let him join them. He would be a cop who was joining the resistance, maybe the only cop.

"The people I work for do not value human lives," Carl said.

"Took you a long time to realize this, but why now?"

"Remember what you said to me when I almost killed you?" Carl asked.

A gasp went through the men. It was just what Carl wanted. He wanted them to know what they owed him. He saved Graham, and the fellow, in turn, saved most of them.

"There were many things I said," Graham replied.

"About robots replacing humans," Carl said. "The robots... they seemed to have such... such hateful disdain against humans. I mean kids were shot down, and this goddamn robot went to shoot them again. The fuck! Why?"

The crowd was stunned into silence. They could not believe this was coming from a cop. Carl did not care what they were thinking. It was how he felt. He had been trying to hold it back, struggling to convince himself that he was working for the right people, trying to maintain law and order, only for the government to send him on a murderous spree against women and children.

"I cannot answer that," Graham said.

"I cannot too... that is why I am here."

"And not because your people are after you?"

"They are not my people. Not anymore."

"What changed?"

"I have just told you the fuck what changed!"

The crowd of men did not look like they wanted to fight Carl anymore. If anything, they looked like they were willing to accept him into their fold. It was a silent agreement, a silent acceptance, one that did what words could not do. In their eyes, they felt they had seen someone that was in support of their course.

Mira

Her world seemed to be crumbling down slowly, and that was what made it worse. It was one thing to be very sure that a misfortune has befallen one, it was another thing to be afforded the chance to hope. She wanted to go see Roland dead for herself, to see her love one last time, but her parents would not allow that. She had no choice but to stay up in her room, lock the door and stare deep into the wall—she could see the memories there.

"Roland," she whispered. She feared for her sanity, but most of all, she feared for the loneliness that would soon enclose her. She and her parents lived in different worlds, they, with their science and she with her pettiness and stubbornness. She hated science because of what they had turned into: another child that was more important than their biological one. Roland made her see science in another light. If they knew what the man they hated too much had begun to do in her life, then they would have understood him; they would have loved him. Or maybe they knew. Maybe that was why they hated him because, they knew he could do something that they could not do. She was ashamed of them, both of them.

"I will never forgive you," she said of them, banishing their thoughts away from her mind.

Somebody knocked on the door. She ignored the person, still sitting completely still. Her mind traveled off again. Maybe she should not have left Roland all alone in that scary house. She killed the first intruder herself, didn't she?

"You selfish, petty girl," she mumbled. All she was thinking of was herself.

Because of the luxury, she felt she would enjoy here in her parents' house, she waved Roland's concerns away, making light of them. She told him she would never leave him. At least that much was the truth. She was in love with him in a way she had never been with another man. Maybe, it was because of the way that he condoned her excesses without being judgmental of it; the way he asked her to do things without really asking her to do it. She had concluded that her boyfriend and fiancé was, in fact, more brilliant than her parents could ever wish to be. He had every damn thing that she wanted in a man. He still had it apart from the most important thing: life.

The knock came again, this time jolting Mira from her thoughts.

"Open the door, Mira," Phil said.

He had returned, Mira thought. Why though? To mock her for the kind of man that she chose to give her heart to? If she had a chance, she would do it over and over and over again till she was tired of loving, and she knew she could never get tired of loving Roland.

"Mira!" The man called again. There was a mixture of concern and irritation in his voice, the very thing that distanced Mira from her parents.

"Go away," Mira said.

"Phew," Phil sighed. The fear was no longer there. It was only a mild irritation like he was dealing with a little girl. "I want to talk to you, Mira."

"Talks do nothing... go away."

"It's about Roland."

Mira paused suddenly. She swirled towards the door, her eyes wide, her face animated.

"What about him?"

"Open the door and let me in."

"I don't want to see your face," Mira objected.

"We found Roland."

"What?"

"Will you open the door now?"

Mira pulled the bolt away before she engaged the system lock and unlocked the door. Her father was standing at the door, looking serious. She had never seen him look this serious in any matter that concerned Roland. It was always an irritation.

"Do you want to see him?" Phil asked.

"Is he okay? Is he fine? Where did you find him? Yes, I want to see him. Tell mom to take those monstrous bots away from the door."

"Come," Phil said instead of answering any of the questions and led her to the bed. He sat her down slowly and stared into her eyes. "Roland is not in the best condition," he said.

Mira's heart skipped again. Her heart had been skipping so many times today that she feared it would soon explode and she would die.

"Where is he?"

"Still in the countryside. The medical team is with him, but I don't think he can make it..."

"What?"

"...not without help anyway."

"What must be done? Where is he?"

"You are his fiancée. He has no other family."

"I want to see him."

"And you will... soon."

"I want to see him now!"

Phil paused as if he was considering his options. "Okay, okay, we will go and see him now. Then you permit for the doctors to work a procedure that would bring him back to health."

Phil stood up from the bed and stared at his daughter with concern. The look could have been similar to the look that the biblical Jacob must have given to Isaac before taking him on a trip at the end of which he had to be sacrificed.

"Come on," he said and walked through her door.

She followed him, not bothering to put on any other piece of clothing apart from the pajamas she wore to sleep from the night before. Phil turned and saw her, then he shook his head.

"No, you can't dress this way," he said.

"Can we just go?" Mira begged.

"Find some clothes," her father insisted.

Mira ran back to her room to choose a piece of clothing. She ran back after hurriedly throwing a blue t-shirt on and pulling a black Jean trouser over her hips.

Together, they walked towards the door. There was no sign of Melinda downstairs. The bots too did not approach the two as they headed for the door. But it was not until they were out through the door that Mira heaved a sigh of relief. She was beginning to hate bots, annoying things.

CHAPTER 13

Dora

The safe house they were hiding in was not really safe. Dora knew that soon they would have to leave if they did not want to be caught by whatever it was that attacked them at the café.

She looked over at Barry Stivers. He looked more shocked than scared. He was probably expecting something like this and had tried to prepare his mind for it, but somewhere along the line, his mind failed him. So, he was shocked and not afraid.

"Are you okay?" She asked. He was her target after all. She wanted him. It had been a while since she had a man in her life, but this was not the way she wanted the man in her life.

"I'm fine," he said, sighing.

The safe house was someone's abandoned house. It blended in with the stories and rumors coming from town about people disappearing for long without saying anything to their neighbors. Then after some time, they would resurface, looking younger and smelling different.

Barry did not know what to make of the news. But he knew that the people who owned this house would be coming back soon, and being found in someone else's house, hiding like a thief, did not sit well with him.

He stood up and walked to the fridge. He had caught a glimpse of it as they went around the house, making sure that they were the only ones in the house.

He opened the fridge. What he wanted was a bottle of water, but the only thing the refrigerator provided was bottles of juice. He took one, hoping that there was nothing else apart from the juice in the bottle. He was too tasty to allow his paranoia to get the best of him.

"That is risky, you know," Dora said as she headed to the fridge and took out the canned food she saw there. She settled on the sofa and dug into it. She ate hungrily, with a purpose, as if she knew what she was doing, as if she had been in this kind of situation before.

"Have you done this kind of thing before?" Barry asked.

"What kind? Saving your life?"

Barry blanched, remembering he had not even thanked her for saving his life and he was about accusing her of breaking into people's homes and eating their food.

"Thank you," the scientist said, swallowing his shame.

"You are welcome... try to eat. We could be tracked to this place, you know."

Without a word, Barry searched for something he could eat in the fridge. He was not really feeling hungry, but his body was shaking with emptiness, and he figured he needed the strength if he was to make it out of this godforsaken town to the towns where the drones worked. He had designed the drones, and he knew they could be trusted.

As he dug into the cereals in front of him, his phone started ringing.

"Fuck! You still have your phone!" Dora screamed.

Barry understood her worry. "My phone cannot be tracked," he said.

"Oh," Dora said. Sometimes Barry behaved like he could not even take care of himself, and Dora forgot he was a great scientist, the one leading the charge for a brighter future for the whole of humanity.

Barry took one spoon of the food and accepted the call.

"Hello," he said.

"Hello, Barry, where the hell are you?"

"I'm trying to stay alive," Barry replied.

"Nobody could track you... what happened?"

"I pulled everything off, senator."

"Don't call me that!."

"Why? Are you afraid?"

"What has come over you?"

"The fear of death. Who the fuck attacks a man when he is eating!"

"You were attacked?"

"Oh, you did not know? So much for having the situation under control."

Dora ate in silence, listening to the conversation. She could hear from both ends as the speaker was quite loud and the doctor did not seem to care. It was working. She was pushing her way into the doctor's trust. Anyway, who wouldn't trust someone who put her own life on the line just to save the person? Not her though, but that was probably because she knew too much about these things. Doctor Barry as old as he was, was still very green in matters like this.

"Come in, doctor, let me get protection to you."

"No... I would rather remain in hiding."

"How then would we get on with the program?"

"That has always been your concern, Senator..."

"Don't do it, doctor!"

"I thought the line is secured."

"What has come over you?"

"I am trying to protect myself, and you know what that means, right?"

"You seriously cannot be thinking what I think you are thinking."

"Oh, I am."

"The government would never attack you for working for them."

"I will send the coordinates of the places I buried these muons once I feel safe. You already know the procedure."

"Come on doctor, you..."

Doctor Barry Stivers ended the call. He turned back to his cereal and continued crunching it, sparing a moment to look at Dora. She was not looking at him, but he knew she had heard everything. Only one location was known for muon-catalyzed fusion. This was the countryside where he had spent more time than he would have wanted. The other places were scattered all over the top countries of the world. They were the countries that had come together to make his brother's dream a reality. He sighed when he remembered everyone thought it was his dream.

"Are you okay?" Dora asked.

"Have you ever felt like an imposter?"

"A couple of times, yes."

"Do you shake it off?"

"I just keep doing what I was doing."

"That sounds tough and long-suffering-like."

"Well, isn't that what life is?"

**

Dora

Dora finally got a chance to sneak into the toilet and make her calls. She had had a nagging feeling somewhere in her heart when she thought of the attack. It had been so close and sudden that if her reflexes were not as good as she had honed them to be, there would be two dead bodies back in that Café by now. If her people were responsible for the attack, then she had to warn them in clear terms, to stay the fuck away. Humans were always the problem.

"Hello," she said into the phone.

"Hey," Jax said into the phone. He sounded relaxed. If he was acting, then he was pretty damn good at it. "How's the mission coming along?'"

"Good... we were attacked."

"What!"

"Yeah."

"You think we have something to do with this?"

"You have always wanted the genius dead, and me? Well, I am just collateral damage for the big fish."

"What the fuck are you talking about? You are the best that we have."

"Then, why did your men try to take me out?"

"It was not my men," Jax said.

He was so adamant that Dora had to think of something else. Did the government have any reason to kill off one of their own? Maybe he was done with their project and they did not want to leave any loose end.

"Well, this shot is complicated. I don't know what to think. We were almost taken down."

"The men have been here for a long time. The last time we went out we lost too many men. I have not had the mind to embark on anything since then."

"Well, later then."

Dora ended the call and stood looking at the wall. There was something that she was not seeing yet. Her men were not seeing it either, but she was sure it would play out, sooner or later.

Heather

Why the fuck would he use me as a bait?!

It had seemed funny at first. At a point, it had seemed brilliant to Heather, how Andre would allow her to lead the men on, then he would come out from behind to take them out. Then, she started thinking of bullets sinking into her flesh, or the pulse guns that create a hole in people's heads. It was frightening to just think of what would have happened if any of those men were fast. She would have been lying in the cemetery with the dead. That was foolhardy.

She saw Andre approaching with a rifle slung over his shoulder and ran up to him.

"That was stupid what you did there... very stupid!"

"And yet, we're still alive, aren't we?"

"I could have been dead. They could have shot me before you did anything.

"But they did not, did they?"

"Stop being stupid, I feel like shooting off your head right now."

"You have a weird way of professing your gratitude."

"Fuck you."

"I could take that too, but not here. We need to get out of here. I have a car at the end of this pathway."

Heather had no choice but to follow the wayward fellow who took stupid risks that paid off. She swore to make him pay for making her seem like she was crazy. That was not saving someone's life. How could he put her in harm's way and say he was saving her life.

The car, a blue, old Mercedes sat somewhere in the middle of the woods, waiting for them. It was easy to see that it was not among the new generation of cars, probably for obvious reasons. The government was in charge of all those, and Andre did not look like he trusted the government. He pulled the door open and got in. Heather pulled the passenger door open and got in too.

The car drove off, meandering through the pathway and finally coming out onto the road. Heather watched the road and fell silent. Many thoughts were going on in her mind at the same time, all of them seeking her attention

She did not know which one to pay attention to. There was the feeling of being abandoned, of having no parents anymore because she could not understand who those people in her house were. Her parents had always been strange, but it seemed science was further messing with their senses.

"Where are we going?" She finally asked.

That single sentence contained all her worries and the thoughts bouncing around her head. She turned to the driver whose eyes were fixed on the road.

"The question is, do you trust me enough to come with me?" Andre asked.

"No... I don't trust you. You could set me up to be your bait. That is stupid, you know?"

"Still going on about this?"

"Admit it, you were crazy."

"I am crazy, that is me. That is how I survived. I went to your sister's funeral when the drones could have easily killed me. No, I didn't tamper with the drones, I couldn't. I guess some of the drones still function properly."

"What do you mean?"

"I think something is happening in The White House. I think something is happening with the government. Emotionless beings are taking over. I don't know exactly what it is, but I am going to find out."

"Emotionless beings?"

"Yes, a certain cop had his car mow down resistors, women and children, anything that stood in his way."

Heather was lost for words. She had not really been concerned with what was happening in her own country. She did not really care. She preferred staying in the countries considered underdeveloped. People were not being sacrificed for the survival of others.

"That's terrible."

"Maybe it is something they are taking. Rumors said there are plans to destroy the earth as we know it while people who feel they should inherit the new earth would hide somewhere. Once the destruction is passed, out they come."

"Is that not far-fetched?"

"Not really," Andre said. "Your parents might be among the ones I'm talking about. They led me to this place."

"What do you mean?"

"Don't they look changed to you?"

"Changed?"

"You will understand later."

The trees passed by quickly as they embarked on a journey across a lonely road. For some reason, Andre was moving the car towards the countryside. Heather felt she understood. Everything was just moving too fast. She had become like someone without parents in such a short while, and she could not wait to watch the rest of the video.

CHAPTER 14

Laura

The room was empty, but the scent of the girl in the room was rife. She could smell it. It was the scent of someone strong. Laura shook her head. The only time she had perceived that kind of strong scent was when she went after the man that was her husband now. No, not her husband that the world was now seen, the other man, the one that had to be replaced.

Her eyes went round the room, trying to pick cues and traces till they came to the curtain. Of course, she had realized that was what had happened. The girl was not one to simply lie down and take every instruction from them. She was unlike Marie, poor girl. For a while, Laura actually thought of leaving the girl as she was. There was no need for replacement, but that was a mistake. It was also why the girl had to die.

"Johannes!" She shouted.

The girl was brainy too. The last evaluation from the house sent her IQ rippling through the roof. Must be the combined genes of both parents. Laura was annoyed that she did not have both genes. She was just Laura. The woman was brilliant, but she was not the greatest thing in science. Oh well, it did not matter. They had to remake the girl, change her so she could do their every bidding. If she was still out there running around, how would they convince people that the one with them was the right one? Besides, they did not have everything they wanted from her.

"Johannes! Get up here!"

Heavy footsteps announced that Johannes was making his way to the room. He stood before the open doorway and stared into the room.

"She ran away," he said, needlessly.

"Apparently," Laura said. "We need to find her.'

Johannes nodded.

"What would you like me to do?" He asked.

It seemed a bit odd, but it would not be noticeable. Dumb humans would probably put it down to the humility of the husband and the sign of strong love and bonding between the couple. They would not, in their little minds, ever fathom the fact that something they made was growing and taking over from them. Laura came into being before Johannes, and as they were both alphas, she was naturally the leader, the one who had garnered more experience in the world that they were supposed to infiltrate.

"Track her, see if there is anyone helping her. Then, come back and report to me," Laura said.

Johannes nodded.

"We have to know how much she knows."

Johannes went to the open window and stared down it. Laura watched till he went over the window, then she turned back into the room and started sniffing things.

"Marie," she said. Why was she getting the scent of the dead girl here? There was another scent, a distinct scent. It was almost recognizable, then it faded. She struggled to get the scent back to her nose, but it was gone and had no intention of coming back.

Laura settled into the lone sofa in the room and dug into her memory. Even there, the scent was fragile. If she delved too much into it, it would simply break up, dissipate, and recollect, it would be an uphill task.

She moved past the scent and went back into her memory. She had a file for everything she had ever done to further their cause and bring about the new age. Her favorite was serving hot tea to the man that was supposed to be her husband.

A car had brought her to the house during the noon, and she immediately recognized the house from the thousands of programs that had been stored in her head. She was the replacement, the main thing.

She sat in the house that day, waiting and waiting till it seemed she was waiting for Godot. *Ha-ha, waiting for Godot.* These literary expressions were in her mind. There were so many of them that she entertained herself with when she got bored by running through them.

When the car carrying the man she was supposed to send in a bag to the company building stopped in front of the house, she was all pumped up and ready.

"You didn't pick my calls, Laura," the man said as he walked into the room and found her sitting there like a strange apparition.

He was about to walk past her when he stopped. It was strange, the way she was just sitting there, saying nothing. What he did not know was that it was also deliberate. She could act as naturally as the obsolete woman she had come in to replace, but she had some plan in her head, something she could not wait to carry out.

"Are you okay?"

"No," she replied.

The look on his face was that of confusion. He had probably never seen his woman in that state before. Considering how many years the couple had stayed married, she concluded that the man was daft.

"What's wrong?" He asked.

"Come," she said.

She walked slowly, shaking her backside and causing Laura for having such an unremarkable backside that she could do nothing with. Nevertheless, Doctor Johannes followed him. In that little moment between life and death, he would have probably wished he had not followed her. He would have wished he discovered something suspicious enough to make him run away from the house.

Laura stood from the sofa and walked down the stairs till he got to the living room. It was airy, one of the things she liked about the couple they were replacing. Someone was already at the door.

Johannes stepped inside, looking unkempt. He had grasses stuck to places on his clothes and his hair, even in his glasses.

"She has already made it over the fence," Johannes said. "There was someone with her, some scent. I could not really fathom what it was."

"Some scent," Laura said dreamily.

Detective Shaun

After the call from Aaron, Shaun knew there was more here than met the eyes, but it was difficult for him to pick out. Lobo, the robot was in charge and the only human who should be in change was behaving like a fool. He wondered if he could call the man out and ask him what is happening, but Lucas seemed to be avoiding him. It was like avoiding trouble and staying on a low.

He walked through the investigation, and all the time his mind nagged at him. Something was warning him to be careful. He could still remember Aaron's voice on the phone.

When he retired to his room, one that he had chosen out for himself, he sat at the table, staring into space.

"Something is off," he kept saying. He had a piece of paper in front of him and a pen. But the more he thought about what was off, the more whatever it was kept evading him.

"Think, Shaun, think," he said, gritting his teeth.

The first name he wrote down on the sheet was Lobo, then Lucas before Aaron. These three knew things that he did not know.

"I have to see Lucas," he decided. He knew it was risky, both for Lucas and him, especially, for him, but he knew he had to do it. He had seen where the robots ended people's life, and he wondered why the man was so happy in creating something stronger and faster than he would ever be. What if these things got out of control?

Shaun had long ceased to make his position and fears on the growing robot industries known. More and more policemen were being taken to paperwork where they grew fat in food and staying idly in front of a table without doing anything while the bots went out there, garnering experience.

Shaun turned off the light in his room first, then he snuck to the window to find out if people were spying on him. He would not put it past that quiet Lobo that seemed to have the intelligence of his own. *Programing, my foot!*

Satisfied with the knowledge that there was no one lurking about the street that night trying to keep tabs on him, he walked quietly to the door, pulled it open, and let himself out into the hallway.

There was no one here all the way down to the end of the hallway. He was supposed to be in a hotel provided by and paid for by the people that had invited him for the investigation, but he was already afraid for his life.

His life hand brushed against the side of trousers to make sure that the small pulse gun he had kept there was still in place. He loved these guns. They were not like the obsolete ones with which one could manage to hit a robot and have the robot laughing at the end of the bullet. This one boreholes in humans and robots alike. If he was fast enough to hit the robot, then he was safe.

The hotel lobby was deserted apart from the receptionist, also there was a robot who looked up lazily as Shaun walked past.

Shaun knew where Lucas lived. He was not certain if the man had wives and children. Well, he had just been transferred here and he was hating it already. Of course, he was transferred here because the bigger cities were demanding bot officers. They had no idea what they were getting themselves into. Even Shaun had no idea, but he did not like it in the least. *Damn bots! Fucking bots!*

He got down and headed for his car. Before he got inside he made sure to look at the backseat, ready to pull out the gun at the slightest, perceived movement, and start firing away. There was no one there, not even on the floor between the seats. He shut the door and took a deep breath.

"You are becoming very paranoid, Shaun," he said.

When he started the car, he looked around again to make sure he was not being followed, then he guided the car into traffic and set it on course for Lucas's house. The human second in command looked more like a servant than a cop.

He stopped when he was still two blocks away from the man's house and parked by the side of the road. Again, he observed silently with his headlights out. Cars were whizzing by, at intervals, and the place was mostly quiet.

"Well, here goes nothing," he said.

He got out of the car and walked casually towards Lucas's house. His porch light was on, so he did not walk to the front of the house. He took the side, making sure to look around again, and ensure that he was not being followed. Convinced that he was not, he accessed the house through a window, breaking it from the outside, and hoping that the noise was not enough to wake up the occupants of the house.

He stood in the darkness in the hallway and waited after he had gained access to the house. His ears were attuned to the highest frequency as he tried to catch any sound drifting by. There was none, just the night sounds of crickets in the flowers from outside.

He began searching from room to room.

Barry Stivers

He sat so still that he could be mistaken for a statue. He wondered what Dora would think of him now. She would probably think of him as a naive person, giving away such sensitive information when he did not even know if there was a mole in the government.

"Hey," the woman called him from behind. He swirled around quickly.

Dora stood up before him, her eyes not missing one beat. The single bulb in the room cast her shadow against the wall. Her gaze was intense as she tugged at her top and pulled it off. Then, pulled off her trousers.

Sitting on the bed, Barry swallowed as the gown came off her. He could not find his voice. They had just escaped death and there she was, baring her firm breasts for him. His mouth slowly hung open like it did the first time he saw her naked. Her skin was tanned and flawless. Her breasts were full and bouncy, and he could not stop himself from imagining how they felt in his hands the first time. She wore a G-string pant, but no bra.

"What are you doing?" Barry asked, breathless. He was still feeling troubled.

"I want to remember you," she said. "I want a memory to take with me."

"Memory?" He asked.

Her only response was to grab her own breasts and squeeze them while she licked her tongue. It drove him mad. She had a tummy that stood the risk of disappearing into her body, and her hips were curved with a pleasing roundness.

"Come," she said, stretching out her hand. He took it and she drew him up. The room was small, but there was enough room for them to stand together, pressed against each other.

Dora pressed Barry into her bare body, her hands on his shoulder, feeling the fabric of his cloth against her nipples. She smelled his body, felt the tension in his body, saw the trembling of his lips, but there was something else. The air was rippling with desire, and as their bodies met and melted into each other, she felt warmth burning within her. His breathing became labored as if something was stuck in his chest. The chest heaved up and down, endlessly.

"I still remember the first time," she murmured, her lips traveling up his neck and close to his ears. She was on tip-toes, so they stood at the same level with her body still pressing into his.

Barry could see her face clearer now. It was frighteningly fierce like there was a lot on her mind that she wanted to do to him. He did not mind. The vision of the room started fading before him, flickering out of sight. The only thing that was real was Dora, her wrath, and her body.

"You're beautiful," he tried to say. It came out in a grunt before she pressed her index finger against his lips, effectively shutting him up.

He did not speak again. Instead, he leaned closer into her as if he was trying to join their bodies as one. His hand went around to her backside, out of control now, running along the pant edge before slipping under to grab her backside. They were soft like he remembered.

He trembled a bit as his hand traced along with the rise of her backside, she raised a hand to touch his face, running it against his cheek. He suddenly leaned forward and kissed her breasts. She stifled a moan. The action had been sudden.

She leaned towards him and kissed him on the lips. The kiss was one long, passionate, slow kiss that she drew it out while freeing him from the shackles of his jacket and pulling his trousers low. He groaned when her hand brushed against his manhood.

"I thought you wanted to leave," he said

In response, she glared at him and squeezed his manhood lightly, then stroked it. Then, she continued kissing him, preventing him from talking or moaning. Unable to stay idle, his hand moved down towards her center. She caught it, making him slow down. She wanted to be in control, but he did not know how long he could hold himself. He desperately wanted to fuck her. She was stroking him towards insanity.

"I will miss this," she said. It was a husky, drawing sound from her throat. Barry did not hear her. Before he could ask, she pushed her lips against his.

She spun him around so his back was against her body, and continued stroking him, pulling the trousers all the way down to his knees. His knees got weak and wobbled like jelly. She held him firmer and stroked harder and faster. Then, she knelt before him and took his manhood in her mouth. Barry's groan was loud because he was not expecting that. She stroked and sucked, keeping her eyes on his face. The pant still hid her center from his sight. She pulled him deeper in, gripping his butt cheeks as she continued sucking the life out of him. Then, finally, she stood up.

He found himself looking into her piercing eyes, consumed by lust. Her lips were delightfully wet and inviting, and he wasted no time in going for them again, grabbing her tiny waist between his arms, as if she would run if he failed to hold her. She welcomed him, his head between both of her hands. His hand moved down from her waist to her backside. He squeezed, gently at first, then ferociously.

"You want me," she said, flapping her lashes like an experienced seductress that had done her work well.

Dora closed her eyes, and he finally slipped the pantie off her, revealing her center. Overcome with sudden strength borne of interest, he lifted her so her nipples were level with his mouth, then he ran his tongue around them, one first, then the other. Dora arced her body, with her legs around Barry, and her breasts formed the top of the arc. Her head hung down and away from her boyfriend while her breasts presented an irresistible offering. Barry took her protruding, right nipple in his mouth and sucked deeply. This time, Dora could not keep down the moan that burst from her lips. He bit the nipple softly between his teeth and ran his tongue slowly over it.

"Fuck me," Dora muttered, pulling at Barry's head as she tried to drag him down to the bed. She started to force her nipple deep inside his lips, pushing her breasts in his face. He bit down hard on the nipple, causing her to scream out loud, then he carried her to the bed that had been a silent observer.

He laid her down on the bed and silently admired her body. She had a shape like an uneven hourglass, her waist down forming the bigger proportion against her upper body. Her complexion was tanned, and her eyes were glazed over with passion. She licked her lips sensuously, fanning awake the crackling embers of lust in him.

He forgot there was danger as there was no way he could resist this kind of temptation lying in front of him. Between his legs, his muscles arced and throbbed. His hardness dangled heavily between his legs, still laden with memories of her lips around it and the other times they had been in bed. He lifted her from the bed again and hung her upside down, so the wetness of her womanhood was to his face, and her own face hung low in front of his swinging cock. She wanted to ask what he was doing before she felt his lips on her center, probing, sucking, eating, and dipping into her. His hands were around her, locking her in place, while her legs were wrapped around his neck, so she would not fall. Even then, the shock was still unexpected, causing a tremor to run through her. He continued thrusting with his tongue, and she lost it. She hung on tight as if for her dear life while shock after shock built up from her inside. She moaned them all away loudly, her control was abandoned. He was enjoying her moaning, so he sucked harder because he wanted her to go completely crazy. She was struggling to be free of him now, not knowing what she was doing, but he held her tight and kept at it, licking, thrusting, and nibbling. It seemed he had found another person inside of him, one bent on giving cruel pleasure, like a punishment. She was the one who had looked like she wanted to punish him at the beginning. *Now, look who is getting punished,* he thought.

She grabbed his cock, which had been dangling in front of her, and sucked it deeply, going as fast as he was going. It seemed like her last resort, her last grab at sanity, and she was beginning to affect him, to regain some type of control. He collapsed on the bed, his lips still in her center, and his cock still between her lips.

He then aligned himself up against her on the bed and rubbed his hardness against her. She moaned. She moaned again when he slipped into her, ready, wet and slippery, smooth and expansive enough to take everything in. She felt him growing inside her. He filled every space inside of her before he began moving slowly. With long, slow thrusts that brushed against every side of her hole, he made her wetter, made her want more, desire more, moan for more. Then, he increased his speed. Her voice was fluctuating between moaning and screaming. Each thrust came with a deep grunt from Barry's throat. He sounded like a beast. The faster he moved, the quicker she lost herself. All she wanted was for him to keep going, to keep ravishing her body the way he was doing. She wanted to enjoy this ride as much as she could, get to the end of it, and store it in her memory. Maybe that was all she would remember him with. He did not know it, but the world was done. One last meal, she thought. She felt the first tremors build up and wash over her body along with goosebumps. The second one followed shortly, and before long, she was shaking all over, her orgasm rocking her body hard.

The ceiling faded into nothing. The room drifted away. There was only her and Barry floating on fluffy white clouds. Barry continued moving, faster, as he himself was close. He could feel a fountain building up in his groin. He moved roughly now, and Dora had to reach out and grab the bedsheet. Still moving, Barry bent towards her and bit her nipple before sucking deep. He wanted to make her forget their argument, to wipe the slate clean. She quaked again, unable to hold herself. Her fingers dug into Barry's back. It was as if Barry's shaft was still increasing inside of her with every thrust. She felt herself moving dangerously close to the cliff again.

Before she climaxed for the second time, she felt Barry tremble. She shook for the last time and Barry fell on top of her.

She was the only one that knew this was the last night. In time, the world would be done.

CHAPTER 15

Levi

I nside the house, Ashley led Levi straight to her room upstairs after she had locked the door.

In her room, they stood looking at each other. The tension of coming close to death was slowly wearing out. They gravitated towards each other. Having been so close to death, their bodies were trembling with unattended passion.

Suddenly, the girl slipped down and he almost caught her, but she was quick. She pulled open his fly and slipped her hand into his brief. He groaned, feeling himself floating away on a cloud. The girl was too eager to prove herself, but from the way she handled his hardness, he realized that she must have watched a lot of porn or had had a lot of practice.

She slipped his hardness into her mouth and started sucking furiously. It was so sudden, so daring that it was all he could do to keep himself from shouting. The sound of a car horn passing through the street brought his attention back to the present. Ashley was busy on her knees, gripping his butt cheeks and sucking on his cock as if her life depended on it, as if she was trying to impress him.

As Ashley sucked, the hardness became longer and bigger. Levi had one massive dick that could not fit all the way into her mouth. But Ashley found that what she was doing to him was affecting his speech and movement. She sucked harder till he gripped her head.

Ashley pulled his dick out to take a breath, but Levi pushed it back in quickly. This time Ashley had no control of it. He was fucking her mouth, holding her head in place with his big hands. She could not talk with all of that cock in her mouth, fucking her throat. Levi had his hands around her neck now, moving his waist like a dancer; forwards, upwards, roll to the side, thrust. There was something beautiful about the way he moved, like a song that every girl would love to dance to. She took a shaky breath in and gripped the sofa so hard her knuckles turned white.

Finally, Levi pulled his cock out of Ashley's mouth and turned her around. He was so fast that she did not know when her clothes left her body and he pushed her down in front of him. She was on all fours now and he was kneeling. He slipped into her, slowly. She moaned with a shaky voice, gripping tightly to the seat of the sofa in the house. He let her feel the width of him before he started moving slowly.

For her, it was pain and pleasure, but the pleasure blinded her from feeling the pain. It was the debilitating one, the pleasure she felt. She could hardly move. Levi breathed deeply behind her, and the pounding started again. Ashley tried to hold it in, but she could not. Her moans filled the room.

As Levi slammed into Ashley, he could not believe this was happening. They were only neighbors who had not spoken to each other before now. The girl's moans were all the encouragement that he needed. At first, he had thought that she would not like fucking in people's houses, or even know how to fuck. He should not have worried. The girl knew what to do. She arched so perfectly that her back was a deep valley as he took back shots, slamming into her from the back.

When the position got a bit boring, he got up from the ground and went to the sofa in the room. She followed him and leaned into him as he sat on the sofa in the middle of the room pushing him deeper into sofa, till he felt he was going to be swallowed up by the sofa. He tried to sit up, but her entire weight was on him. Her breasts, now freed from her tight bra, pushed into his face. It seemed the girl was enjoying the escapade more than he was.

He realized just how shapely his new friend was now; a thin waist had two massive breasts and one big revolving backside on him. It was hard to breathe with her firm beauties on his face, restricting his airflow. The nipples called to his lips and he answered. He could feel the weight of her ass and hips on his center.

She slipped his cock back into her wetness and started riding, gasping and moaning in turns. Her warm, pink hole gripped unto his hardness in ways that shocked the stimulation out of him.

When Ashley had ridden enough, she slipped downwards towards his manhood, where the cock shot upwards in all its glory.

When she slipped his dick in between her lips, Levi got lost. Her hand reached upward for his nipples. Then, they began to play with them, kneading, twisting, touching, and rolling. She was something else. He tried as much as he could to gather his thoughts and his wits about her, but instead, he found himself spiraling out of control.

The lady's lips made slurping sounds around his cock as she focused on the tip. Just when he felt like he was going to let off his load, she stopped sucking and massaged a huge vein at the back of his cock. He felt the sensation die down. She did it three more times, toying with him before she slipped him back into her heat.

He had forgotten completely about the danger that they were both in forgotten that Rami had been kidnapped. As far as he knew, he was alone in this new world with this girl and would give an arm to remain here.

"Oh shit," she cursed as the dick went all the way through. She let it fill up her insides, every part of her. Her eyes were on Levi, her hands were on his big chest.

She began with a slow rhythm as if she was getting into the feel of things, then she started riding hard and fast. He was lost. It took 7 minutes, and he had to lift her up away from his cock while he groaned in the pleasure and agony of finally getting to climax.

"Where did you learn to do that?" He asked.

She simply smiled at him. He was certain she was going to become a constant feature in his life. For the moments, the worries were gone, the lies were forgotten, and he could breathe freely again.

Shaun

In Lucas's house, there was darkness. The only source of light seemed to be coming from the porch light outside. Shaun waited for a while, while he willed his eyes to get used to the darkness. His ears were busy too. He must have caused some racket to get through the window. If Lucas was a light sleeper, then he would be up and about, looking for who broke into his house. He hoped Lucas was not.

Finally, after waiting for a while and discovering that his eyes had gotten used to the semi-darkness, he crept forward. The house had rooms downstairs, but he knew Lucas would not be in any of these rooms. Yet, he opened them and checked one by one. Slowly, he would push the door open, cursing under his breath if the door made too much noise. He did not want to be caught in this house by the incapable Lucas who had a robot take his job off his hands.

After going through the room downstairs, he proceeded to the rooms upstairs. He wondered why one person would live in a big house like this all by himself. *Does he like bringing girls over for a drunken party?* Shaun remembered when that was all that he cared about, partying long into the night with asses and tits in his face. People grow, and he had grown. He was done with all that now and had serious stuff before him. Serious stuff like finding out what was wrong in this fucking name with such a creepy name as Waterloo.

The first two rooms were empty. Shaun hoped that Lucas had too much faith in his own ability to protect himself and had his door open. If his door was not open, picking the lock might draw his attention. Now, he would not want that. Catching Lucas unaware would be the best. If it was possible, he would get out of here with the information he wanted and without sacrificing his identity.

The third room had the door slightly ajar. Shaun noted the difference and preferred for a hail of bullets blazing through the door or a charge by an awoken

Lucas. When none of that came, he pushed the door open slowly, gritting his teeth when the door sang a little. The song was not enough to wake the figure that was stretched out on the bed.

By now, Shaun's eyesight was used to the semi-darkness. There was light coming from the glowing cloud outside. Before Shaun slipped into the room, he worried about silent alarm systems that he could not see, one that would send out an alarm to someone without him even knowing. It made him move faster. He had to be out of the building before anything happened.

The figure on the bed was Lucas. He could see the bobbly hair. There was too much on his head. *He needs a haircut.* In the darkness where the hair could not be differentiated from the head, it made his entire head look big.

Shaun moved close to the sleeping cop and placed cold metal against his skin. It was enough to wake him.

Lucas

At first, it was a dream. Then, the cold feeling against his skin became more concrete. He tried to pull himself away from it and continue sleeping. But none of that worked. The more he tried to get away from it, the more the feeling of the coldness against his neck became real.

"Wake up," a voice urged.

"No," Lucas murmured sleepily.

He could hear Martha from afar, hear Cody crying and reaching out for a hug. But he could not see them. It was confusing. He knew Cody wanted a hug, yet he could not see her.

"Wake up, officer," the voice said again.

Officer! The word threw Lucas out of sleep. He was about springing up when the force of a hand pushed him back down on the bed. The cold feeling had come from his dream and was against his neck. He blinked several times, trying to understand where he was. Everything was so confusing. It felt like he knew this place and he did not.

"Lucas," the voice that had pulled him out of sleep called.

He wanted to turn towards the voice, but the cold steel pressed forcefully into his neck. With a startling shock, he realized what it was.

"No... no, no, don't kill me," he pleaded, sleep completely deserting his eyes.

He was in his room now, he realized, at fucking gunpoint. *Who does that? Who breaks into a police officer's house at night?* Some cameras could catch the person and the robots would not waste time to waste the person's life. They did the best investigations.

"You are going to provide an answer for every question I ask you," the voice said. "It is for your life."

Somehow, the voice sounded familiar, and somehow, it did not.

"I have a family!" Lucas cried. His scream got him a smack in the head from the butt of a gun. He yelped in pain, then became silent, nursing his wound.

"Good, don't shout," the intruder said again. "Why do you have a robot as your superior?"

"I... I don't get this..."

"Do you want to die?"

"No."

"Then, don't play smart. A robot can easily replace you. Answer the question."

"It's the directive."

"From where?"

"HQ."

"There are humans there. Why would they keep a robot as your head here?"

"Maybe that's where humans should be."

"Are you kidding you now?"

"Shaun?"

"Shut the fuck up!"

"Shaun, what the fuck are you doing?"

Finally, he had managed to place the voice and trace it to the other. Shaun must be out of his goddamn mind to try to pull this off.

"I ask, you answer."

Lucas heard the man swearing softly under his breath.

"There is no need to threaten me with a gun. You cannot shoot me."

"You would be surprised at the length I can go to stay safe from robots."

Dora

They were both lying on the bed, tired from too much fucking. Dora was having mixed feelings. The man could be anything, but he was also a good fucker. She could feel his light breathing as she lay on his chest, that gentle heaving up and down. He did not fuck like a scientist. He fucked like there were no rules, no procedure to follow. Her kind of man.

She looked up into his face. His eyes were shut. He was not bad-looking either. If the world was not poised to end, perhaps she would have stayed with him, had something with him that they could build for the future. But the world had to end in order for humanity to have a chance at survival. There were so many powers, so many forces in play. There were rumors of machines taking over. These rumors had been downplayed time and again by the defense ministry, and at one point, by the President himself. If the rumors were true, then ending the end would ensure that these machines would stop functioning. It would give the strongest among them a chance to get up from the ruins and start all over again. She hoped whoever it was would not mess it up this time.

Barry stirred and Dora quickly shy his eyes. She did not want that man to know that she had been gawking at him. Barry fell silent again and continued sleeping. Dora opened her eyes. She had the locations, the coordinates. They would need every branch of their organization, The Greater Earth movement to carry this out. Even then, it would still not be enough. They would have to travel to some countries where they had no members. No, she was not crazy. It was the world that was crazy, and it needed to be reset. There were still rumors flying about that some countries were killing children. If one had two children, one had to go. Dora had not really seen these herself, but their information network was so vast that she had reason to be concerned about the development.

She extricates herself from Barry's hands and stood up to watch her naked body before the mirror. For a woman who was in her mid-thirties, her body was beautiful. In fact, it was like the blooming body of a teen who had finally grown completely into a woman. She was proud of it.

She did not spend much time before the mirror though before she hurried towards the restroom, snagging her phone off the table. Quickly, she dialed the number she had crammed. After the call, she would delete the call log.

"Hello," a voice called from the other end.

"I have found the nests," she said, sticking to the code language, as she was afraid the call might be monitored, although there was no reason for the government to. Still, she could take no chances with the oppressive governments of the world today.

"All of them?"

"All of them."

"When will you move?"

"I will help you find them tomorrow."

"So be it."

She ended the call and sighed. The world was making them do things they ordinarily would not have conceived of. Who would have known that death was the answer? That in order for humanity to survive that they all had to die.

She washed her face at the sink as the scenes of last night replayed in her mind. Together with the scenes, she could see Barry's face popping up time and again, and her heart skipping beats. He was out there, and she was going to see him once she opened this door. She was supposed to be a strong woman. This feeling was not even supposed to exist. All she had to do was to put it aside and do the work that she had taken upon herself to do. She had met with trials and tribulations and all that shit, and none ever made her think twice about what she had committed to doing. Maybe it was because this one meant the end of a lot of things, and she could not help but wonder how a void would look like without her, how she would stop existing and just fizzle out into nothingness.

She opened the door and walked into the room. Barry was not there.

Heather

She woke up. Then she panicked, realizing she had fallen asleep in someone else's house, and the person did not even know who the fuck she was. She quickly looked around the room, discovering that it was dark. When she had tried to turn the lights on earlier, Andre had cautioned that she stayed her hands and left everything the way it was. Everything except the refrigerator and the kitchen. They could take whatever they wanted from those places and eat to their fill.

Her eyes slowly got used to the darkness inside, and the reflection from the porch light. They went to the other sofa in the room and she found Andre lying stretched out. She could not tell if he was asleep or awake, and she really wanted to talk. It was a mixture of confusion, abandonment, and helplessness. The people that she called her parents were now colder. It was almost as if they had been changed from the inside.

She turned away and stared at the ceiling. There was just too much to know within a short period. And all through that short period, she had to be careful about the people that she confided in, otherwise, she could end up like her late sister, Marie. The girl was not supposed to die.

"Fuck," she muttered.

"Can't sleep?" Andre asked from his side of the room.

Heather turned towards Andre. The man was still not looking at her, preferring instead to stare at the ceiling. Heather sat up. She was tired of everything. If she could, she would return to her parents, but the uncertainty surrounding her sister's death made it necessary for her to trust a complete stranger instead of her parents.

"What is really happening?" She asked.

"You don't follow the news?" Andre asked.

"What news? We have been running for two days."

"See how far I came for you?"

"What the hell do you mean?"

"I don't stay around here, you know. I'm not part of anything. I am just me. I have been observing your parents for a long time."

"Why?"

"I suspected something was wrong with them. I was not wrong, and anyway, if you ask what's happening, then you should know that a cleaner and the most powerful energy catalyst has just been launched. Already going through trials in most countries. You know what I mean."

"What energy?"

"America, Britain, Russia, Germany, even China are in on it. Although America wants them out. It's going to take something more than the grumbling to get them out."

"It's out?" Heather asked disbelievingly. She could not believe her parents did not tell her.

"This muon-catalyzed energy can be used for just about anything. It can be used for weapons, lots of it. Weapons that would have wide-reaching consequences."

"My parents helped make that?"

"I'm afraid they did."

Heather could not think straight again. She knew that her father hardly showed any emotion these days, but back when she was a child, she remembered him very well. He was nothing like what he later became. He smiled easily, laughed easily, and got sad easily. But these days, his face was always gloomy.

"Damn."

"Right, damn is right because this thing that they are looking at all over the continent could become one massive bomb that would take out the entire world."

"What?"

"The damn thing is unstable."

Barry Stivers

Call me crazy, I don't care. I want to marry her.

Barry was not thinking straight anymore. Maybe it was the sex, maybe it was the way she leaned into his body after the sex. The sleep and the cuddling

It had been long since he made love in that way with reckless abandon. He was pushing 40, and life was not getting simpler. Having someone in his life at this time meant the person had seen him and thought all about it before letting him in. She was not that young either.

He let himself into the shop he had seen on their way to this place. It was still early morning and he did not think that there would be people interested in shooting him.

It was a thrift store.

"I want a ring," he said, walking up to the dealer.

The man had not been replaced by any bot yet, and Barry did not know how he felt about that. He refused to admit to himself that he felt comfortable when robots were not around him. The drones maybe he could deal with, but the robots who wanted to speak and talk like humans made him think of a sinister aim buried beneath all of that ambition of recreating humans.

"What kind of ring do you want?"

Barry did not have much money in his pocket, but he knew he had enough in his account and could use his fingerprint and face scan to make the purchase, but he did not want that. He was not yet completely out of Waterloo, and the guys who wanted him dead could track him to this shop and end him.

"That one," he pointed at a simple ring, hoping it would not be costly and he could pay for it with the cash he had in his pocket. All he needed was a symbolic gesture.

He had thought about it. The woman was in love with him, and he had not seen any person quite like her. She came to that Café to save his life, almost as if she knew... wait, what? Knew. Could she have known that some people were planning to attack him?

He paused. The seller was saying something, but he was not listening. What if she was planted to make him give her his trust? Was that why she gave her body so readily? But, fuck it, she looked like a woman in want. He was in want as well, and they satisfied themselves. What was this doubt?

"Are you taking it?" The seller finally asked.

"I would like to think about it," Barry said.

"Do you even have a way of paying for this?"

"Of course."

Barry walked outside. He was stunned by the discovery that he had made. He sat down on a seat by the road and reclined his back against the rest. Slowly, he began analyzing everything. Why was she there just at that point in time?

Was it a coincidence? Did she know what was going to happen? Damn, and he had been making sensitive calls before her. Her face bothered him because it showed the right amount of concern and unconcern at his business, which either meant the woman was a good actor or she was genuine.

"Fuck this," he said finally. He did not even trust the government that had promised to protect him, yet he had given them the sensitive information that she was afraid of letting someone that saved him know.

He walked back into the shop.

"I will take the ring," he said.

CHAPTER 16

Mira

The helicopter ride was the longest of her life. She thought she would just get on the helicopter and in no time, she would see herself in Waterloo. But it did not work that way. The clouds crawled past, and the wind gently touched her face. It was as if every element was conniving to be deliberately slow.

Doctor Phil had his eyes in front of him, glasses covering them. Mira could remember him without the glasses. It was almost as if those glasses were part of his face.

"How long before we even get there?" She asked for the umpteenth time.

"Mira," the man said, turning to his daughter. "Calm down, I think he will live, okay?"

"Okay," Mira replied. She was calm now, and she had already convinced herself in her mind that Phil was the better parent. Melinda had her hatred. There was nothing to love about her mother. She was as vain as she was, and topped hers off with her arrogance and the stupid thought that she knew what was best for her daughter.

Finally, the helicopter found a place to come down, swirling wind and dust were all over the place. Mira waited until Doctor Phil let himself down and followed him across the plain towards the laboratory. They were both running very fast as they ran towards the building.

In front of the building, two men wearing lab coats welcomed them.

"Doctor Phil," one of them said. "So, kind of you to come down from the city."

Phil shrugged and smiled. "Well, my daughter loves this guy. How is he?"

"Stable, but he is under."

"Are the tissues responding to treatment?"

"Yes, the injuries have healed. We could not wait for authorization before embarking on that. He would have died if we did not quickly salvage the situation."

"Good work, boys."

Mira nodded at the men before she followed her father into the building. It was a big one, maybe too big to be a Waterloo where many homeless people ran to so they could ravage people's farmlands and stay alive at least. Life in the city was becoming tougher by the moment as the population soared. The employed were being swallowed in numbers by the unemployed. There were so many bills to pay, but of course, Mira could not relate to any of these things. She was glad she did not have to.

"Where is the subject?" Her father asked the receptionist.

Subject? Mira thought. Why was the man calling Roland *the subject?* What was going on? Before Mira could clarify, they had been pointed to a room at the far right side, down the hallway. She followed Doctor Phil and they got into the room.

The first sound that greeted her when she entered was the beep-beep of the life support. There were red lines on the screen and they flowed like gentle waves, very close to fattening.

"Roland," she said, in tears, and walked over to the bed where she saw Roland's face. He looked like he was sleeping, and had not just recently been a victim of assassination.

"Who would want to hurt you?" She cried.

Doctor Phil stood by the side and let the girl have her time with her lover. It irritated him, but he knew it was something he would have to bear. Mira's tears were streaming down from her eyes, staining the bedsheets and whatever fabric it came in contact with. When she turned to look at Doctor Phil, she discovered that his father's mind was far away. *Is there still hope for Roland?*

"Will he be okay?" She asked.

Detective Shaun

He must have fallen asleep on the couch in the room before he realized that the sun was up. His adventure last night had yielded results. It had also exposed him. If Lucas was the pushover that Lobo made him look like, then he would have reported him to Lobo. That would be terrible. Waterloo was a countryside that he did not even know if it was on the map.

When he woke up, he quickly sprang up and reached for his gun. It was in the same place he had left it. He looked around, expecting someone to break through the door and come looking for him, but no one did. He sighed and stood up from the seat. Some cold water from the fridge calmed him down before he proceeded to the bathroom to take his bath.

He would have to make an appearance at the precinct so he would not be suspected. It was a risk that he had to take. Shaun had lived his life on taking risks, calculated risks. So far, they had worked out, but he knew there was always a first time, a time when nothing works out and it all comes crashing down. He hoped it would not be today.

Once he was done with taking his bath, he quickly pulled on fresh clothes and stood before the mirror. He and Lucas had come to some kind of understanding last night. He promised he would help the cop get his wife and daughter back because of the information that he got from Lucas. In exchange, Lucas would cover for him. Lucas already had the trust of the bots that worked at the precinct.

"The world is going to be shit when humans now have to earn the trust of robots," Shaun muttered. "Shouldn't it be the other way round?"

He walked outside and found his car waiting patiently for him outside. But his eyes did not dwell on his car. They moved quickly across the street where there was an SUV parked. The doors of the car opened immediately he got outside the house.

It raised enough alarm, and Shaun already found his hand pulling his weapon. He stayed it and waited for the men to walk towards him.

There were two men and one woman, all dressed in black suits and wearing glasses. The way they walked, he realized immediately what they were. It was unnerving, seeing all of them so lifelike and making their way towards him.

They stopped about 10 feet from where he was standing and the female smiled at him.

"You must be Detective Shaun," the female said.

"Who are you?" Shaun asked.

"Detective Becks. Becks Hans."

"Just the kind of stupid names they would give bots," Shaun muttered.

"Hurtful, but it does not matter. I am here to replace you. You have been taken off the investigation of Mr. Roland Hughes."

"What? Is this a joke?"

"I'm flattered that you would consider my kind capable of making jokes," Becks said and turned to go back to her car, together with the men.

"You couldn't wait for me to get to the station?" Shaun asked.

"I felt that I should give you a heads up," Becks said before she got into the car.

Shaun watched the car, Rev, up completely stunned. The car's engine roared before the car completed made a U-turn and headed up the street, leaving him in its wake.

"No, thus fucking can't be," he said. Whatever that thing was, it did not even let him see an ID.

He walked over to his car and got in. He had to get to the precinct, although he suspected that his business last night was now public knowledge.

The car roared and followed the trail up the road. Earlier this morning, he had been hesitant of getting to his workplace, but after meeting Becks, he knew he had to call in.

The precinct loomed in no time before him, and he found a parking space. Then, he walked up to the entrance.

"I will have to search you for weapons," the bot at the door said.

"My weapon is government-issued. What the hell do you mean search me for weapons? I work here.

The bot paused and made a show of thinking, which was actually going through its database, then it turned back to Shaun.

"I can't find your name in the database."

"You did not ask for my name."

"I know your name."

Shaun thought of going into the precinct without his weapon, but he quickly realized how all of these could be a setup. While the new bots were arrogant and believed in their abilities to replace humans, they were not stupid. They knew the things he had done with a gun; they knew the things he could do with a gun, so they were not taking any risk.

"Search again, I was assigned a case here. I was recently transferred."

"Maybe you have been transferred again," the bot said.

Shaun could swear that the thing smirked. He turned around and walked back to his car. This should not be right. Putting people's faces on AI intelligence had to be wrong. What was this country turning into?

He got into the car and sat down, his eyes on the door. Maybe there was a way he could sneak in there when the guard would go for a break. *A break? You have got to be kidding me.* They were bots and they fucking had no need to rest.

"Shit," he muttered. He had to know what the hell was going on in there. The place pulled him like gravity.

Maybe he could take the bot out. All he had to know was how they worked. The government would not be happy with what he wanted to do, but they would appreciate him in time. They would realize that he saw the future before anyone of them could.

"Don't do it."

Shaun started. His gun was already out, in his left hand, the barrel watching Lucas silently. *The fuck! How did he get close?*

"I got close to you without you noticing me, and I was not even sneaking around," Lucas said. "Imagine what they could do to you. They all are the best of mankind."

"The best of mankind would not hold your family hostage."

"Maybe, it is for the good in the long run. You know sacrifice a little and…"

"Your family is little? Have you lost your mind?"

"Lobo asked about the bruise on my face. I told him I was in a bar fight. I'm suspended for today."

"He can do that?"

"He can do whatever the hell he wants. The programs on these computers are incredible. Man is a god."

"Man?"

"That's how they see themselves. Listen, I think you should leave the town. Find something else. Maybe even go on retirement if you can afford it."

"What are you saying?"

"You can't save me. You can't save anybody. Go home and spend your time on something else."

"Since you are a coward, my emphasis is on breaking up this little ring of knuckle-head robots."

"As long as the rules are concerned, they have done everything according to the book. Go home, Shaun."

Lucas left the car and started walking away. Shaun wanted to call him back, but he did not want to attract attention to himself. So, he watched him walk away.

"So much for the deal," he muttered.

It had not been really much of a deal anyway. Lucas was at gunpoint. Was it not the same thing these monsters were doing for him?

He was about to turn the key in his ignition when he suddenly paused.

"No," he said. He had not seen Lucas's move his hands suspiciously even though he knew that he could have easily missed it. He held his breath.

Lucas, however, did not strike him as someone that would want to kill him or anybody for that matter. Still, if he was properly motivated, who knows? He could do it.

With his heart racing, he turned the key in the ignition, there was no sound except that of the car kicking to life, and when he relaxed, he realized that he was still alive.

The roads were busy for a countryside road and he had to move slower than he thought as he headed back to the hotel where he was staying. He was going to sign out and leave the building for the bastard robots. Before that, he had to make a call to Aaron. He cleared by the side of the road and picked up his cellphone.

The call connected almost immediately and Aaron's voice came online.

"Hello," he said.

"What the fuck is going on here? I have been replaced, is this a joke?"

"Who is this?"

"What the fuck!"

"Can you stop swearing and go straight to the point?"

"The detective you fucking transferred to Waterloo."

"Becks Hans?"

"What in the fucking hell. It's Detective Shaun."

"Shaun?"

"Yes."

"Never heard of that name before."

Almost immediately, there was the sound of a big lorry horn as the heavy-duty vehicle bounded down the highway.

Shaun turned too slowly. He wanted to pull off his body and change it into the one he had in his mind. It responded too slowly. Before he knew what was happening, the lorry was just right behind his car, the horn louder than ever, doing more to disorient him than to warn him. Then, it came immediately. A sound like an explosion of metal upon metal, glassed showering the street. Then, dead silence.

CHAPTER 17

Heather

U nstable. Unstable. Why would anyone work with something that has the potential of taking out the whole world?

Heather wanted to doubt Andre. She desperately did. She wanted to believe that she just had bad parents, not despicable human specimens who did not care about what their project was doing to the world. She wanted to believe that she was dreaming, having a nightmare, and that when she would wake up, Marie would still be alive. Her father would have the biggest smile for her and stop walking around all the time with the gloom on his face. But it seemed nothing of the sort was going to happen.

Andre sat down.

"I need water," he said suddenly.

When Heather looked at him, she discovered that he was sweating profusely. A moment ago, he had looked like the calmest thing that she had ever known, and now, he was sweating and unable to stay still.

"Are you okay?" She asked.

"Water, get me water."

Quickly, she rushed to the refrigerator and came back with a bottle of water. Andre popped it open quickly and poured the content into his mouth. Heather got another bottle and he finished that too. She could not help but notice how much heat he was giving off. His temperature seemed to be soaring through the roof for no reason. It was frightening to behold.

"Are you okay?" She kept asking. Andre leaned against the sofa.

Heather could almost swear that she could see vapor coming off of his body, but she was not sure. When she went to get the third bottle of water from the fridge, she discovered that his temperature had reduced as suddenly as it increased. It was confusing, but his eyes were already shut and he seemed to be sleeping.

Heather looked outside. The day was gradually coming around to dispossess the night, and cars had begun passing through the street. There was no telling when the real occupants of the house they were in would come back to their house.

"Andre," she called.

But Andre continued sleeping. He was breathing so slightly that she was afraid that he had died. She felt his pulse. It was strong. He murmured a little in his sleep and continued sleeping.

"Fuck," Heather said.

She paced the room, always making sure to look through the window whenever she got close. She did not want to be taken by surprise.

The sound of a car passing outside drew her attention. The car was not driving by; it was slowing down. She ran to the window and looked. It was a black SUV with tinted glass and unmarked. The doors were pushed open before the car even pulled to a stop and out they came, people wearing black suits with dark glasses over their eyes. There were four of them, three male and one female.

"Shit," Heather muttered and ran to the sleeping Andre. "Wake up! They are unto us!"

Andre did not bulge from his sleep. Heather ran back to the window. The potential intruders were walking up to the door now. It was clear that they knew people were in this house.

As Heather turned around to shout at Andre again, she found him standing. He cracked his neck and his eyes glowed briefly before it stopped, or so she thought.

"Come," he said, taking her hand and pulling towards the hallway. The house should have a backdoor or a window or something. It was better to find if and flee than turning to face the people who were clearly coming for them.

"I think there's a tracker in you. I blocked the one on your phone," Andre said.

"Who are those people?" Heather screamed.

"You know."

Yeah, she did, but she did not want to believe it. She did not want to believe that her own parents could send people as deadly as that to come find her.

They heard the sound of the door being kicked down before Andre broke open a window.

"Go on," he said and turned back.

"Wait, what? Where the hell are you going?" Heather asked. There was panic in her voice.

"Just climb through the window... I will be with you soon."

Heather watched him walk down the hallway. *Oh well, if he wants to die, he is welcome.*

She helped herself through the window. Immediately she made it through the space, she wished she had not. About 20 feet from where she landed, she found a female figure waiting for her.

"Heather," the figure said. The voice tried too hard to be natural that it failed. It sounded eerie for want of words to her.

"Who are you?" Heather asked.

"Your replacement."

She was walking towards Heather now, covering the ground quickly. Heather waited till she was very close. The strange female threw a lunch and Heather parried easily. She had learned how to fight on one of her journeys, the journeys she hated for herself. But there was another punch on the way. Heather also defended this valiantly. Then, more punches followed, giving her the chance to create an attack of her own. Finally, one of the punches hit home like she had feared it would, and she stumbled on the ground, rolling back to her feet again.

When she woke up, she was confused. She was standing before her, staring at her with a look of complete irritation. But that was not the source of her confusion. There was actually no difference between her and the her standing before her. In her confused state, she was too slow in throwing her jab, and instead caught a blow with her lower jaw. An uppercut followed and she found herself sailing through the air before she landed on hard earth with an oomph.

She layed there, hoping she had not broken anything. When she heard the footsteps of her *replacement* coming to where she layed for the kill, she remembered she had taken a gun from Andre after berating him about making her a bait. She reached towards her trouser waist for it, pulling it out, taking the safety off, and firing in one fluid movement. But her opponent was faster. She had seen the bullet coming and quickly swirled away from it before it could get to her.

Heather spun around fast looking for her. The movement was a blur, a flash. Before she could bring the gun up again, it was knocked out of her hand. But she clung onto the hand that knocked it off, pulling the enemy towards herself. The other her was not expecting the head-butt she gave her.

The other Heather tumbled to the ground. At the same time, Heather heard a thud beside her and swirled around quickly, only to discover Andre. He had blood and bruises on his face and shirt and had the rifle raised towards Heather's attacker. Two shots rang out immediately she got to her feet. One of the bullets hit her, but she managed to get back into the SUV.

Andre held the gun and aimed, but he did not shoot. He watched as the car tires screeched and the car sped down the street.

"Shoot her for god's sake!" Heather screamed.

"I can't... That is you," Andre replied.

"You saw her?"

"I felt her."

Heather was confused. Ever since Andre's temperature did the strange thing it did inside the house, he had been acting strange.

"You felt her?"

"Yes."

"Where are the others?"

"Dead, but we have to get out of here."

"Damn right... we have to."

"The chip in your hand, we have to remove it too... it's a tracker."

"There's a chip in my hand?"

"Things mothers never tell us."

Dora

The room was empty. There was no sign of Barry, and the bed yawned emptiness from where his full body had only recently filled. Dora stood for a while at the door, getting all manner of emotions running through her. Rage, anger, fear, love, regret, nostalgia. If anyone from her group had been here to kidnap or kill the man she had found her heart slowly melting for, she would make sure that person is the sacrifice that the earth needed to survive. The earth would hear the screams of pain as she would tear the person limb from limb, patching him or her up again and again till the heart gives out.

The thought she had about the punishment of whoever had taken care of the confusion that Barry had brought to her emotions seemed to calm her nerves. She walked to the window and stared outside—there was no sign of Barry.

She still had the towel wrapped around her waist, so she went to change into something simple: a pair of hose and a short gown. The hose went all the way up to her waist and gripped her figure in a way that made her feel sexy and comfortable.

Then, her attention turned back to Barry again. What if Barry had run away from her? What if he had found out what she was actually here for and decided to get away before she broke his heart?

"Fuck," she said and sank into the bed. The thought was paralyzing.

She was caught between two things now: following her feelings and seeing where this led and doing what she had always wanted to do by bringing the end of the world nearer, so there would not have to be a complete annihilation of the human race.

What have you gotten yourself into?

The question bounded across her mind, demanding an answer that she could not even give. She did not know what she wanted again.

The door opened then, with her mind still in a state of confusion. At the door, the reason for her confusion stood with an uncertain smile on his face. He gently closed and locked the door before turning back to look at her. She was scared. He looked like he was about to do something that would deepen the confusion that had already started germinating in her mind, so she decided to get rid of the silence. Silence was like a vacuum for words. If nothing was said, it would only provide an avenue for him to say what he wanted to say.

"Where did you go?" She asked, trying to keep her voice from screaming her concern. Keeping her emotion from her voice was a tasking thing, but she managed it, keeping it cool.

"Out."

"Don't you think that's a bit careless since some people want you dead?"

"No, not for what I got."

Jesus! He is kneeling down.

"I know that I hardly know you, Dora," Doctor Barry Stivers said, staring straight into Dora's eyes. "But I already know what I want and for how long I want it. I would like to think that you want the same thing, seeing as you went back to that Café specifically for me..."

Don't say it. Don't fucking say it.

"The world is hanging in the balance and might even fall apart. Apart from the irresponsible thing I did in handing the government keys to the end of life, there are other things threatening life. The world could end today..."

You don't know the first of it.

"If the world is ending now, I would like to know that I had something with you. Will you marry me?"

The question. It finally came. She had been running from it all this while, trying to convince herself that she felt nothing of worth for the man that was just meant to be a paw in a bigger man, a man she was supposed to use and move on. She blinked so many times that she felt her eyes were going to disappear. He still knelt there, expectant. Her heart was beating. His eyes were pleading, and time was slowly strolling by.

Levi

He woke up the next morning with memories of the previous night hanging like cobwebs across his mind. It was mind-blowing, the night he had had, so much that he decided it was a dream.

When he turned to the other side of the bed, the emptiness told him his thoughts might not be far from the truth. But he wondered how a dream could be so intense that she could feel Ashley's lips around his manhood. Whoa! He was naked. He quickly hurried under the cover and stayed there, looking around for his clothes.

Discovering himself naked meant that something had gone down between him and Ashley. He was in her house after all. Her room. He remembered that the girl's parents were out, and she did not even tell him when they were coming back and panicked. Quickly, he rose from the bed, but when he was reminded of his nakedness again, he slipped back under the sheet. Then, he listened. Someone was singing a song from somewhere in the house.

He reached to the bedside table and grabbed his clothes. He had finally discovered it was neatly packed and kept there for him. He took a little while to slip into it, then he came down from the bed and started towards the door.

The room was strange. Being here frightened him. What if last night had happened only in his mind, and like in one of those freak movies he had watched, somehow, he had teleported to the girl's room naked.

The sweet melody that the voice carried with it lured him down the stairs. He continued moving towards it. The Voice belonged to Ashley, clearly.

When he made his way to the living room, he saw Ashley through the big window that connected the kitchen to the living room. She had a tiny pair of shorts; they barely covered her middle. Then, she had a red singlet that was suspended just before her tummy.

He found himself watching her body, then looked up to find her looking at him strangely.

"Who are you?" She finally asked.

"Who am I?"

"How did you get in here?" She continued.

"Ashley..."

"You know my name, get out before I call the police!"

"But..."

"What were you doing up there?"

The questions confirmed Levi's biggest nightmare. It felt like a strange movie, one that he wanted to skip quickly. As he still stood there astounded, Ashley burst out laughing.

"You need to see the look on your face," she said.

Levi took a deep breath, realizing it was a prank. Ashley laughed for a while, and when Levi did not join in, she looked at him worriedly.

"Wait, you do remember, don't you?" She asked.

"Of course, I remember," Levi replied. Forgetting last night would be impossible.

"You must be hungry."

"Mom must be worried sick about me now," Levi said.

"Mommy's boy eh? Why are you in such a hurry?"

Levi sighed. "What are you up to?"

"Scrambled eggs and bacon... you will like it."

Levi did not know if he would like it. But when the meal came, he wolfed it down with Ashley and drank the water she offered. It was only after they had both eaten to their fill that they remembered Rami. They were not really sure what had happened to him.

"Maybe we should report to the police," Levi said.

Ashley scuffed. "The police? Who do you think was responsible for the raid?"

"The police?"

"They do it all the time, secretly. I heard they are taking people to their labs to be experimented on."

"Where did you get this from?"

"You don't have to know."

"So, you think we cannot tell the police anything?"

"No, we can't. If we do, they will know we were the ones there that night, and we would be targeted and they make us disappear."

Levi's heart sank at this. He did not like Rami one bit, but he did not think anyone deserved to be kidnapped and used for whatever experimental purposes the government decided. Who was the government anyway? A bunch of humans like them.

"So, we do nothing?"

"Sadly, we cannot fight these people. We can only do our bit."

"Our bit?"

"Yes."

"I have to go now."

"I will walk you home."

"You know you don't have to."

"What are you talking about, I do."

So, together they went down the stairs, through the front door, and towards the tenement building that housed at least 200 people.

When they got to the front of the tenement building, the silence there tried to whisper to Levi, but the only thing he felt was soft, invisible hands raising goosebumps along his skin. The place was oddly quiet.

"Where is everyone?" He asked.

Ashley did not have the answer to the question.

The people that loitered around the lobby of the house were missing. The caretaker's seat took charge in his absence, and nothing breathed.

"Maybe you don't have to go in there," Ashley said.

Levi could see the fear that was in his heart reflecting in her eyes. He seriously considered her offer but knew that in the end, he would be forced to go in to find his family.

"I have to," he said and started up the stairs.

As he went along the way, he feared the worst. He feared that the feeling of abandonment that he felt now would be intensified when he finally saw what he was rushing up the stairs to see.

"Mom!" He screamed.

He could have taken the lift, but it was not in order. There was no power in the building.

Finally, he got to their apartment and barged through the door. The door was even open, and the house was deserted. He went from room to room, shouting the name of his sibling and calling his name.

The silence mocked him.

CHAPTER 18

Levi

"We have to go. We have to leave this place!"

Ashley's voice rang out in his head, but he was not listening. He was looking at the place he had called home since he was born, looking at it, and there was nothing even remotely homely about it.

"Levi!"

She was screaming and trying to drag him out of the place, but he stood still like a statue, unmovable. The more she pulled at him, the more he stood where he stood. He did not feel like moving from where he stood. In the background, he could hear the sound of a tractor outside. It frightened him, but not enough to push him from his dazed state.

"They are coming to destroy this building!" Ashley shouted again.

It had been in the courts for a long time. Apparently, the government worked the way it wanted. Without the tenants in the building, there was no need to worry about the courts or the people fighting back.

"We have to go!" Ashley kept shouting. Still, Levi did not move.

The building trembled as it was attacked from the foundation. Ashley ran to the window and started waving. If they could saw her, then perhaps they would hold on. But they did not. Most of them were robots anyway. They milled around the house like ants, just recently there had not been people. It was like a war zone, this time the troops were running over abandoned grounds.

"Hey! There are people up here!" Ashley screamed.

From the ground, none of the robots looked up. They carried on destroying the building like they did not hear anything.

"Are you deaf, you empty, iron-headed things!" Ashley screamed again.

In response, the building trembled again. Ashley was panicky now. She ran towards Levi and dragged him to the door. This time he left himself to be dragged across the room towards the door.

"No!" Levi screamed.

"We have to get out of here! Can't you hear the destruction outside?"

"My family!" Levi screamed, reaching for the doorpost.

"They are not here! We have to find them!"

That did the trick, pushing away Levi's objections. He allowed himself to be pulled along, down the steps and away from the room where his childhood had been built on. The building trembled again, threatening to collapse. Ashley was muttering silently. It had to be prayers for the building to hold till they made their way downstairs.

Carl

After the initial tense situation, the crowd seemed to realize that Carl was a worthy addition to their rank. It was like the coming of Saul to the apostles. He had killed a lot of them with the help of the government, and he was highly skilled in combat. Graham decided that killing him would cost more than keeping him.

"He is one of us now," Graham said to the gathering crowd of men, women, and children.

They nodded in affirmative, but some looked without certainty at the man that was supposed to be one of them now. In the eyes of some, the memories of dead, loved ones stood out. It was saddening and frightening. It was also harrowing being on the same team with a man that had brought most of them nothing but pain and sorrow. Still, they knew that they needed his help. The government was pulling the carpet from under their feet and getting closer to squashing their resistance by the day. They needed someone with experience to fight back the government.

"Come, my friend," Graham said, taking Carl's hand and leading him away from the crowd of people.

Among the crowd, Carl saw new brothers and sisters standing around in what used to be a dance club when the world was not yet going to hell. Also among the crowd, he saw enemies that would remain just that for a lifetime. He did not think there was anything that he could do that should make these people have a change of heart for him. No amount of apology would be enough to bring back their dead, loved ones. No amount of making up would do anything for them. They would keep hating till they had a chance to get their hands on him, and logic was not going to be of help.

Carl decided to keep his eyes away from them. Those were the really dangerous ones. They would wait for him to turn his back to defend them, then they would knife him. It would not matter if they would be killed right after from the very thing he was defending them from.

"We need your help," Graham said, taking him through the crowd of people. "We have to break into a secure lab. We figured out where the location is, and the weapons there, mostly experimental would be good for us."

Carl nodded.

"What do you think?"

"I will have to take a look at the building plan," Carl said.

"We don't have that."

"So, how were you planning to get in?"

"You."

"Fuck this, without the building plan, you wouldn't even know the safest way to get into the building."

"Carl, Carl, my friend. Look at the crowd behind us..."

Graham paused for emphasis. They were in a single room now away from the dance hall where the crowd of people that made up the resistance milled around. The only thing demarcating them from the people was a glass wall. It muffled out the noise too.

Carl turned to look behind him. The crowd was there. He still could see the look of hope in their eyes, especially in the eyes of the younger ones. Hope was a beautiful thing. So was a decorated flower vase. It is easy for it to shatter if it is placed in the wrong place from where it can fall to the floor. If it shatters, picking up is the most difficult and harmful thing. That was the thing about hope.

Mira

After seeing Roland and watching his chest heave up and down, Mira found her mind returning back to normalcy. But there was something strange and odd about this place. It looked nothing like a hospital. There were so many equipment's there that she could not recognize. She had been in hospitals before, seen extreme situations, but nothing as extreme as this. There were so many pipes around, slipping in and out of Roland's body. It was almost as if... as if they wanted to use him for an experiment.

She turned to his father.

"Is he going to be okay?"

"Certainly, Mira. He will be fine."

They were sitting in the lobby of the building alone. There was only one soul down there with them. No one passed through the place for as long as they were there. No one else came in through the shut door.

It felt strange. If this was a hospital, then people had to be coming in or at least going out.

"What is this place?" Mira asked.

"A secret facility hospital," Phil replied. "The doctor will be out soon, and he will explain everything."

"Explain everything?"

"Yes, the procedure."

As if on cue, the door opened and a man wearing a white gown walked into the lobby. He came straight to where father and daughter were.

"Doctor Phillip," the man greeted, stretching out his hand for a handshake.

Phil took the man's outstretched hand and smiled perfunctorily into the man's face.

"I'm really sorry about what you have to go through." This time, the man spoke to Mira. "But we would require you to sign a few documents so we can begin the procedure on bringing back Mr. Roland to life. It is important that you take a quick decision..."

"You should not force my daughter into making decisions that she is not ready for," Phil said grumpily.

"I'm really sorry, it is just that..."

"It does not matter. You should not force my daughter into making fast decisions by..."

"Where are the documents?" Mira asked.

"Are you sure you want to do this?" Phil asked.

"Will it bring back Roland?" Mira asked the doctor.

"Definitely, he will be brought out from the coma.

"

"Then, bring the documents, I want to sign it."

Phil sighed.

The doctor led Mira to the receptionist's table and got some documents from the woman sitting there. The woman offered a tiny smile at Mira before she turned back to face the computer screen as if she did not want to be distracted in the least from what she was doing.

Heather

There was blood everywhere, but Andre was doing his best to stop the bleeding, and it was eventually stopping. Heather was wide-eyed. She could not believe that her parents could put a tracking chip in her, and leave it there even when she became an adult, albeit an adult that walked away from them.

"Did my sister have this chip too?" She asked Andre. He seemed to know more about her and her family than Heather would ever get to know. He would know about her sister.

"She had one. If you had another sibling, that one would have probably had one."

"When did they put this stupid chip in?"

"When you came back recently. It's a new technology," Andre said, holding the little chip in his hand and looking at it. They had stopped by the roadside to lose the chip, and the operation had been successful.

"What?"

"Yes, maybe you were sleeping..."

"I'm a light sleeper."

"Then, you were most probably knocked out by some substance."

"Substance? I don't think my parents would..."

"I don't think those are your parents."

"What?"

"You've not heard of the replacement program, have you?"

"Replacement program?"

"Yes, everybody thinks that Doctor Barry is a genius; that he is at the forefront of everything. Maybe he is not. I think he is caught in between. He can't call the bad out because he is embedded in the system."

"What are you talking about?"

"A crazy scientist's plan to live forever, to make the earth habitable."

"Muon-fusion..."

"No... that is just a front for creating bio-robots that would not need to be recharged in the future. They would just... keep on living."

"I don't get anything you are saying."

"Listen, humans are being replaced by machines. They are fast and efficient that your mom might actually prefer one to you."

"Don't bring my mother into this."

"Okay."

Andre turned around and got back into the car.

"We have to keep moving."

As Heather got into the car, she waited for Andre to continue from where he stopped, but he looked like he had completely forgotten what he was talking about, preferring instead to focus on the road. Instead of continuing their journey, Andre made a complete U-turn and headed back the way they had come.

"What are you doing?" Heather asked.

Andre chuckled.

CHAPTER 19

Detective Shaun

Discovering that he had been put off the job had him stuck inside his seat in the parking lot as he considered his options. He fished around in his dashboard and came up with a packet of cigar. He lighted one quickly, sticking the long roll between his lips.

The first inhalation brought calmness to his nerves, something that he solely needed. Fighting against creatures that he knew nothing about was no way to be welcomed into a new place. He had his suspicion, and Aaron would think of this suspicion as ridiculous. In fact, so would many others. But then, what if Aaron was part of the conspiracy, the ones that wanted to rid the earth of real humans and fill it with these unreal things that had their appearance.

It was the perfect recovery plan for the earth. They did not eat, therefore, they had no need to excrete waste from their body. They were powered with one of the cleanest energy sources around, and he had heard rumors that, in fact, the muon invention was not going to be used for farming and every other energy pursuit, which would make things easier for humans. Rather it would be used to power more of these robots, so they could last forever and create more of themselves if they wanted to. The new level of evolution. It was all bullshit, but he had to confirm.

This was all before the lorry slammed into his car from behind.

**

Now, he laid in the forest, having escaped from the car unseen. Somehow, he had managed to pull the car down open at the last minute and jump off the car into the bush. He had managed to move as fast as he could before an explosion rocked the day, an explosion that would have had him dead.

He laid on the ground, looking up into the ceiling that the treetops formed in the forest. The sun was having a hard time getting through, and he was thankful for that. His mind failed to focus on anything but instead ran all over the place. He thought about the death that he had so narrowly escaped, thought about what the world was turning into, and wondered if what he wanted to do was worth it. Who were the real humans remaining? How would he know? Some of the bots were so lifelike that it was impossible to tell them apart from the humans they represented. Lobo was almost like that, but not quite.

"Aaron," he muttered. Then, he shook his head. For all he knew, the bastard was in on this. He was probably the one that had given his location away and almost had him killed.

Still, grappling with his thought, he brought himself to a seating position, looking around the greenery. He had to act, and fast. The longer he took sitting here to wait around, the more these things take over. He decided he had to hack into the system and open the case file on Roland. That would probably tell him how it all started. He was told that Roland was close to death, then he was yanked off the investigation, and now, he was nearly killed.

He waited till it was dark, then he sneaked out of the woods. While he had been in there, the sound of the fire service department, manned, of course, by robots had filtered down to his hiding place. He had tried as much as possible to stay out of sight, so the story about his death would be believable. And when he saw the state his car was in, he decided they would probably think the fire was too hot that nothing of him could be found. Well, except the cigar piece he was smoking.

The lorry had come from behind.

He moved past, heading towards the police station. There would be guards standing there, guards who were robots, and whom he had no problem killing. Luckily, he still had his pulse gun strapped to the band of his trousers. It had not fallen off after he dived out of the car.

He paused a building away and observed the guards. They were hardly moving. The only thing that was moving was their eyes.

"Well, what does one expect from a fucking robot?" Shaun said bitterly.

Finally, one of them moved. He said something to the other and quickly walked inside. Taking out just one of the robots should not be a problem for him. He started sneaking towards the guard. At a distance, scared of the robot finding him, he stopped and took aim. He went for the guard's head and recorded a perfect headshot as the guard swooned and fell to the ground. He hurried forward quickly and dragged the guard to the side of the building and out of sight. If other cops sees a dead cop in front of the precinct, then his mission here would be effectively ruined.

He was about to walk away when he suddenly saw the eyes of the guard light up. It was glowing red, and some codes were running in his eyes.

"Fuck," Shaun cursed, his gun quickly springing to his hand. He was about to pull the trigger when a fast blow from the guard he thought he had ended knocked the air out of his lungs. His gun went a different way, and he was sprawled in the ground, breathless.

The guard stood up and walked towards him with a speed that bellied the size of the head. The hole in the head was also rapidly closing up like the guard had some magical, healing power. It was true.

Shaun tried to get on his feet, but got a kick against the side of his body. He was thrown on the ground again, farther away from where he had fallen before. The red eyes of the guard glowed brighter, stronger as if it was enraged. The head was almost completely healed now.

Shaun sighed. Death by a robot was the most shameful way to go.

Carl

He could not afford to fail these people, not after they had taken him in as one of their own. Using his knowledge of safe houses where weapons were kept in storage, houses that were made to look ordinary in order to forego suspicion and attacks, such as the one they were planning to carry out, he drew a map from memory. He hopes it was the right one, and the building was not different from other buildings he had led his men into in the past to get more weapons.

"Here," he said, handing Graham the map. "We will get in through here." He pointed at a point on the map.

It was a door that was mostly unguarded. All it needed was for someone to press the pin and the door would slide open. There were a couple of combinations he had gone through over the years, but he knew it was not going to be any of them. That was why he would need a sticky tape and hope that the place had been opened recently. With the tape, the heat maps of hands that had opened the door in the past would be revealed, and all he would do would just be to follow them.

"There's a door here?" Graham asked.

"Yes."

"Can we get it open?"

"We will have to try."

Carl was beginning to admire the resistance. They were becoming smaller by the day, but they kept demanding that the government do the right thing. Increase interest in healing the earth and leave the pollution that comes with too much science and advancement. They were proposing a return to nature, one that had been soundly ignored by the government of the day. Still, they were resolute, going into things unplanned.

"Okay," Graham said, his eyes holding all the hope that he had for his people.

Carl realized with a sudden fear that that hope had been transferred to him because of his knowledge of the people they were fighting.

"Before we go, I have to show you something," Graham said, pulling Carl aside.

Carl wondered what it was all about until Graham pulled his wallet out of his pocket. He extricates a little picture from it and showed Carl.

"Her name was Anna. Annabelle," Graham said, fighting to hold back the tremor in his voice.

"Your girl?"

"She was my girl till the federal forces broke into my house and took her off. Some of my people found out what they do to the children they take away."

"What?"

"Replace them."

"What?"

"These people are not fighting for humans. In the news, abductions like these are not reported. The government does not take note of them. The only thing the government cares about is profits!"

"Profit? What if the entire government is replaced by these crazy robots?"

"There has to be someone in charge, someone that started all of these."

Laura

She was in charge. Or so she thought. These things were not always the way people thought they were.

Barry Stivers. The name annoyed her, but she knew he was instrumental to her plans. If she was to get the whole world down on her knees, then she needed his invention to power her robots. She would not be here to see the new earth.

"In the beginning, God created the Heavens and the Earth," she murmured.

She sat in her laboratory, lost in thought. She had done it. What was more? She had also given them independent minds and made them hate the human race.

At the thought of the 'human race', her first daughter came to her mind. She did not know what she was up to, and she did not care. Much had been said about a mother's love for her child, but Laura seriously doubted that she was a mother at all. Even Marie, the obedient one. She had considered coming out to take Marie with her. Hiding underground till the AI's were done with the human race would have been the best thing to do for Marie, but she died. She killed herself.

Laura watched one of the screens from where she monitored her own part of the earth. There was static on it. Apparently, Heather had gotten close to the information that led to her sister's death. She had not stopped there, but gone as far as getting rid of the chip in her hand.

"Silly girl," Laura said, wondering what her obsession was with the girl.

If she was the woman she thought she was, then she was not supposed to be bothered about what Heather had found out or not. Sooner or later, anyway, she would meet her death at the hands of the people that had the new earth.

Laura coughed. The coughing continued like it would not stop, heaving discomfort from the depth of her belly. She continued coughing till she went to the sink in the room and coughed out blood.

She sighed, her end was coming nearer. Everything was moving too fast, and she knew she had less than a year to stay. She wanted to see the new earth before she died of this strange illness that had ravaged her lungs. The promise she would see in robots who would not pollute the earth, who had minds sharp as a razor, and who were terribly efficient, would give her a good rest. She would shut her eyes to death, knowing that she left the earth better than she found it.

Her mind turned to Barry Stivers again and the drones. The drones were supposed to identify threats to human existence, but they had not seen this one coming. How would it be when the robots had the same DNA as humans. That was perhaps the only downside to the robots. In other ways, they were the pinnacle of creation, what humans should be.

Barry Stivers' stupid drones would not be able to identify the threats till the threats were ready to take them all out.

CHAPTER 20

Barry

he said yes!

S His heart could not stop beating too hard. He could not believe that they were about to become something more than just strangers who found each other's bodies attractive. They were going to own each other, and he would make sure he loved her for whatever was left of the world.

"A small wedding would do," she said when he asked about it. "Just the minister, then you and I."

It was the same thing on Barry's mind. He so frighteningly echoed in his mind that she was afraid that she was reading his mind.

Impossible.

"Your parents?" He asked. It was crazy. He did not even know her parents, and here he was asking for her hand in marriage. Maybe, it was not too late to know anyway. He calmed his mind when he realized she probably knew just the same about him, and she had said yes.

"Long gone, Barry. Are we doing this or not?"

Are we doing this or not? Sounds like a business deal.

"Of course," he said. "I want to do this. Strange as it may sound, I love you. I feel like I have known you for ages, and with the world hanging in balance, I think I'd like to spend the rest of my life with you."

She stared deep into his eyes.

"I would love that too."

They had found another room in a modest-looking hotel, one where someone with the prestige of the scientist was not supposed to be found.

Barry turned away from her and stood up to walk towards the fridge. He had bought wine for this special occasion, and felt this was the right time to take it. There were glasses atop the refrigerator, and he rinsed them for use before he came back with everything to the bed.

As he slowly sat down, Dora turned on the TV. She seemed to be interested in what was happening around the world, making calls and watching the news wherever she could. Barry had not bothered asking who she was calling. In time, she would let him know, he knew. For now, all he had to do was to enjoy the exclusivity that they had created.

The Prime Minister of England has been overthrown. I repeat, the Prime Minister of England has been overthrown. The royal family has fled from the country. In what is possible, the swiftest coup in the history of...

"Yes!" Dora screamed.

For a moment, Barry saw another woman, other than the one he had fallen in love with. She was fierce, looked angry, and showed so much passion. It was like a moment of revelation, and he was sure there were a lot of things still yet to be revealed, but Dora sat back down, and calmness settled over her face once again like a veil.

"What was that?" He asked.

"England is free," she said.

Carl

They gained entrance more easily than Carl had thought. There were ten of them, strong-looking men who had more than themselves to fight for. Carl felt at one with them. Before, he would feel strange watching them, wondering why they were doing what they were doing before he would quickly mow them down. To him then, they were the enemy that should never be allowed to rear up their head.

Thinking about it made him feel a certain responsibility for the ones that were there with him. He would rather die than let them be killed.

"Which say?" Graham asked, coming up behind him.

Carl stopped before a crossroad of hallways. There were three options to choose from, so he stood there, trying to remember, trying to make up his mind on the way to choose.

"Give me a moment," he said.

The men lined up behind him, men who had no business trusting him, but who did trust him.

"That way," he said, and started moving on straight ahead. He heard the sound of footsteps following him. The men were trying to make their footfalls soft, but if one listened well enough, it was easy to pick out.

Carl was convinced about one thing. The authorities would not know that he was here. They would not be bothered to change their security procedure since he was already dead. That had always been their way of functioning. Kill off the erring officer and have their secrets remain secret.

Following memory and intuition, he walked down the hallway. It led them into a hall. It was dark. At the end of the hall, there should be a door. It was behind this door that the weapons they wanted could be found.

As Carl walked into the hall, he found that there was something different about the place. There were rows and rows of tanks hanging from the ceiling. The tanks were enough to contain a full human and there were about a hundred of them. The light in the hall was on, and a closer look further confused Carl. It also popped something open in his mind.

Replace them.

There were humans in the tanks. They looked like humans at least, but he was not sure that was exactly what they were the conversation he had had with Graham kept coming up in his mind.

He got closer and watched one of them inside the tank. What he saw frightened him. It was him. What were the odds?

He was lost for words and kept staring like he had seen a scary, mind-boggling apparition.

"What is it?" Graham asked, coming up to stand beside him.

Graham too was struck dumb by what he saw. The resemblance was eerie. Then, there was another possibility.

Graham quickly turned his gun on the Carl and pulled off the safety.

"Now, who the fuck are you?" Graham asked. There was fear and a little trembling in his voice, but for someone who was potentially faced with a robot that could easily kill him and 8 of his men, he showed great courage.

Detective Shaun

On the ground, the detective thought about his end, and how quickly it had come. Maybe he should have simply left the town and went to the city where there was more sanity. If he got killed here, he knew very well that no investigations would be carried out. He would probably be erased completely from the records. It had already started. Aaron was pretending like he did not know him, like he was not the one that sent him down here. It made him wonder if this was the plan all along. Would the robots have let him leave town if he wanted to? Would they have waited for him at the exit of the town and gotten to him?

The robot-cop standing over him had his eyes glowing brighter and brighter. There was tension hanging in the air. An expectation that waited for something, maybe an explosion, maybe the spurting lightning bolts from the eyes.

Shaun turned to the side and saw his gun! He was shocked as hope began flooding back into him. Then, he tried to keep a straight face while he went for the gun. It was the fastest move in his 10 years old career. He simply rolled over, picked up the gun, and turned quickly back to the position where he expected the cop to be. That one seemed to be rooted to the spot while the red glow in his eyes kept increasing. Without waiting for any reaction from the robot, Shaun squeezed the trigger multiple times in his direction, moving at the same time away from the spot where he had been lying.

Immediately Shaun moved, rays of red laser shot out from the eyes of the robot. But the lasers were not sustained. The root fell to the ground with holes puncturing its heart. Shaun was breathing heavily now. There was no time. He could not afford to hide the body of the dead cop again. Besides, he did not know if the creation would wake up again if he tried to hide it.

He got up and snuck into the precinct. He walked with his suit and looked like he pretty much belonged there.

In the hallway, there were some robots walking past. He kept his head down and walked past them till he got to the control room that he was looking for, he slipped in to find a robot at the desk.

"Hello," he said as the robot tried to get up from his seat. He blew a hole into the robot's chest. There was no noise, no sound of the booming explosions that obsolete guns brought about when one used them.

The computer was already open. All he had to do was type in the name of the man he wanted.

Mr. Roland Atkinson. Deceased. Program Robocop.

"Robocop, what does that even mean?"

Carl

At the end of the barrel of many guns, which could very well spell his end, Carl remained calm.

"They have not gotten to me yet," he said. "Why do you think I left the force?"

"Maybe you did not. Maybe you were created to drag out the resistance."

"And you think I could not do that simply by moving in with more robots and gunning you all down. I have always known where you stay.

Graham considered this. "Maybe you want us alive."

"I could still have kidnapped you with robots while you sleep."

Graham put his gun down now. He remembered when the cop let him go without any reason. Just a warning to stay away from trouble. How could he forget? His offense had been a treasonable one, and most officers would have shot him where he stood.

"Put your guns down," Graham said to his men.

Carl could read the fear on his face, hear it in his voice. The resistance leader was taking a great risk in trusting him, in believing that he was really who he said he was when, in fact, he could be anything.

The men slowly put their guns down, and the tension that hung in the air seemed to dissipate a little.

Carl could still feel it in the tenseness of the muscles around their lips. The men's nerves were all over the place. He did not blame them. He felt the same way. Some of them were observing more of the creatures in the tanks. Replacements that was what they all were. Carl thought of destroying the thing that was meant to replace him, but decided against it. The robots could not be killed with obsolete bullets. They had to be shot straight through the heart with a pulse gun. It would blow their power system off their chest. But that was only if the shooter was fast enough to know where the robot would be at a certain time. But without the pulse guns, they had no chance against these creatures.

"We have to keep moving," he said, leading the way.

He could see the door at the end of the hall and could not wait to get there. Behind him, the men hesitated a little before Graham led them towards him.

At the door, Carl felt there was something strange, something off-putting about this place. The door was open. The door was never open. Never. The weapons had to be kept safe at all times, and only authorized entry was allowed.

"Wait a minute," Carl said, looking around. His eyes went to the tanks. There were over a hundred of them hanging down from the ceiling. Carl suddenly had a rush of sight, a vision where the tanks suddenly burst open and the robots slid down from them to attack. He pushed the door open an inch. The room was empty.

Fucking trap!

"Retreat!" He screamed. "It's a trap! We have to get out of here!"

The men swung into action immediately, all of them running down the hall towards the door on the other side. Carl risked a look behind him, and what he saw spurred him on. It was happening exactly the way he had seen it in his mind. The tanks were bursting open, but they were opening from the one far from them, the ones behind them. Carl knew it did not matter. The robots were fast, and the perceived distance gave them false hope, one that propelled them on, and gave them dreams of reaching the door and sleeping through it. Carl was not sure they would get there.

Just when they were close to the door, the light went off.

CHAPTER 21

Heather

The car was running back down the highway. "Where are we going?" Heather asked, turning to her companion.

Again, Andre chuckled. Heather hated the fact that she was not in charge of her destination of the vehicle taking them there. She wanted to wrestle the control of the car from Andre and take the car to somewhere she would be comfortable with. But that was the problem. She did not know where she would be comfortable. She had no idea which place was safe and which place was not. Andre had more knowledge on the matter than she did.

"Why did you turn back?" She asked again.

"We have somewhere we should be," Andre said. "We can't get there by sticking to our former route."

"Where?"

"Somewhere we can meet some old friends."

The car continued on the road, eating it up and springing over the ground like a skipping antelope escaping from danger. Heather turned to look back on the route they had abandoned. She had felt that it would be the best route to get out from the city and away from her parents, but maybe she was wrong. Andre knew best.

"Here is a fun fact," Andre said.

Heather turned back from watching the road to look at the most trusted person in her life right now, a stranger.

"What?"

"Once they track the chip to where we got rid of it from inside the city, they would continue up the road, believing we got rid of the chip and carried on. You see why we had to abandon the route now?"

Heather was surprised she did not think about that. But then, she was not used to being on the run especially from her parents.

"Who are these old friends?" Heather asked.

"You won't know them," Andre replied.

Heather turned to stare out through the window again. Whatever Andre did not want to tell him, he would not. She could not convince him to. She did not know how his thought process worked. He was a stranger as far as she was concerned.

"One is a cop," Andre finally said. "The others are a part of a resistance group. They have been fighting the government since it became tyrannical."

Heather had not realized that the government was tyrannical. In her formative years, she had been cocooned under her parents' own tyrannical care and did not have time to see the world. When she finally set off on her own, it was to be vested in a fight against her own parents again and, of course, here. Far away from them, she could feel a part of her fighting for them. Then she remembered her sister who did not even get to fight before her life ended. It brought a bitter taste to her mouth.

"Was she happy?" She suddenly asked.

Andre turned to her. The car was moving, but none of them was bothered that Andre's eyes were not on the road.

"She was happy for a while," he finally replied, then turned back to the road to keep on driving.

The rest of the journey happened in silence. The driver, a stranger that got more mysterious as their journey progressed. The passenger, a lady who was at the end of her wits and her trust for humanity, a confused and grieving mess.

The trees passed silently as they got into the quieter territory. Then, Andre pulled over to the side of the road.

"What's happening?" Heather asked.

"We wait," Andre replied.

Shaun

Armed with the information he had gotten from the police records, he snuck out into the night. He had to go in search of the deceased fiancé, Mira. Maybe talking to her would ensure that she did not permit the people working behind the scenes to use Roland's body for their nefarious purposes. He still did not know what to think about robots replacing humans. It sounded far-fetched, but he had almost been killed by a self-driving truck and Aaron had claimed not to know him anymore.

Outside, he got to his car before the alarm in the precinct was raised. He started up the car engine and guided the car into the road. He had to find where Mira was staying. Maybe from her, he would find out where they had kept Roland and know what the hell was going in there.

The night was cold, and freezing wind whisked along the side of his car, slapping him across the face. This time, yesterday, he was still a cop fighting to show that humans were superior to robots. He still had not had any attempt made on his life. But now, he was an outcast, and he did not know how deep the rot had grown. There were people with a great deal of power that wanted a robot to dominate everything about their world, and he wondered where that left people like him. Who, in their right minds, would want to be controlled by a robot?

The car headlamps pierced through the night as another scary thought seized Shaun's mind. What if this robot takeover thing was not limited to the forces? What if people were being replaced by these robots and the whole town was already full of them? It was a scary thought, but one which gripped his mind nonetheless.

Mira

Signing the papers was the easy part. She did not even bother to read what was in them. She wanted Roland to come back to himself as fast as possible.

Sitting in the lobby no longer cut it for her. She stood up and walked towards the door.

"Where are you going?" Phillip asked.

"Outside, I cannot sit here anymore."

"Be careful out there," Phil said.

Mira nodded and pushed the door open, and out she went.

Outside, the darkness was almost complete apart from the lights all over the place. The road was also abandoned, and since she had been inside, she had not heard a single car drive by. It was as if the road was sealed off from the rest of the town. She tried to remember meeting any gate on their way here, but her memory failed her. Then, she remembered she had been flown in by helicopter and chuckled. The things worry could do.

Sighing, she walked to a seat under a tree and sat there. The open-air gave her some peace from the worries that had been tormenting her mind. For once, her mind shifted from the worry about Roland's health. They did not allow her to see much of him when she went in with her father. They had made her to hurriedly sign the documents that would ensure that Roland's treatment would continue. Her father did not seem like he wanted her to carry on with it, but he caved too easily.

"Psssst."

The voice startled Mira. She swirled around, trying to find where the voice was coming before she decided it must be her mind playing tricks on her. She had not seen anyone walk up to this place.

"Psssst," the voice called again.

This time, when Mira turned around to look, she found something in the woods. She froze.

She could barely make out somebody's hand waving at her, trying to call her over. She was confused. There were a lot of things she wanted to know about this mysterious place, and the strange man hiding in the woods seemed like he had something to say. Mira stood up and walked casually towards the hedge where the man was hiding. He was hiding in a way that kept him away from the sight of whoever might be observing her from another part of the building.

She got to the hedge and realized it was a middle-aged man.

"You are picking flowers," the man said. "Don't give anyone the impression that you are talking to me."

She concentrated on both the flowers and the man at the same time.

"My name is Shaun, Detective Shaun. I'm not supposed to be alive," the man said. His eyes showed he came with a piece of important news. "You are Mira."

Mira wondered how the man knew who she was, but she did not give it much thought. People knew whatever they wanted to know these days. It was easy.

The man was gazing intently at her, almost as if he was expecting her to move. When she did nothing but looked confused, he sighed.

"This is a risk," he said. It was a difficult one, but one he had to take anyway.

"What is a risk?"

"Talking to you. Your fiancé is being treated here," Shaun said.

"Who are you? Who do you work for?"

"Nobody, don't let them do anything to his body."

"His body?"

"He's dead."

"What? He's alive... I saw him."

"That's not him, it's his replacement."

Shaun

His replacement.

It sounded strange coming from him. He had always prided himself on following the laid down rules, on believing only the believable things. This one was strange. It was like a horror story written by a child whose future would be sufficiently messed up by his thought processes at a young age.

"His replacement?"

"Yes,"

"I don't understand."

"You don't, let me just say it this way: the person coming back is not Roland. It is someone else, a robot."

"Roland is not a robot."

"Roland is dead."

"How did you get in here?"

"It does not matter. They are changing your fiancé into something that you would not recognize."

"I will call security."

"Get it into your head, Roland is dead. Why is he not in a hospital? Why is this place hidden out here? Have you thought about it?"

The woman seemed like she wanted to talk. Her eyes seemed to be taking into consideration what Shaun was saying, but then, a curtain drew over her eyes.

"You will have a lot of explaining to do for the security," she said.

"Security, why do you think this place is so closely guarded?"

Again, Mira appeared to be at a loss for words. Her eyes were misty and lost. She worked her mouth to see if something would come out, but nothing did.

"Your father is coming," Shaun said. "I will find you again."

With that, Shaun disappeared behind the thrushes, moving fast. He hoped he had made his exit as dramatic as it was in his head. He did not know why he was interested in a dramatic exit in such a time. As he rushed through the thrushes he hoped that Mira would not get the funny idea of calling the security. He had managed to bypass them just to meet her.

Mira

The stranger disappeared through the woods, and she stood there looking after him. It was hard not to think about what the stranger had told her. The secluded facility made it even harder. Everything pointed to the man telling the truth.

"Shaun," she murmured as if she was trying to commit the name to memory.

"What are you doing out here all alone?"

The voice startled her. She jumped and turned around to see her father standing a little distance away from her.

Why is he suddenly so caring all of a sudden? Why is he interested in Roland?

CHAPTER 22

Levi

He could not think straight, not after what he had seen. Or was it what he did not see? He was already full of guilt and grief. He had left his family for a night of fun with the girl that was now standing beside him while they watched the building he had called his being demolished.

"Your parents would soon be back. They probably left the house because of this," Ashley said.

Levi desperately wanted to believe her, but he found doubts clinging to the sides of his mind. The mother he knew would have called him and told him about this. The heads-up would mean he would not have to climb up there and risk getting killed. He could not even remember how they had managed to make it down from the floor where they had found themselves. There was nowhere he knew that his family could have gone to. They hardly left the house anyway.

"They will come back for you," Ashley kept saying.

His mother and his younger brother, the two most important people in his life. He sat on the front step of Ashley's house and tried to hold back his grief and fear. His worst fear was that the worst had happened, that they had been killed. He remembered the raid at the uncompleted building so clearly. These raiders never went to the rich neighborhoods to haunt people. They came down to this place where nothing could be done if they were found.

"I don't know," he said. His voice was weak. His mind had not even gone to where he would sleep for tonight. The shock of meeting their house empty had not faded. He did not think it would fade anytime soon.

"I know," Ashley said. "It is not as bad as you think. You would see them soon and you would wonder why you were ever worried."

The evening tumbled into the night, and the light faded from the sky. Darkness descended on the verandah where Levi still sat on the step. There was still no sign of his mother coming for him.

It was around 10 p.m. that Ashley finally spoke to him.

"My parents are not coming back today too. Come on, let's get inside."

Levi was not interested. He was tired of everything. It was this house that he had gone into while his people were made to disappear.

"No," he replied. "I will sleep outside here."

"Why? Come on in. They will know you are here."

Levi showed up with anger clearly showing on his face. The accusation was there somewhere, and Ashley shrank back on seeing it.

"I would have been with them if I had not followed you," Levi said bitterly.

"I saved you, Levi. Being with me meant whatever you think happened to them did not happen to you."

"Indeed, what about Rami? You saved him too?"

Levi turned and walked away from Ashley. If she followed him, he would tell her exactly what he thought of her. As if she knew what was on his mind, she stayed put.

Carl

Carl was the last person running back towards the door, but he got there before the other boys. He was faster with Graham following closely behind.

When he got to the door, he realized with a sinking feeling that the door had been slammed shut. He tried to pull it open, but it did not budge. More robots were running towards them. Far behind, one of the robots jumped on the last man and tackled him to the ground. The rest of the men opened fire on the robots.

Carl kept pulling at the door. He knew that shooting these obsolete bullets at the robots would not cause any harm to them. It would only infuriate them.

"What's the holdup?" Graham shouted above the din.

"The fucking door," Carl replied.

Quickly, he bent towards the keypad and typed in the password that had let them gain access into the building. It was only after keying in the last digit that he remembered that the entry and exit passwords were usually different. He could not get the mark off the keypad again as he had already contaminated it with his own hands.

"Fuck!" He cursed.

"What?" Graham asked again.

The shots were getting louder. The men were getting more frightened. The bullets were doing barely enough to keep the robots at bay. They were advancing even with the bullets tearing into them.

"We are stuck," Carl said. His mind was getting to the outside. If it was this terrible inside, how would the outside be? There would be cop cars waiting for them, more robots with pulse guns. Carl could see the slaughter in the eyes of his mind. They had walked right into a trap, and he had messed it up further by not committing things to memory. In his defense, he had not always had to use the exit code. They slipped in and out with the door still open.

"Fuck!" He cursed again. This time he cursed in unison with Graham.

He brought his gun around and trained it on the robots. More of them were jumping out of their tanks, and there was about 50 of them now swarming the intruders.

"Shoot at their hearts!" Carl screamed. He wondered what good it would be. The robot's body was built as a protective shield against the old bullets. The chest area was especially thicker than other areas as that was where the central power was positioned.

Guns sang, bullets whizzed and the robots were kept at bay till they overwhelmed the men. Carl had already seen it coming. The ten of them, perhaps, could take down one robot. But when it got to 2 robots, the odds were shifted in favor of the robots. Here, there were not 2, but more than 50 robots, and they had the singular intent of ending them all.

Carl saw Graham go down. The robot that was on Graham was the one with his facial features. He watched Graham grapple with his lookalike and was about to join the fray when another robot slammed into him from nowhere. This one was a lady, half his size and ten times as strong. He had no chance. Blows rained on his face, disorienting him. There was no chance to admire the robot and the way it looked exactly like a human.

Then, the wall exploded. Another explosion flung the robot from him.

"Come on!" Someone screamed.

But Carl was still too disoriented to do anything. His eyes were pulling short when he felt strong hands grab him and started to pull him away.

Heather

Old friends. Whatever that means.

Heather could not measure how much time they had spent in a spot waiting for the so-called old friend, but she wanted to be on the move again. She felt that the longer they stayed in one place, the easier they would be caught. Surely, someone like Andre should know this better than she did. Why stop here?

"When are we moving?" She asked for the umpteenth time.

"Soon," he replied, his reply was no different from the last one hundred times that she had asked.

"Don't you think we will get caught if we stay in a place?"

"Not today, Heather," he replied. "We are not getting caught."

The car started and Heather was startled. She had not seen his hand around the ignition. When he noticed her staring, he simply shrugged and pulled the car onto the road.

The road was deserted like they were heading to a reserved area, yet there were no roadblocks, only drones flying around overhead.

Andre pulled the car close to a big building and pulled to a stop.

"Get into the driving seat," he said.

"What are you doing?"

"Just get in, there is no time."

Andre got out of the car and walked towards the side of the building bearing something he had produced from the dashboard of the car.

From her position, Heather watched the strange man who aimed to have been Marie's boyfriend, wondering if she had not been brought out here by a mentally challenged person. What if everything had all been in her head, and this guy, Andre, was the one fanning the embers of her craziness?

It was a crazy thought, but it bid her stop, so she could think about it properly. There was no time to. The part of the wall where Andre had been standing, suddenly blew apart.

Again, Heather was startled. Her eyes searched around for her companion. She found him running through the hole that the blast had made in the wall. At the same time, she heard the sound of gunshots.

She was instantly alerted.

What is the crazy stranger trying to do? She wondered.

Then from the dust and darkness, Andre emerged, carrying a heavy-looking man over his shoulder. He pulled open the backseat and dropped the man into it.

"Go!" Andre screamed.

The car tires screeched as Heather pulled the car back into the street, many thoughts on her mind about the battered man that Andre had brought with him.

Barry Stivers

The preparation for the wedding did not take so much. Humphrey, the trusted reverend that Barry Stivers knew from the old days was in the same room with them. Barry had asked him to make sure he was not being followed. He was to look out for people, robots, and even strange drones. This was 2055 and anything could happen.

"Do you take this man as your husband and do you..." Humphrey was saying.

"I do," Dora replied quickly.

Barry loved her high spirit. It made him realize that he was not the only one who wanted this to happen and happen fast. He could hardly wait to go through his own path before Humphrey gave them permission to do what they had been doing for a while.

"You may kiss the bride," Humphrey said.

He leaned towards Dora and the latter grabbed his head. The kissing started. There was too much passion, too much hunger. Dora was kissing him as if she was trying to remind herself of why she had made the decision she had just made.

Humphrey watched both of them, smiling.

After the minister was gone, Barry looked out through the window at the road. They were in a room facing the entry to the hotel just the way Dora wanted it. She was still afraid of people attacking them with the element of surprise. In this way, they would be able to see their attackers grouping outside before they could make their way into the building. Barry knew the type of people to look out for. People from the government.

Dora got up from the bed, walked to the window, and drew Barry back to the back.

"We just got married," she said. "They should respect what we have even if it is for one night."

With that, she pushed him into the bed and got atop him. The next few minutes saw their clothes fleeing their bodies, their moans and groans filling the room as they came together, hands moving all over the place, feeling each other out. They were in love with each other and it was clear to see.

Just before Barry penetrated, his phone started ringing.

"Leave it," Dora said and pulled his head to her, hooking him with a kiss and wrapping her long legs around him.

He slipped in with a slippery wet sound, eliciting another moan from Dora. The phone continued ringing, disapproving of their sexual union.

When Barry started moving, the ringing stopped. Dora gripped his head so tightly that he felt the head would fall off. Then, she left his head to dig her fingers into his back.

Sweaty bodies, moans, and groans, a dance as old as time. When both of them breathed out in unison, having achieved their climax, the phone started ringing again.

This time, Barry fell to Dora's side and picked up the phone. Dora snuggled up to him.

"Who's this?" Barry asked.

"You have not been keeping in touch," a voice said over the phone. It was easy to notice that the voice was trying to keep the edge away.

"I don't see any reason to," Barry said.

"Your work is not done, doctor."

"I have to be alive to finish it, don't I?"

There was a sigh over the phone before the person tried again.

"I apologize for that oversight. Your security is the topmost priority for us. Tell me where you are so..."

"No, not a chance."

"We have to see Barry. You have to tell us what you know. You have got to be debriefed."

"I think I made a mistake telling you where those plants were. The government does not deserve it. I have been hearing some rumors. What really are they going to use my inventions for?"

"Forget about the rumors. For old times' sake, let us meet. Somewhere open where you would be comfortable. I am not your enemy."

"Maybe you are not, but I don't think the government is going in the right direction. I think we have a lot to worry about. There may be moles in your organization."

"And I hope to fish them all out."

Barry wondered idly if, perhaps, his friend was the mole. He had heard about the news in England, the state of affairs, and of the US government plans for invasion. He had known his friend for a long time since high school, and they had only embarked on this dangerous mission together because of trust. But as his friend grew more important in government circles, they drew apart. He was afraid that the man might have been compromised. The dangerous thing he was doing to secure a dying future for millions of humans all around the world was looking more dangerous by the day. Muon-catalyzed fusion was a delicate thing that could blow up in anyone's face. The energy was unmatched.

A series of explosions caused by the instability of the process could cause the earth to fall flat on its knees. It frightened him.

"Tomorrow, 12. The overhead bridge close to Luton hotel."

"Alright."

Barry knew why he deliberately mentions the hotel. Maybe it would shift their attention from where he really was if they thought him that dumb. It was worth a try.

He dropped the phone and turned to his wife, Dora.

"Who was that?" Dora asked.

"Work," Barry replied.

He thought about how odd it sounded telling her 'work'. She knew nothing about his work, and he knew nothing about hers.

"They want to see you?" She asked.

"Yes, they do."

"Are you going?"

"I have to see Drek. He might have something he cannot tell me over the phone."

"You don't think he might be with those behind the attack on your life?"

"Drek? No," Barry said quickly, but the thought stuck on his mind. There was no harm in considering everyone as his enemy.

Dora continued staring at him with worry and concern in her eyes. It was not the hopeless kind of worry. It was the worry with the thought of locking Barry in a room so he would not go out. Barry knew she could do exactly that.

"I'll be fine," he hastened to assure her. He needed to see Drek. He could learn from the way he moved the thoughts in his head, or so he thought.

CHAPTER 23

Carl

There were voices in his head, voices outside of this body. Then, there was the shooting and explosion and robots running all over the place. He saw Graham. He was screaming as his neck was being torn open by one of the robots. The robot was huge, designed for a fight with muscles and limbs way stronger than anything he had ever imagined.

Graham's voice box was busted. His scream died in his throat, and with that the hopes of his people. The robot was onto another one of the men. The bullets that the remaining rained on him were like little pebbles falling on a rock. It pulled the hands of one of the men all the way from being enclosed around his gun till the hands were spread wide apart. Carl thought he knew what was coming next and he tried to close his eyes, but found that he could not close them.

Watch this, see everything, you coward, a voice in his head taunted him.

The robot began to pull the man's arms further apart, eliciting screams of pain and anguish. The man's struggle was nothing— it was useless.

"Let him go!" Carl screamed.

The robot continued pulling the hands apart.

"Let him go, you freak!"

The robot finally pulled the hands out of their sockets. Blood spurted all over the place, and the victim collapsed on the floor, physically and mentally defeated. A blow to the head from the robot fractured his skull and ended whatever little life that he had left. He fell on the floor, dead.

Carl watched, horrified. There were things that he could not 'unseen'. This was one of them. The robot slowly turned its sight on Carl, eyes glinting red, codes flipping through his eyes. Carl was frozen where he stood. So far, he had not been able to gain control of his own body, and he was not sure what he was going to do if the robot turned on him.

The robot turned to him.

"Fuck," he cursed.

The thing started running towards him, one step, two steps, bounding off the ground and eating up the distance between them with frightening speed.

"No!" Carl screamed.

The hall faded from his view, and he found himself gazing at the roof of a car. The car was struggling over on an uneven terrain, judging by the way the car lunged to one side, then to the other.

Someone looked at him from the front seat.

"He's awake," a woman's voice said.

Mira

Mira walked back inside the building with her father, still thinking about what the strange man said.

"Are you okay?" Phil asked.

"I'm fine," Mira replied.

"You are pale, did something happen?"

The man turned to look back at the hedge of leaves and flowers.

"I'm okay, let's get back inside," she said, walking faster. Somehow, she felt like protecting the man that had come to her, at least, she knew what the hell was happening. The look on Phil's face was not nice, and she was afraid he would report to the security if he felt that someone had managed to sneak into the property.

Mira had not seen any security person yet, but she was sure they were around somewhere. A facility kept hush like this one would surely have enough security to mow down people who wanted to gain entrance into it.

"The procedure has started," Phil informed his daughter.

Mira, once again, felt the strangeness in those words. Why was her father so interested in seeing that Roland got the treatment, someone he had loathed all the time that they were together?

They sat back down in the lobby, and Mira felt uncomfortable. With the way Phil came out for her outside and quickly followed her back inside, it was almost as if he was monitoring her. She had never known her parents to care so much about what she was doing. They would rather have guards following her in case there was any trouble, but they never followed her themselves and showed little interest in what she wanted to do with her life except where Roland was concerned.

"What made you change your mind?" She asked Phil.

"What?"

It was obvious that Phil was lost in thought and her question had succeeded in dragging him back to the present.

"What made you change your mind?" She asked again.

Phil raised his eyebrows in confusion.

"About Roland," she added

"Oh," Phil said. Then, he stopped talking as if his exclamation was all the answer that she needed for her question.

Time passed slowly, agonizingly while Mira debated within herself if she was to ask the question again.

"I could not bear to see you in that state," he said. "I was afraid you would... you could do something crazy, like taking your life."

The words hit her square in the face. The man knew how she thought after all, and his answer was believable. She was thinking about taking her life. The courage was lacking, but she was slowly building it up before he came.

He nodded at her when she continued staring at him. Then, he reached out and squeezed her shoulder. Strange, because her father had never done that, would never do that. Yet, people change. Situations brought out parts of people that seemed to be absent from existence.

The flurry white coat announced that the doctor was put in the lobby.

"Would you like to see him now?" He asked them.

They are done?

Shaun

His heart still pounded after escaping from the facility. What he had wanted was to go through the facility and find out what they did there. He was sure he would find a lot. But he knew that would be pushing his luck to the extreme, and he would get caught. He could not imagine being used for the replacement program. The biggest fear he had was the fear of being replaced. That was why he hated the robots that tried to do his job. It was why he would not stop his fight against these robots.

All he needed to do was to find the idiot at the top of the chain. It was this person that was controlling the robots. Once he found the person, he would be able to bring down this program and let the world carry on towards a path of recovery.

He got to his car and opened the door. Immediately he pulled the door shut, he felt the cold feeling of steel against his skin.

"You have been sneaking around a lot."

It was Aaron's voice. Still, oddly, it did not feel like it was Aaron holding the knife against his throat.

"Aaron, what the fuck are you doing?" He asked, pretending to play along to give himself some time.

"Stop it," Aaron said. "You know exactly who I am. How prepared are you to become the same thing?"

"What are you talking about?"

"You are going to drive into this facility. You will like it since you want to know a lot. Say, you would probably die with your knowledge. Start the car."

"I can't start the engine with your knife against my throat."

The blade moved away from Shaun's throat. Apparently, the thing now replacing Aaron had much faith in its ability to subdue his victim. Shaun felt insulted. He started the car, and at the same time wondered how quickly he could get to his gun. Not fast enough. The knife would be buried in his back before he could get to it.

The car revved up and he pulled it away from the bush where he had had it hidden.

"Everyone has a computerized car except you. You are obsolete," Aaron said from the backseat.

Shaun looked at the rearview mirror and increased the car speed. It went from 0 to a hundred almost immediately.

"Slow down," Aaron warned, but Shaun was not listening. He headed straight for a tree standing by the side of the road, at the same time pulling his door open.

"Stop!"

He was already out before the car hit the tree, rolling on and on, over the grass, and away from the car.

When he came to a stop, he reached for his gun to make sure it was still there with him. Then, he rose to his feet, panting.

CHAPTER 24

Barry

hey were lying in bed.

Dora looked worried even with all of Barry's reassurances. He expected her to. She did not know much about what he was doing. Even if she had made plenty of research on him, there was still a part of him that he kept a secret, from the government, from his friends, from everybody. It was for the good of the world. If anyone knew about these things, they would use him against his will. What was that they said about power? Absolute power corrupts absolutely. He was the one that was well-made for the role he had now. With his little interest in power, he would not be able to abuse any.

"I don't like this," Dora said. "We just got married and you are putting yourself in harm's way, like you care nothing about me, about how I feel."

"Believe me, I am not in danger. They should be afraid."

Barry said it with more conviction than he meant, and Dora's face quickly pulled together in a puzzled frown.

"I don't understand," she said. "Do you have some hidden power no one knows about?"

"Even better," Barry said, hoping to pass it off as a joke. Maybe, it was not the right time for a joke, but he could not afford it for her to be suspicious of him now. She would go sneaking about and who knew what she could find? Maybe after some years in their marriage, he would let her know who he really was.

Dora's phone started ringing then. Barry watched her intently. Her face was transformed from worry to tenseness, then quickly back to calm and expressionless. These changes occurred too quickly, almost too quickly that Barry was barely able to pick them out, but he did. Apparently, Dora had her own secrets too.

"I have to take this," she said as she walked towards the restroom.

Once again, Barry wondered what the both of them were doing. Why did they get married when they had not fully trusted each other? Maybe, it was the raw passion they felt, something that Barry had not felt in years. He was grateful for it, but he could not control his thoughts in moments like this when he wondered if it was better for him to be alone. She shut the door behind him, and he felt the sensation of being locked out of her life. He was not yet in where he wanted. Maybe companionship was enough.

He turned away from the restroom and walked to the window, all the while wondering if he could go to the door to eavesdrop on her conversation. Some of the doubts he had had previously about her were lingering in his mind. It was nothing that a round of passionate lovemaking would not wash away. And he longed for the lovemaking more than he longed for clarity.

Maybe he would stay back and let Drek wait for him. After all, he owed them nothing, and they had not kept their side of the bargain. They had failed to keep him safe.

Dora

"I have told you to stop calling me at odd hours," Dora whispered into the phone.

"Well, I think you need to see this."

A message came into her phone and she clicked it to see a link. The link revealed an article on US forces invading Kuwait for the alleged development of muon-catalyzed weapons. There were other links too, of Germany, France, and China invading other smaller countries and accusing them of trying to usurp world peace.

"The world does not deserve to go on," the voice said.

Dora felt the same, but there was something else, something bothering her, so she remained silent on the phone, thinking.

"We have to move. The muon factories would give us enough power to take out the earth."

"Is it really necessary?" Dora asked. Her voice was small.

"Fuck," the person at the other end of the line swore softly. "What have they done to you?"

"Nothing," Dora replied quickly. "Can't we wait?"

"All of us went over this, and we know how it ends. Humans cannot win. Good cannot defeat evil. The governments of the stronger countries are becoming more evil by the day with the discovery of how much power they can wield. Mankind has reached the pinnacle of its development. We are retrogressing now, going back in time."

Dora sighed. She could not bring herself to say that she had been married newly, and even though there was a world of difference between her and the man that she had chosen to marry, she still wanted to spend time with him. Everything was happening too fast, and she was now scared of losing, a fear she did not have until she met Barry.

"Meet me at the crossroad by Luton place. I will give you the coordinates. The lines are not completely safe."

"Okay."

The line went dead at the other end. Dora spent a minute listening to the silence at the other end. That was exactly what they planned to turn the earth into after the big blast. They had been looking for the right bomb, trying to get access to atomic bombs, but they had failed so far because it was closely guarded. Now, they had their chance with this new invention.

She came out from the restroom and found Barry seated on the bed. He was lost in thought and did not see her get out of the room.

"Penny for your thoughts?" She asked cheerfully, thinking about the resemblance between them and the couple in an old movie she had watched: Mr. and Mrs.

He looked up as she came to sit on his lap.

"You wouldn't want to know," he said, looking into her eyes.

There were lines on his forehead, lines of worry. Dora could not bring herself to think of the end.

"Why?" She asked.

"It is mostly boring thoughts."

"Can we make it interesting?" She asked, going for his lips.

It was this yearning that was messing with her mind, this inability to stay away from his body. She could not stop herself.

Carl

The car was moving. It was easy to realize that he was in a car, which was a complete change from the scene in his dream. He looked around quickly, trying to access the situation and find out if he had been captured.

He pulled on the door handle, only to discover that it was locked. Quickly, he smashed the window, and the car screeched to a halt by the side of the road.

"Carl!" The driver called. "What the hell are you doing?"

Carl paused in the middle of his escape. The two at the front were staring at him in the backseat, but they made no effort to hold him back. They simply stared at him like he was mad. He stopped.

"What is happening? Where am I?" Carl asked. They seemed human enough to him. There was more color on their faces than the one he had come to notice that the robots had.

"You were almost killed downtown," the man said. "That was a foolhardy mission. There is no government facility that is not guarded by robots."

"Robots," Carl said, thoughtfully, remembering. They had been thoroughly dealt with and decimated. "Did you see any of my men?" He asked suddenly.

The man shook his head sadly. "You are the only one that made it out of there."

He would not have. He was not supposed to. As the panic about his safety faded and sadness intermingled with grief set in, he felt the pain of the bruises on his face together with a slight headache. He did not know if the robot's hand was made with stone. His hits were accurate too, enough to disable him. He wondered what would have happened next if he were still there. Then, he looked up. The man and the woman were still staring at him.

"Why?" He simply asked.

"A favor, for an old friend," the man said.

"It is useless. We are all going to die anyway. We are no match at all for these things," Carl complained, touching his face gingerly. He could not believe he was once happy to work alongside robots of all things. He hated all of them now with passion, and he could not get the gory image of Graham's death off his mind.

"Maybe, we don't have to do," the man said. "Maybe all we have to do is survive. My name is Andre. This is Heather. We are your new friends."

"I don't need friends."

"Everyone does," Andre replied. He turned around to drive while Heather continued looking at Carl.

"Can you do us and yourself a favor?" Heather asked. "Try not to jump out of the car. I don't know why Andre saved you, but he probably thinks you will be useful."

Useful? Useful at what?

The car tires screeched as they gained traction and sped off down the road.

Dora

She waited until Barry was out of the room, then she went before the mirror to look at her face. She did not spend much time there before she walked towards the door, got out, and shut it behind her.

She was barely able to keep her body from trembling as she walked down the hallway. What she was about to do would get her labeled a terrorist if any human survived. She hoped none would. She hoped life would come back to earth after many years, and that whatever creatures found the earth as a habitat, that they would use it better than humans, that they would be better than humans, and that the spherical entity would be glad to have them.

She walked past a few people on her way to the lift, people stared at her so strangely that she wondered if what she wanted to do was plastered across her forehead. Or maybe it was her mind, playing with her. This had never been done before, probably would never be done.

As her mind traveled all over the place, she got into the lift. She was alone. With death so near, everything reminded her about death. The lift made her worry that it would be unscrewed and send her on a free fall to her death, something she did not have to worry about as the floor level was not that far below.

She thought of the building collapsing while she was still in here. That would do it, but the world would carry on destroying itself and she did not want that. She had to be alive to finish what she started.

The lift stopped and she made her way to the lobby battling with her mind. Many people, especially those in the government, would see her as a fanatic. Perhaps, even Barry would think of her as such, but she was far from that. This was one of the reasons she had been hiding her true self from the man she had fallen in love with. He would probably report her to the police once he learnt about her plans. So much for love.

Outside, she headed towards the junction where she was supposed to meet Little. Across the street, she saw him standing by the side, his hands in his pocket as he glared at someone lighting a cigar. He was in the middle of people milling around the place as they went about their business. Always, getting outside reminded Dora that the world was on the verge of being overrun by the human population.

She stood by the side of the street and waited until Little's eyes fell on her. His face registered mild recognition before he walked across the road to meet her, his bald head glistening in the sun.

"How are you doing?" he asked, looking genuinely concerned.

"I'm okay, Little," Dora replied, wondering again, as she had so often done in the past, why the bald-headed man before her was called Little. He was anything but little as 6 feet with a body mass like a gorilla's.

"I'm worried that you are going in too deep," Little said.

"Here are the coordinates," Dora said instead. "Copy them, and worry about setting these places off at the same time."

Barry

As Barry walked towards the meeting place, he wondered about the call that he had seen Dora take. It would take a lot of time before the both of them would get used to each other. There was hardly time. They had none. The world could turn over at any moment, and that was clear for him to see.

As he made his way through the street, his mind settled on Drek. He had seen Drek losing his soul little by little, and he had himself to blame for that. He had shown Drek the way. They had to have a man in the government if they wanted to get the government to listen to them. It was true that the idea taunted as the world's saving grace was not his, and that he felt like an imposter sometimes, still, he was a genius. No one knew this more than Drek. Drek insisted he would do everything to make him heard, and he believed him. Now that he thought of it, perhaps it was not worth it. The same class of greedy bastards were still up there. The same men who got drunk on power and wanted nothing more than the furtherance of their own nefarious goals.

He pulled his hat tighter around his face. The sun had grown hotter in the last few years, the signs of a dying world. Pollution was still climbing despite collective efforts to keep it down. Barry felt that the governments were just deceiving themselves.

He got to the meeting point and sat at an open-air Café. This place was open enough for his liking. If the government agents tried anything, there would be people around to witness it. Even though they had the power to do whatever they wanted, they still wanted the goodwill of the people.

He ordered for a hot chocolate and sat there sipping it silently while looking around for his friend. He wondered if he would recognize him when he sees him.

He was almost done with his cup of chocolate when a shadow fell across his table. He looked up and saw Drek smiling down at him. Drek sat across the table from him.

"I have never seen you taking chocolate, Barry," Drek said.

Barry shrugged, taking his time to look around and make sure he was not surrounded. There was not one person that seemed off in the neighborhood.

"It's okay, Barry. I came alone like we discussed."

"Okay, can't be too careful."

Barry turned to find his friend staring at him.

"When did it get to this? We are supposed to be friends."

"True, senator."

"Come on, cut it out, Barry."

"You call me doctor and I can't call you senator?"

"Not here," Drek said quickly, looking around.

Barry knew what he was afraid of. He knew what every person in the position of power in the US was afraid of; "assassination." Drek had tried to keep a low profile since his project kicked off.

"I see."

"What happened to the trust?" Drek asked.

"I was almost killed."

"Thank goodness you were not. Now, we need to rebuild what was damaged."

"How do you propose we do that?"

"Follow me to the office building."

"No."

"What are you afraid of, Barry?"

"Dying for nothing."

Drek sighed. He looked around like he was at loss on what to say. Barry let him. He was not going to make him feel comfortable like he always did in the past. He had almost been killed and Drek did not look too remorseful about it.

"Your protection is guaranteed."

"You told me that before. Guess what? It was not. I would have been killed if I was not saved by a stranger."

"A stranger?" A look of curiosity came over Drek's face. His eyes widened slightly before he got it under control again.

"Yes, a stranger who is surprisingly skilled."

"Does that not seem suspicious to you? The appearance of this stranger just at the time you were being attacked."

"Maybe, do you know what else seems suspicious to me? The silence of the fucking government on an assassination attempt on their top scientist."

"Come on, you knew this was a secret endeavor. No one has to know you are the one that started all of this. You wanted that yourself."

"Perhaps that was a mistake. It means I could easily be gotten rid of by the government whenever they want."

"What do you think we are? A bunch of murderers?"

"Who knows? The news makes the rounds you know?"

"What news?"

"Convenient disappearance of loud critics."

"Surely, you cannot pin all that on the government."

"Why not? It is convenient for you."

"What do you think of me, Barry?"

"I don't know."

There was a lull in the conversation of the old friends, a coldness and indifference were trying to creep in between the friendship and none of them was making any effort to push this coldness back.

At length, Drek got to his feet.

"The bosses want you in the office tomorrow," he said.

Barry shrugged. His mind was already made up. He was not stepping foot into a building belonging to the government. He still wanted to live a little longer.

He watched Drek walk away and poured the remnant of his Chocolate drink into his mouth.

The bosses want you in the office tomorrow.

It almost sounded like Drek was sent to capture him and drag him back to the office.

Finally done with his drink, he stood up and turned to go, only to meet a mountain of a man standing before him. The man wore a hoodie and hid something in it, but Barry could clearly see the barrel of a pulse gun staring at him. Pulse guns were silent, and the man would be gone before anyone knew he had shot him.

"You raise an alarm, you are dead," the man said.

CHAPTER 25

Dora

hen she got back from her meeting with the bald-headed Little, she opened the door and was shocked to find Barry seated on the bed. He did not look surprised in the least, as if he had expected her to be gone after him. He did not look up when she came inside, and she was immediately hit by a wave of guilt.

She walked to the bed and sat beside him.

"You went out," he said, matter-of-factly.

"I want to tell you something," she said taking his hands. "I have to tell you."

He turned to her. The tone of her voice had alerted him as to the importance of what she wanted to say. His attention was completely on her.

"You might already know this, but I have been following you," she said.

"I know."

"You do?"

"Yes, I know that you have been following me."

"What else do you know?"

"That you are in love with me."

She smiled.

"True that."

"What do you want to tell me?"

Her smile grew wider.

"That I'm glad I met you, and that the time we spent together means a lot to me."

He caught her smile, and he was even wider. She loved it when he smiled like that. It was strange, falling for the man she had been shadowing. But she did even before she got very close to him. Maybe because he was just like a pawn in the scheme of things and did not know what the government was trying to do with his invention.

She kissed him and walked to the bed.

"We have to leave," she said. "We have stayed here too long."

"You are right," he said. That was another thing she loved about him. How agreeable he was. No matter the bone of contention, he always managed to find a common ground for both of them. He made efforts for them to stay together.

Dora suddenly wished she had not given away the locations she had heard from her husband. She suddenly wished she had more time to spend with him, that the world as they knew it was not coming to an end by her own doing.

"I need to take a bath," Barry said.

Dora watched him walk into the bathroom. She knew that was her cue to move. How would she have the face to stay with him till the end knowing that she was going to kill the both of them, and that he knew nothing about it. That would be a betrayal. She knew that the more she stayed with him, the more she would be pushed to let him know what was going on.

She looked around for a pen and a piece of paper. Maybe she could find some compromise. She would be putting everything she had worked for at risk, but she wanted him safe.

Barry

She was acting strange.

As the water ran over Barry's body, he knew that there was something on his wife's mind, something that Dora was keeping from him, but he could not bring himself to ask her. Usually, he never did. He let the person mull over it and decide if he or she wanted to share. He hoped she would want to share soon. The suspense was killing him.

He was sure that telling him he was the best thing that had happened in her life was not what she wanted to say initially. Her face had looked like she had seen doom and condemnation when she called his attention. He had braced himself for some bad news before she suddenly switched off. What about getting to the room to find it empty? She had sneaked out after he left. No, no, he was not limiting her or encroaching on her freedom or whatever. But what happened to telling him where she was going. He told her where he was going to, didn't he?

As he rinsed himself and turned off the tap, he realized that the room outside was quiet, too quiet. Dora had not called him since he got into the bathroom. He listened intently. Then, he dried his body and hurriedly pulled the door open.

The right thing to do would probably be to stay in the bathroom and keep straining his ears to see what he could pick out, only coming out when he was sure there was no one around and the silence did not seem odd anymore. But he got out anyway, throwing all caution to the wind.

An empty room stared back at him. He stood there for some seconds trying to understand before his eyes went to the note on the bed. It was placed in that way for him to see it immediately he got into the room from the bathroom.

"No," he muttered.

His mind had already told him what it was, but he did not want to believe it. How could something be so certain and yet so uncertain? He matched across the room, dripping a little before he snatched up the note from the bed. His fingers made the note wet.

I meant it when I said I was glad our paths crossed, the note began and Barry's breath caught in his throat. This was certainly not how he had expected this marriage to go.

I have done something you would probably consider terrible, and I can't bear looking into your eyes because of the judgment I might find there. The world is coming to an end, you know. My group and I are making sure of that. The injustices in the world can no longer be reversed. Terrible things have happened, and have continued happening. The world needs a rest and a reset button.

Thank you for helping me find it. Maybe you should find a bunker underground and hide till justice is done. You don't have time.

Xoxo. Your wife, Dora.

Stunned, Barry continued holding the paper till it slipped from his hand. He had always prided himself on seeing ahead, but not at this moment. He might have seen robots gearing up against humans and might have known the government intended to use his invention for making weapons. But he had no idea that someone else was planning to destroy the world, and that person was his wife.

Levi

He slept outside, on a park bench. It was a risk, but he did not see himself going back to Ashley after pushing her off.

By morning, the rage had subsided and what remained was guilt and grief. He still did not know how to go about looking for his people. So, he walked the length and breadth of the park that was just behind the bench he had slept in, looking lost.

Maybe he would find them here, squatting somewhere just like he did for the night. Why had he not thought of it? But the more he walked around the park, the more he felt despair.

He decided to walk to the river nearby. Perhaps, watching the water would calm his nerves. He highly doubted it, but he had nowhere else to go and was trying out everything.

Ashley barged into his mind. She had called him while he angrily walked down the street, warning her to stay away from him. It was crass, but in his defense, he was feeling really bad. Imagine having sex when his family was still missing. Ashley would not understand. Her parents were never at home. She practically lived on her own.

Levi came to the river and sat on the plier that ran into it. His legs dangled in air and he let them slip into the river. The water caressed his feet as they flowed past.

He sighed. Ashley being here would complete the feeling of bliss that the touch of the water brought to him, but her presence would also remind him that his mother and younger brother were missing.

"Well, look who's in our spot today," a voice called from somewhere behind him.

He swirled around to see Ben, Harry, and Freddy. They were teens like him, but the three looked older than their ages, or maybe they were actually older than they swore they were, especially Harry. He had a full beard covering his face and shifty blue eyes. Freddy was the tallest, but the one that could be easily controlled. He had a goatee instead of a head and was the tallest student in the class. He had fists that could punch through a wall. Ben was the smallest, yet he was the crudest. Once he had insulted a female teacher by asking her to 'suck my cock'. The result was not pretty, but he survived it and became some kind of a legend in the school. As Levi turned around, they walked out from the crowded park space and met at the plier.

"You hardly ever come here," Freddy said. "What changed?"

Levi shrugged. He never really talked to these guys. They lived in the same neighborhood and went to the same school, but they seemed to have a gang of their own, the very thing Levi's mother always warned him against.

"The demolition brought him out here," Harry said.

"That was terrible," Ben said. "Knocking down your house like that."

"Why would they do that?" Levi asked no one.

He imagines Jeremy seeing him with these guys. He would curl his lips up in disgust. Jeremy hated these guys, but Levi felt indifferent.

"Maybe they don't like fags in houses, pretty boy," Harry said.

They stood around him, and Levi suddenly felt uncomfortable. He got up from his sitting position.

"Excuse me," he said when he discovered they were in his way.

"Did you hear anything?" Ben asked, turning to Freddy.

"No, did you?" Freddy asked, turning to Harry.

"Just something humming, a mosquito," Harry said.

The three turned their attention back to Levi.

"Jump into the water," Ben said.

"What?"

"Go on, do what he said," Harry said.

"Did he stutter?" Freddy asked.

"This is not right," Levi asked.

"Who cares?" Ben replied.

"I need to find my family."

"Pretty boy wants to report us to his family," Harry said, chuckling. The others joined in the painfully agonizing chuckle, laughing at nothing. It infuriated Levi, but he knew he had to keep his peace if he was to come out from this unscathed.

"No, no, my family is missing."

"Jump into the fucking water," Harry roared.

Levi cowered from him, moving back till the next step would send him over the plier and into the cold water.

"I can't swim," Levi finally said.

"Don't you fucking lie to me," Ben shouted. He rushed Levi. The latter did not see him coming. Freddy was shouting at something and pointing at the sky.

Ben collided with Levi, pushing him away from the plier and into the water. On his way down, Levi saw what Freddy was shouting about. It was a bright light in the sky, outshining even the sun. Levi was sure if the sun had eyes, it would be blinded by now. Then, he hit the water.

There was a loud noise above water level, voices screaming, and running footsteps. But they were all drowned out by a loud explosion. The kind that shook the foundations of the earth and turned the river into a storm as Levi was still struggling to navigate through it. He lost control, and was pushed about by the force that had hit the earth.

When the bright light hit the water, there was no noise anymore. Levi had the sensation of death moving towards him. Then, the brightness introduced a darkness so complete the boy did not realize he was struck unconscious.

CHAPTER 26

Mira

S he was led to the room with her father beside her, tension and anticipation seizing her speech for all of the time it took to walk down the hall. The doctor was trying to initiate a conversation with them, but neither she nor Phil was interested. It seemed that they both shared the same concern about Roland.

"Okay, don't be too shocked. He is still getting used to being alive," the doctor said and pushed the door open.

The two of them rushed into the room. Roland was standing by the window. His stance looked strange, and he did not turn immediately after they entered the room. Mira wanted to rush up to him immediately, but Phil held her back.

"Roland?" She called.

The man at the window turned to look at her strangely. Mira was confused. She felt it immediately: this was Roland and this was not Roland.

"Mira?" Roland called.

That cleared her doubt for the time, and she quickly dashed forward to run into his arms, brushing Phil's hand away.

"Are you okay?" Mira asked, looking him over.

He nodded. His nod was somewhat mechanical and reminded Mira of the robots they had back at home. Those ones were not humanoids, still, they had some semblance with Roland now.

"I am fine," Roland replied. "And you?"

"You are back from wherever it is coma patients go. Why wouldn't I be fine?"

She hugged him again before she found out she was the only one doing the hugging. Roland's hands went gingerly around her back. She did not want to pull away, but she did. Roland was not behaving the way she expected him to.

She turned to the doctor, puzzled.

"He's fine. Just a bit disoriented," the doctor said hastily. "He would need to get home and spend some time in familiar surroundings, and he will be back to full soundness of mind.

"Are you saying he's crazy?" Phil asked, a note of alarm creeping into his voice.

"You have nothing to worry about, sir," the doctor said.

It took less than half an hour to get Roland's things. Roland moved about as if he had not been injured fatally and almost died. He looked fit as a fiddle and that confused Mira even more. What sort of treatment would heal a fatal wound that fast? She wanted to ask Phil, but decided not to. Not now anyway. She was just happy that Roland was back with them.

When they got to the helicopter, the pilot was already there, and the blades above the helicopter had started slicing through the air. They followed Phil, crouching a little as they made their way to the helicopter.

Phil sat at the front with the pilot while Mira sat beside Roland. He was still looking about strangely like he was seeing everything for the first time. There was hardly time to point out any of the tall buildings to him. He just looked at them till they were out of sight, then he would turn to another high-rise building.

Beside him, Mira observed his every movement, perturbed. He was no longer obsessed with her. His hand was not around hers. He was not touching her. In fact, she could as well not be there. Something was wrong.

What did they do to you? She thought before she turned away.

Then, she remembered the man that had snuck up to her there. He had told her not to sign over any right to the hospital, that they would make Roland worse than he was. But she did not think much of it at the time. Maybe the man was onto something. If only she had listened and asked him to explain more. Perhaps she would know exactly what was wrong with Roland. But the man had said that he would find her, and right now, she wanted, more than anything, to be found.

"Are you okay?"

Mira turned around quickly to find Roland's eyes on her. It was Roland alright, but the voice, the texture, the mannerism, everything was off. Mira wondered if it would ever be the same again. She missed the Roland who tolerated her excesses without making it seem so obvious.

"I'm fine," she said. "I'm okay. Do you eh... do you remember what we are?"

"Of course, I am your fiancé. You are my fiancée."

He said it so casually that it made Mira afraid and confused. Was it that she did not mean much to him anymore? Did his brush with death make him realize that loving was not worth it?

But Roland had already turned to the window again. He behaved as if he did not want to be here, as if he was brought back to life in opposition with his wishes.

"What's that?" Phil asked the pilot from the front seat.

Even though Mira did not want to look, she found herself leaning forward to see what her father was looking at below.

Bright lights were erupting all over. There was no other way to describe them. The lights were bright and dazzled Mira's eyes. It felt like the explosion was spreading.

Suddenly, the red light in the helicopter started flashing. The pilot was grappling with the control. Mira was shouting. Only Roland remained calm. Seeing him calm made Mira frightened. She felt like she was looking at a psychopath.

"Get us up! Get us up!" Phil shouted. His voice was shrill and loud, unlike the one that Mira was used to.

The pilot strained against the control and Mira stuck out her head to see the fast-spreading explosion climbing up towards them.

Once she stuck out her head to look, the helicopter was hit with the first wave of shock. Mira's hand slipped and she tumbled over the door and started falling towards the white light.

Her screams trailed her fall, coming after her. There was nothing to see except light. She fell into it and disappeared from sight.

Heather

The car pulled to a stop and the three of them got out of it. They had been driving for a while and would love a little rest, so they could stretch their legs. They were heading towards the countryside for reasons best known to Andre.

The place where they stopped was abandoned completely, and they looked like they were the only people to have passed by this place. To both sides, there were mountains and spotting openings to what could be a tunnel and a cave. Carl's eyes were immediately drawn to it.

"How beautiful is this place," Andre exclaimed. He looked like a child struck with wonder at the sights of the beautiful things he was seeing.

Heather did not know what was to be admired about the landscape, maybe because of her mind. There were the mountains on both sides, then trees and the woods growing on both sides as well. As far as she could see, that was all this place was about, and she did not see how it was to be admired.

"I want to take a look," Carl said and walked away from the two. He walked to the side of the road and climbed the mountain till he came to an opening.

"Sure, go ahead," Andre said, watching Carl.

E.S. Dawson

"What is he doing?" Heather asked. Her hands were raised to shield her from the rays of the Sun as she was not under the shed of any of the tall trees around.

"Exploring," Andre replied. "It calms his nerves."

"How would you know that?"

"I know a great deal about people."

"Really?"

"Yes, like you. Haven't I convinced you with what I know about you? About your parents?"

"You know nothing about me."

"You would be surprised."

"Try me."

"Othniel. Why do you think you two did not work out while in Ghana?"

"What?" Heather felt her mouth opening like a door with loose hinges. As the implication of what Andre said dawned on her, she found that her vocabulary was severely impaired. There was not one word there that made any sense right now.

"Yeah, just before you came back," Andre finished.

"Who are you?" Heather asked.

"It's not time for you to know yet."

"Did you really know my sister?"

Andre chuckled. "She thought me what it meant, what it really meant to be human."

What it meant to be human?

331

"Care for a smoke?" Andre offered, pulling out a packet of cigar from his pocket. He let Heather take a stick dreamily and put the stick to her lips.

Then, he turned and stared at the opening in the mountain again. Carl was no longer in sight.

"Let me go see our friend up there. Maybe, he needs some help."

He handed Heather a lighter and turned towards the mountain. Heather watched him leave, still unable to contain her surprise. There was no way anyone was supposed to know about her relationship with Othniel. She kept it a secret even where she was. How did Andre get to know?

Carl

He no longer felt safe.

Anything could be weapons positioned at strategic places to snuff the life out of him. The robots could have rescued him from other robots just to make his death more painful. Maybe they should have left him where he was about to die rather than drag him out here to live with all the pain and guilt. He could have left the resistance alone, but he had led their strongest men to slaughter. He had to go back to the remaining and do what he could to stand by them.

The thought, however, died as quickly as it had formed in his mind. There was no going back to anyone.

They would never accept him back if they learned that 9 of their best men died and he was the only survivor. He would be declared an outcast. It was better that he was here while they thought of him as dead. At least, they would take solace in the fact that he sacrificed his life for them.

The thought brought relief as well as shame to him. He was a coward, always had been. He had many chances to put things right, to fight against the government, but he did not. And none of that bullshit about not knowing that he was not on the side of the truth. He knew all along. He knew that mowing people down because they were resisting the government was wrong, yet he could not bring himself to stop doing it.

He still had his gun with him. Hands trembling, he emptied the bullets and fixed one into the chamber. He rolled it, clasped the gun into place, and set the barrel against his head. He was sure if he pulled the trigger that he would meet his end. If he did not meet his end, then he would know that whoever was in charge of fate was a gambler, just like him.

He shut his eyes and pulled the trigger. The clicking sound of emptiness announced that he had won the bet with his life this time.

The tunnel seemed to be closing in on him, but he did not mind. He felt safer here than he had felt for a long time. Maybe his companions would get tired of waiting for him and drive off. He was counting on it.

With the world disintegrating this way, people hardly had the patience to wait for anyone.

He walked deeper into the cave till he came to a larger opening. He sat down here, marveling at the purposeful work of nature in digging a habitat into this rock. If he could, he would remain here shooting at his head till the one bullet would do the job.

"Carl?"

Fuck!

It was the man, Andre or whatever his name was. Carl had thought he looked crazy the first time he saw him. He was the kind of person that would climb up here looking for him.

"Go away," he said.

"We have a journey to make, Carl. Come on out, we are waiting for you."

"You guys can leave me here."

"Not gonna happen."

Footsteps announced that Andre was traversing the tunnel and coming towards the cave. It was then that they heard it. It sounded like some kind of faraway explosion. Carl became quiet. More explosions followed, then the rock trembled. Carl had a vision of the rock breaking apart and burying him alive.

Someone zoomed through the entrance of the cave with an alarming speed. Carl was shocked to find Andre in the same place with him as the mountain started colliding on itself.

"We have to leave," Carl said.

The mountain thought otherwise. Huge boulders were falling off from the side, blocking the exit. Carl started laughing. Finally, fate had come for him. She came pretty late.

Heather

Outside, Heather lit the cigar stick and inhaled. Her hands were still shaking as she worried over how Andre got his information. That could mean that other things about her were out there, ready for harvesting by anyone, anyone like Andre.

He was strange, Andre, very different from anyone she knew. It was easy for him to infiltrate the burial ceremony of the child of a senior government official without the drones picking him out. She wondered what other things he could do that he had been hiding.

When she let out the smoke from her cigar, it came out forming an 'O'. It had been a while since she smoked and she welcomed the warmth inside of her.

There was a rumble in the sky. When she looked up, she noticed that a bright light from an explosion was covering the sky, spreading across it.

Her eyes quickly went to the entrance of the cave where she had seen Andre enter. The two were not yet out of the cave yet. The sky rumbled some more and she saw a roll of dust covering the atmosphere.

"What the..."

Before the next words could come out of her mouth, the cloud rolled over, coming with a strong wind that blew her over the car.

A loud explosion followed and Heather was no longer able to see anything.

Detective Shaun

He was on the ground for a couple of seconds after reaching for his gun. Then he knelt on the ground and waited for the humanoid to get out of the car. The rage he felt at their attempt to replace him eclipsed his thoughts about safety.

As he expected, the thing was not yet dead. But when it came out, it was clear that it was not human. Parts of the head had been slammed in, and from there, Shaun could see wires crisscrossed in the form of veins. The hollow was close to its eyes.

"You never listen, do you, Shaun? Fucking headstrong bastard."

Shaun could see that the robot had been weakened from the crash as it dashed towards him. He raised the gun, positioned it at the heart of the crazy thing, and pulled the trigger.

The humanoid moved before the force could get to it. The hand was blown off. Shaun quickly tried again. This time, he was satisfied with the round hole that appeared in the heart of the creature.

The robot froze, stood for a while before it fell back down to the ground. Dead.

Shaun stood up from the ground with some difficulty. He had some bruises on his body, but it was not enough to hinder his movement. Limping, he moved towards the road. Getting out of here would take a great deal of luck.

He stood by the road and waited for cars to pass. There were precious few passing by. The stupid town he had been transferred to had the lowest population of the towns in the country, and would have attracted more people if they had the right infrastructure. But all they were interested in were robot cops. Fucking bastards.

He tried to wave down a car, but the car drove right past him. The second car did the same and he began to worry a little. He knew how suspicious it seemed for a tale, able-bodied male like he was to be standing out alone towards evening trying to wave cars down. The crime rate was on the high side, and nobody wanted to be a victim of an avoidable accident.

Finally, he got tired of waving at passing cars and started up the road on foot. Maybe there would be that one person that would have pity on him and stop for him. But the more he walked, the more he discovered that he might actually have to walk all the way to the next town.

A glow in the sky caught his attention. He paused by the side of the road and stared. The glow was so bright that he thought the sun had finally exploded and some of the hot fiery rays were falling onto the earth. The motorists were stopping too, bumping into each other.

With the sound of explosions, the brightness in the sky no longer looked like it was a thing of wonder. It seemed sinister, frightening even.

In the moments that followed before the explosion found its way to Shaun, he worried about Aaron, the real Aaron.

THE END

CHAPTER 27

Mira

The clouds were floating nearby.

Her eyes were shut, but she could feel the wind going through her body. Somehow, she could hear the language of the wind. It was wailing at some disaster as it swooped past her, touching her, calling her to come wail with it.

Mira refused to open her eyes. At this moment, what she felt was bliss, and she did not want to feel anything else. It was as if she was hanging in limbo between a past world and a new one. She rolled over on air and still refused to wake up.

The wind blew harder as if it was trying to wake her up. The wind had hands, slippery hands that Kira could feel all over her body. Again and again, it tapped Mira, whispering, muttering, and screaming in turns. Mira murmured and tried to push the wind away.

From afar, anyone watching would be perplexed. There was the body of a lady on-air, rolling round and round and completely naked. The wind was swirling around her, forming some kind of cover. At intervals, she would wave with her hand, although she was still asleep, and the whirring wind around her would be pushed to one side, but they always came back.

But there was no one around to witness such a phenomenon. Instead, all around, the place was in ruins. There was not one building standing. There were ruins and rubble like it was the aftermath of Armageddon.

On air, Mira finally opened her eyes. She was greeted with the shocking realization that she was hanging over 50 feet away from the ground. She looked at the ground and almost lost her grip on my wind.

My grip of the wind? Mira thought, suddenly realizing that she could touch and feel the wind. She could hold on to it as it was swirling round and round her.

"Wow," she said.

The ruins she had just seen below were momentarily forgotten as she tried to understand the extent of her ability. It was strange. In fact, she felt like she was in a dream. Maybe she was in a coma in a hospital...

Memories flooded her mind. She remembered being in a helicopter with her father and....

"Roland!" She screamed, looking all around her.

Without thinking, she manipulated the wind into letting her down slowly on the ground. She did not realize she was completely naked as she stepped over the ruins screaming out the name of her lover.

There was no response except the mocking echo of her voice tumbling into the far distance, rolling on and on and on, making her see exactly how alone she was.

There was no sign of the helicopter either. There are only stones and dust. She could not recognize where she was standing because there was not a single building left standing.

"Roland," she said weakly. Still, there was no response. She had gotten tired of screaming her lover's voice.

With the wind, she pushed the stones here and there, trying to see if there was any remnant of the helicopter pieces. She was feeling the same way she felt the first time she got the news that he had been mugged. She did not know if he was alive or dead.

"Roland, where are you?" She asked.

Again, there was no response. She was beginning to doubt that she would get any. As she walked over the ruins, she realized that her body was almost as white as the clouds.

Heather

The feeling of warmth was coming from deep inside her. It was hot and growing. She felt like she had swallowed a huge chunk of burning coal. Yet, she was not even awake.

Surrounded by ruins, boulders, rocks, and stones, she knelt down, her eyes shut, her soul creating a connection that even she knew nothing about. She was smoking as she knelt down there in the aftermath of a great disaster.

Smoke was coming off her body, and before long, it seemed her body caught fire and was burning. From slow, gentle Flames, her body became a roaring fire, but she was not screaming out of pain. In fact, the flames were leaping off her body, but she was not getting burnt. The flames turned red, yellow, then blue, and her eyes sprang open.

The eyes themselves had pupils that flames were burning inside them. Slowly, she got to her feet, slowly taking in the destruction on every side. Considering the magnitude of the destruction that had been brought here, there was not a soul that was supposed to be alive, yet Heather stood, defiling the human senses.

The events before the destruction were coming into her recollection little by little. She had not come here alone, she realized. With that realization, the flames stopped leaping off her body and died down till she looked like a normal human. She was naked, completely. The pieces of clothes, or what remained of them, that had survived the destruction had been completely razed by the fire coming off her body.

"Andre," she said like someone Judy remembering an old rhyme. "Andre."

She turned to look for the mountain where her companion had gone into, but discovered there was no mountain anywhere. The whole place had been reduced to one plain of boulders, rocks, and ruins. There was no way anyone could survive being buried underneath all those stones. It made her wonder how she was still standing.

She raised her palm and held it in front of her, then she will fire to form. She did not know why; she just did like she had been doing it for a long time.

A dancing, a little flame appeared in her right palm just the way she had envisioned it in her mind. Blue on the inside with the yellow crown. She watched it like she was bored.

"Andre!" She shouted.

Her voice echoed through the empty space all around her. Loneliness was the only companion that she had, as far as she could see.

She started walking through the ruins, confused about where her destination ought to be. She stopped before a chunk of sand and poured fire from her hand. The heat was fiery. Instantly, the sand turned to a glass and formed on the ground. Heather stopped then. She walked past the newly formed glass on the ground and continued moving through the ruin. She was supposed to be dead, she decided. She was not the strongest or the most skillful, but she was here in the aftermath of a destruction that had rocked every part of her world. She did not know how deadly the strike had been. But she knew, from the quality of air that entered her nostrils, that the air was no poisoned. Maybe dirty with all explosion. But she could breathe well.

The next thing she knew she had to do now was to find if there were any other survivors. Banding together was the best thing to do.

As she passed by more ruins, she saw a boulder flying into the sky, knocked off the ground by what was most likely a monster.

Carl

There was no space, nothing. No air.

Still, he was alive. He could sense the cracks in the earth, feel the connection of the tiniest of space from one stratum of sand to the other. The air that was coming in was not sufficient for anybody to breathe through and remain alive. There was a serious lack of oxygen down here, but Carl managed to breathe through the sand. HD could feel every bit of it. He could also feel the silence on the surface. The destruction had been total and complete. There was hardly a soul alive.

Then, he heard footsteps... more like felt footsteps walking above. These footsteps gave off so much heat that Carl thought someone was burning on the surface.

He pushed through the sand till he got to a rock that was blocking him from the surface. Heaving, he struck his fist against the rock without thinking. It just came like a reflex, having somewhere registered in his mind that he could hit something as big as the stone away. He felt no pain as he climbed out from the rubble.

He was about looking around when he noticed that his fist was metamorphosing from a rocky hand back to his normal hand. He did not have time to wonder about this because a woman that he remembered from somewhere in his past called him.

"Carl," the woman called. Her voice was not as soft as he remembered, but he could remember her alright. They were in the same car, driving away from the robots that had attacked him. There was another one. A man... Andre.

"Heather," Carl said. "What happened?"

"The world went to shit," Heather replied. "We are among the survivors."

"Andre?"

"I haven't seen him."

Carl watched Heather closely. Her body still looked like something that wanted to catch fire. She glowed red like a coal fuel warming up to start heating up again. And she was naked!

"Don't ask," she said quickly.

"I was not going to," Carl said and swallowed. It was going to be very difficult to keep his eyes off her body. In addition to the phenomenon of the fire raging through her body, she had a beautiful body, one that he wanted to touch, just to feel it.

"He was with you," the lady said.

"What?"

"Andre. He was with you."

Carl remembered then. Andre. He had moved faster than any normal human should. If anybody was to survive the blast, it had to be him. But a curious look around the ruins that marked the remnants of a world that had ended showed that Andre was nowhere to be found.

Levi

Swimming had never been so easy, and yet, he was not really trying.

Levi found himself adjusting to the movement of the water current and swimming about underwater. It was only after he had stayed there for a long time that he realized that he had been underwater and had not come up for air.

Am I supposed to come up for air?

The life he was living now seemed to him like he had been living it for a long time. He could hear the chattering of fishes, then the menacing transmission of an animal he could not yet place underwater.

He swam to the top and immediately wished he had not. The ruins that met his eyesight ruined his bliss of a great world where he lived underwater. Memories slammed into his mind, reminding him of the bullies that had pushed him into the water, and the blast that had taken everything out.

Tree had been uprooted beside the river. Houses that were not far away had their roofs here, and the houses themselves had been reduced to flat piles of debris.

He pulled himself onto the bank of the river and let his eyes travel up and down in both directions. There were no roads at all. There was no order, none he could recognize. The park that was once standing was no longer in place. The Ferris wheel had been reduced to nothing among the piles of debris.

He walked away from the river without looking at his body. If he had looked, he would have seen that he had the sleek blue body of a wale blended into his human form, and that there were gills behind his ears.

As he walked towards the Ferris-wheel ruin, he saw the first dead, human body. The body looked like a shadow, something that was there and something that was not. He walked towards it and bent down to touch it. Just as soon as his hand made contact, the body disintegrated and became ashes. Levi was taken aback. He looked up to see that there were piles of ashes everywhere. People who had not survived the blasts were everywhere, dead bodies and ashes.

"Fuck," he muttered.

Then, he wondered how he had managed to survive. The three bullies that had pushed him into the river were stronger than he was, yet not one of them survived, at least none that he could see. Maybe it had something to do with the water, he decided, turning to walk back to the water. At the water, he stared down hard, looking for something that made the river special, but discovered nothing. The river was laden with dust and dirt which were flowing downstream. It was just the way humanity had gone. Downstream.

CHAPTER 28

Mira

t was even worse than she had imagined.

For miles around, the only thing she could see were ruins, ruins of places that had once bubbled with life. It seemed like the world had been slammed into sleep, or maybe coma because the silence was too complete to seem like just sleep.

Mira found that floating over the ruins made it easier for her to move. She could pool the air around her and beneath her, and push it where she wanted.

Roland had been brought back to life only for him to die again, and this time, her father was dead too although that did not bother her much. She was more shocked than aggrieved.

As she sailed over the ruins, she could not help but wonder what happened to Roland, what they had done to him. Maybe it was better he was no longer alive now.

She felt something running down her eyes before she realized that she was crying. The loneliness was bitter and biting, and although the wind seemed to obey her every command, it still made her feel cold. She wanted a warm body, like Roland's, to wrap her arms around. But the more she craved his body, the more she realized that she was alone. She was even beginning to miss her father. Her mother had not yet crept into her thoughts, but she would take anything over the depressing silence that stretched out for miles and mocked her best efforts to floats over the ruins faster in order to get to somewhere inhabited by people.

Finally, she got tired of moving and let the wind set her down slowly on a heap of rubble. Again, her eyes swept over the place, bringing her to the realization yet again that she was completely alone.

Some part of the ground quivered, and Mira quickly spun around to see. There was nothing there, just some rubble falling over each other. Mira thought of getting a means of communication when her eyes went to a piece of a broken radio. Maybe it could still work, although she did not know how to work the stuff to send out waves. She could try.

She stood up and floated over to the broken thing. As she reached down for it, a hand shot out from among the rubble, grabbing her own hand and striking shock and fear deep into her.

She staggered, but could not pull free. The wind blew around her forcefully, pushing her back and pulling the rest of the person out from the ground. It was a humanoid, wounded in many places so its insides and the tangling of wires could be seen.

Mira panicked, struggling to free her hand. When she cried for a companion, she did not cry for one that would seize her hand and look at menacing as this one with his red eyes scanning her. It looked broken, but would not let her go.

"Let me go!" She screamed.

The humanoid chuckled before bringing its other arm, naked of any pretense of flesh to Mira's throat. It was too fast that Mira did not see the hand coming. The only way she knew there was a hand to her throat was when she felt tremendous force around her neck choking her life out.

"Let...me...go."

She was hanging on air, trying to move away, but the grips on her wrist and neck were very strong, so strong that all of her struggles were for nothing.

"The war has begun," the thing said.

Its eyes were glowing a brighter red, with every time that passed. It gripped Mira tightly, refusing to let go.

With the last of her strength, Mira willed a whirlwind to form around them. The wind swirled round and round taking them along with it. Round and round they went, still, the grip on her neck was still firm. Mira shut her eyes and willed the wind to go faster.

It moved. The humanoid's grip slowly got sloppy as some parts of its damaged limbs flew off its body, leaving it without legs. When Mira felt the slackened grip, she hit out ferociously, realizing she had more force in her body than she gave herself credit for. The robot went flying from her, swirling round and round in the wind till Mira stopped the wind. All of this came naturally to her. She let herself down a little too hard and went stumbling over the rubble.

When she came to a halt, she looked up to see where the robot had fallen. It had said something about a war. What war? She stood up and trudged over to the robot. It was crawling on its hands now and the red glow in its eyes had gotten fainter.

She kicked it hard on the chest, and felt pleasure as it rolled over, groaning. She would not have known the difference between the robots and real humans if she had not been around both for so long. And even then, there were still some she could not tell apart from humans. Someone was somewhere playing God.

"What war?" She asked. "What war were you talking about?"

The robot chuckled first, then it started laughing, on and on and on as if Mira's words were filled with mirth. But it was not the hearty kind of laughter, it was the laughter of monsters, blood-curdling, blood-chilling, sinister like there was something only it could see that Mira could not see, and this something was dangerous.

"Shut up!" Mira screamed. The robot continued laughing.

"Shut up!" Mira screamed and stamped her feet on its face again and again. But the laughter would not stop until she stamped is heart into the earth, frightened that her leg carried that kind of force.

The laughter died immediately and the robot, tried to point behind Mira, but failed as it slumped on the ground, lifeless.

"Shut up!" Mira screamed again. She hated the sound of the robot's voice and would not mind stamping its head into the ground again.

Then, she heard a bark behind her.

A dog!

Levi

Discovering that he could swim came with some feeling of liberation, but he could not help but realize that the world was no longer as it should be.

"Where is everybody?" He muttered.

He had seen the first dead person. If he would call that dead. It was like an exhuming of the essence of humanity. There was nothing left in the body apart from dust.

From dust, we came, and unto dust, we shall return.

The verse from his mother's Bible came into his head unannounced. He walked along with the ruins uncertain of what to think. His hands were still wet, and when he looked down at them, he saw they were webbed. He continued staring at them in astonishment. The drier they got, however, the more like human's they looked. His flesh was also turning from a pale blue back to the color that he had known himself for.

Am I dying? He wondered.

Of course, he was not. If anything, he felt stronger than he has ever felt before. He felt fitter, lighter. The only thing weighing him down was his thoughts. First, there was Ashley, whom he was not certain he would ever find. He still could not come to terms with what had happened here. He was still waiting to be shaken out of his sleep and his nightmare. Yes, that was what it was, a nightmare. One he had been on ever since he found that his family was missing. That was probably where the nightmare started.

No, it started like a dream, a good dream because of the sex with Ashley. *What about the disappearance of Rami?* Fuck. He did not know how it started. But he knew that at some point he enjoyed it. That session in Ashley's room. They had gone at each other like they had been starved for long. Relieving it gave him the courage he needed to give this other part of the dream. But he was not interested. He was done with dreams and nightmares. He wanted to wake up and go about his normal life.

He pinched himself and waited to wake up. Nothing happened. *What the fuck!* He could not be a fish in reality. Was that not what he was here? What was happening? Again, the memory of the cloud of smoke coming towards them—him and his bullies—flooded his mind. He had quickly dipped himself in water. Not that his body needed much help to do that. He was already sinking as he could not swim. The rest of the boys were shouting, and that was it.

He paused in front of a really big pile of ruins. Something was moving at the top, something like an insect's antennae. It was gigantic and at least twice his height.

Common sense said, "Walk away as quietly, even more quietly, than you had come." But Levi decided it was not time for common sense now. It was time to discover things. The discovery would help him know where he was. It could even force him to wake up.

Filled with excitement unusual for someone who was still missing his family and the lone friend he made his way up the ruins and stopped in front of the antennae.

Strange.

The antennae bent towards him and touched his face. He pulled back. Again and again, the two poles came for him like an excited puppy trying to lick the face of its master.

Levi chuckled, pushing them away. Then, the ruins below him moved. It almost knocked him off balance, but he managed to stay up. There was the sound of teeth clashing against teeth, the sound that he heard when he was cold and shivering and his teeth jammed together. It would have been a normal sound if it was not so loud, which meant that the teeth making the noise had to be giant teeth.

The ruins moved again. This time, it was a deliberate effort to push him off it. The ground moved this way and that, and subsequently, Levi lost his balance before he was flung off the top of the heap. He came crashing down to the ground, rolling and rolling and rolling.

When he finally stopped, he realized that he was on hard soil. He had fallen quite hard.

A shadow fell across him where he lay, a huge shadow that covered him and surrounded him. He scampered up to his feet, frightened. What he saw sent shock waves down his spine.

First, there was a face, a malevolent face where all the intentions to do him bad came alive. The teeth clattering came from this creature that he was finding difficult to refer to as a cockroach, and no, there were no teeth, just fangs, huge fangs that were the same length as Levi's entire body.

"No, no, no," Levi mumbled over and over again.

This definitely had to be a nightmare.

The creature was moving towards him, the harmless-looking antennae moving in the wind. Levi decided that he would have let common sense take over this one, but his curiosity had led him into this.

He got up from the ground and stood there, still watching the monster like he had been struck to the ground. Then, suddenly, as if he had been set free from some kind of spell, he turned and fled.

He was running through the ruins, stumbling, rolling, falling, slipping, but made sure he kept moving forward without looking back. He could not imagine being used as food by a giant cockroach. There were too many things about this nightmare that seemed real to him.

He heard the cockroach scrambling through the ruins after him till they came out to an even terrain. He was running like the wind, but at the back of his mind, something was drawing him to water, any body of water. The monster's legs hit the ground behind him, giving him the impression that he was being pursued by many people.

Suddenly, the footsteps behind him ceased. He continued running, breathing hard and sweating profusely. He had run for a couple of seconds before he saw the body of water before him. He dashed towards it before he heard the sound.

At first, it sounded like a helicopter before he realized what it was. Sickly wings clapping together in air am and coming towards him. It took him all of 2 seconds for the realization to dawn on him. The sound was coming closer.

The fucking cockroach was airborne!

CHAPTER 29

Carl

he was fucking naked.

It was all he could do to keep his eyes off her body. The world was a mess right now, and fascinating as her body was, he did not see the need to keep staring at it. To what end?

The man that had saved him from the hands of savage robots was missing. He was the one that could have explained what had just happened to them as he seemed to know a lot more than any of them would ever know.

"What happened?" Heather asked.

"I think the world has ended and we are the only ones left," Carl replied. Then cursed himself inwardly. It sounded like he was coming onto her. *We are the only ones left. Who the fuck says that?*

"We can't be the only ones left," Heather countered.

"Look around you. Do you see anyone?"

Heather did look around. For miles around them, the only constant thing was the ruins of the place. Most of the trees had been leveled. The mountains that had been on both sides when they got here were crumbled. Only one thing was sure: destruction.

"How did it get to this?" Heather asked.

She seemed to be talking to herself alone, as if she had more insight into the whole business.

"Do you know what happened?" Carl asked.

"I have an idea. Andre told me, but we never knew it was going to happen so soon."

"What was it?"

"The muon-catalyzed fusion. It was made for the unlimited supply of energy it would bring to the world. But, apparently, it is also a weapon of mass destruction."

"Jesus fucking Christ!"

"Yeah. That's about right. It has the power to level the world and it has."

"That's fucked up."

"It is."

Heather started walking away. She did not look like the kind of person that would want to bind with another till they find out what the hell was truly going on. Carl followed her.

"Maybe there are other survivors," he said.

"I thought you said there was none."

"I mean, if we could survive, then there are probably some others out there."

"Have you taken a look at your body?" Heather asked. "I don't know what the hell is going on."

"I don't as well. But we can't be the only ones."

"Or this could all be one fucking nightmare."

Heather

The man was following her through the ruins. She wished the man was Andre instead. She was already getting used to the man and his mystery, only for him to disappear. Well, everybody pretty much disappeared, except this man following him.

Carl that was his name. She noticed he had grown taller. He was a fucking giant now. He was tall before, but now, he was towering over her at 7 feet. She had a body that breathed fire. It was so strange that she did not even know how to start thinking about it. Maybe it was all a dream.

"What do you say, me and you, we go on a search for any survivors. I mean, it would get pretty much lonely hereafter the ecstasy of being a survivor."

"I think we're in a dream," she said.

"How would you know that?"

"That is the only way to explain this. Have you seen your height? Your hand? You hit a boulder of rock that size..." she pointed. "...from the ground. You hit it up into the sky, and you came out unhurried. That is the stuff of dreams. These things don't happen in real life."

"I don't think we are dreaming."

"You are just a figment of my imagination, a creation of my dream. I will stop listening to you now."

"How can you even call me a part of your dream? Where did the dream begin?"

Heather paused and turned towards him. His eyes lingered on her boobs. Apparently, men at the beginning and end of creation would continue being attracted to a woman's body, even when the world was about to end.

He looked up and found her looking at him. Quickly, he turned away, making a show of surveying the ruins.

"You certainly don't look like you are part of my mind. You wouldn't be looking at me with that look in your eyes if you were," Heather said.

"What look?"

"You know what looks. You look like you want to devour me or something."

"Well, you are naked," he said in defense.

"And you are wearing rags. Do you see me looking at you like you have gone mad?"

She turned and continued walking. He followed her. She did not know why. It certainly did not seem like it was because of her naked body, otherwise, he would have made a move. Maybe it was the way she spoke like she knew exactly what she would do.

"Where are we going?" he asked.

"I don't know. We have to find any living survivors. If we find them, we will know what to do."

He agreed.

The Sun was still hanging over the earth like nothing had happened, like it had not witnessed a race wiped off from the face of the earth. Time moved on. As they kept walking through the ruins, their shadows elongated, announcing the end of the day.

Heather was glowing.

CHAPTER 30

December 2258

Levi

I t had taken him a year to realize that he would never see his family again.

He trudged behind the team leader, Heather, who was followed by the windy Mira. Carl brought up the rear. He was no longer a bag of guilt although the feeling comes sometimes when he least expects it. It comes with the memories of the times that he had shared with his family. Ashley was slowly becoming a part of his past.

From time to time, he zoned out, unable to focus on the events happening in real-time. Heather had noticed it a lot and was probably regretting now why she got him on her team. The school of water was the last to be established, following the establishment of the school of fire on February 2258. Other schools, the school of earth and the school of the wind came before it. Being one of the first graduates, many teams were understandably interested in having some of them on their team. That was how he had met Heather again.

"Come on," Heather said, waving them on.

She walked past the giant snake that she had roasted alive from the inside, followed by Mira. Mira was still as lost as he was. Carl and Heather, were the serious ones, the ones who wanted to discover if there were other people apart from those in the southern settlements. He was just functioning without a will to achieve anything. Survival was enough.

"Heads up, we don't know what we might encounter again," Heather said.

She was the one that did most of the talking. Carl did most of the obeying. Levi and Mira were like the children within the group. They were lost. Maybe they died with the explosion which the survivors were calling 'The Event'. An event that was not supposed to happen at all.

He fell in line beside Mira, and the girl smiled at him. She waved her hand at his hair and raised some strands of the hair he had been keeping for the past one year.

"Won't you like to cut your hair?" Mira asked, looking his hair over.

"No," he said vehemently, maybe with a little more force than he intended.

He was keeping the hair as a remembrance of all the people that he had lost. Ashley, his mom, and his little brother. He still met them in his sleep, and he had nothing to say to them most of the time.

"We will be camping here for tonight," Heather said.

They had come to a clearing in the woods. Trees were growing all over the place like they did not care about the near annihilation that the human race had just experienced.

There were ruins of buildings overgrown with weeds. The place could as well have been a city, but nature and the wild were as effective as humans in reclaiming portions of lands.

Everybody stopped. Even Carl, the biggest of them. At first, Levi did not think that Carl should be listening to Heather. He should be the one leading. That was until he saw Heather glowing at night, until he saw him burning up monsters from the inside, the gigantic snake being the latest thing she had ended. It was almost like she was the only one leading them, protecting them, guiding them. Carl simply aided her.

"Gather some wood, Mira," Heather said.

Mira smiled and began to move her hands. Dead woods, sticks, and dry leaves were swirled around in the air. They went round and round, forming a circle around the four of them. Levi did not think the show-off was necessary. She could simply get the fuel they asked her for quickly, so they could all settle down. He was tired after a long walk and could do with some rest.

Finally, the girl gathered the fuel in a single place and performed a cute, little bow for Heather. For Mira, everything was supposed to be fun. It did not matter that they had just narrowly escaped being eaten by a giant snake.

Heather ignored her bow and walked to the fuel she had gathered. She snapped her finger and a flame appeared at the tip of her hand. Although she was their leader and had left the fire school earlier than any of them, she still held the flame reverently, as if she was in awe of the power that she wielded. Levi understood this awe. It was the reason he forgot himself sometimes and played around with the mist on the air, forming them into different shapes. According to Heather, none of them should be out of any school yet, but there was a great need for them to discover if there were other survivors like the rest of them. So they were out here.

Heather threw the flam into the fuel and it cut fire. The flames crackled and leaped around, dancing with themselves while Heather still stood there watching it.

Later, they gathered around the fire and stared into it in the silence. It was the forts night that they were going to spend outside the new world, and they barely knew each other. Well, except the other two. Carl and Heather seemed to know each other pretty well. The only reason Levi knew Heather was because she burned the creature that was after him, the giant cockroach. It had followed him into the water and across, and just when he thought he was going to become food for a strange, giant cockroach, the creature burned from the inside. Heather made sure it became one crispy, burnt animal, completely dead.

"This is depressing," Mira said at length when no one said a word. "Let me make it more depressing. I almost got married."

It was unsolicited and shocking. None of them disturbed the other with their past lives. In fact, they were not supposed to trust each other. One as fire, the other water, another air, and yet another earth. These groups dwelled in different places in the south and had been hesitant to work with each other.

"That... this is... that is just sad," Levi said. "What happened?"

Levi could see that Heather wanted to say something, but she was holding back. Carl was the only one whose expression did not change. He had stopped wondering if Carl was still a human. He looked like a rock. Maybe the earth people were all rocks, people who had lost their emotions.

Mira chuckled at Levi's question.

"The event," she said.

Heather

Nobody was ready for what the world had become. Not even her.

She sat there beside the fire looking around at her team of four. In saner times, these four were supposed to be inside a house, under the heater, getting through the cold season. But they were out here, breathing in contaminated air, which could do nothing to their altered system. Altered, that was what the world had become. Head was tail, and tail was head.

The fire crackled and poured fragments of light into the air. Heather's eyes followed them like the eyes of a trained hunter. Then she looked at her group again. The only person she could count on here was Carl. She could still remember their first meeting. She was naked, and his eyes could not stay above her breasts. He could not stop staring.

Fast forward to a year after, and Carl would hardly stare at anybody. She was shocked to find him this way. They had parted ways when they met people who looked like them. Fire and earth benders, two groups that did not like each other very much. They were the earliest groups. It was a mistake, abandoning him for the very thing that brought about the end of the end, the division. She was supposed to know better, but everyone was afraid, uncertain of what to expect for a world that was just waking up again.

When she met Carl months later following the truce between the tribes, he had retreated into himself and would not talk much about himself. Apparently, he had his own nightmares, his own injuries, and nightmares that tormented him at night. They all did.

"I doubt there is any file on The Event," Carl said, barging into the conversation. It was so unlike him that for a moment Heather thought he was back to his old self.

"I used to have one," Heather said. "It was about clones and bio-humanoids. The muon energy was to power them, so they could live hundreds of years into the future."

"You lost it?" Levi asked.

"Yes."

"How?" Mira asked.

"The Event."

The fucking event.

It seemed that whatever went missing today could be traced back to The Event. In fact, some of the human tribes left, like the water people, used The Event as the beginning of their calendar. The other tribes had reestablished the old calendar.

"But what was in it anyway?" Levi asked.

"A lot," Heather replied.

She still remembered what she had seen on the chip. The betrayal by people she considered her parents. It seemed like a million years away, and it figured, considering that it was in another world another time.

Everything reminded her of Andre. She wondered what had happened to her. She turned to Carl and wondered if she had the same thing in his mind. Did he ever think of the man who had saved him from the certain death the maniacally engineered humanoids presented?

"Let me see," she said, turning her attention back to Levi. "There were humanoids fast replacing humans. Apparently, someone was tired of seeing humans on earth and came up with the bright idea of replacing them with humanoids who would be controlled by computer coded and still be free to make their own choices."

"It did not work," Mira said.

"Yes. Only because someone else decided to kill everyone instead."

"Who?" Mira asked.

"Nobody knows. That is why it is called The Event."

"Like something that happened by itself, huh?" Levi asked.

"Exactly," Heather said.

Carl had become silent again as if the sound of her voices was forcing him to retreat into himself. Heather watched him, wishing they had been together longer than they had been. She had missed a chance to get to know him and the demons that tormented him.

That night, they settled down to sleep, and she offered to take the first watch. Even though she turned Carl down when he said he was keeping watch, she knew the silent giant would not sleep. He could feel things happening thousands of miles away just by placing his hands on the earth. While Mira and Levi settled down to sleep, Heather saw Carl place his hand gently on the earth beside him, then shut his eyes.

She knew what that meant. She was awake and looking out for any strange creature that could happen upon them at night, but Carl would sense the danger first. He always did.

Well, unless it was flying.

Mira

The wind screamed.

She was trying to sleep, but the sound was in the wind. The wind was being forced to do something against its will. Mira could feel it in her sleep. Feathery wings clapping, claws outstretched, tail manipulating the wind.

She sprang out of sleep and found that she was sitting. Levi was lying by the side, snoring gently. Heather had her eyes on her. Carl had his back again a tree, the only sign that he was still alive being the slight heaving of his chest.

"Are you okay?" Heather asked.

"Something is coming," Mira said quickly. She did not even know when she said it. She was looking around like whatever it was, was already there with them.

"I don't see anything," Heather said, looking around with her. "Maybe you had a bad dream."

"No, I know what I feel. Something is coming."

"Nothing is coming," Carl said. His hands were rooted to the ground when Heather turned to look at him. She turned back to Mira and shrugged.

"See. If anything is coming, Carl would have sensed it a long time ago."

"Maybe he cannot sense this one," Mira said.

Carl grunted at the perceived insult. Heather shook her head.

"Go back to sleep, Mira, you had a bad dream," Heather said.

"No. It was not a dream!" Mira insisted.

"I know when I have a dream and I know when I... I see something."

"Have you ever seen anything before?" Heather asked.

CHAPTER 31

Carl

T he inexperienced ones always raised alarm over nothing.

He sighed and leaned further back into the tree. His hands were on the earth. He would feel it if anything was approaching towards them from any direction.

It was a beautiful ability he had developed, but it had its downside. Like the pain, he felt inside. He felt like the earth. There was nothing that passed it by. He had tried going back in time simply by feeling what the earth felt and looking through her eyes, but he had not been able to see past The Event. Anything beyond that brought unbearable pain to his mind, a pain that would not let him continue. The earth felt a lot, and he was witnessing it first-hand. For one year, since he discovered that he did not die, his abilities had been growing constantly, allowing him to act as a guide and a fighter. It came at a great cost, and many people in his tribe had refused to learn past the lifting of stones. They had tried, but it was not easy. Every day came with some bad vibration coming from the bowel of the earth.

He looked over at the girl, Mira, and found her staring up into the sky. The girl was spoiled and he could not imagine someone actually getting married to her, but that was the way of the world. People loved what they loved for whatever reason best known to them.

"It is coming," she insisted.

Carl was alerted. Maybe she knew what she was talking about even though she was the most spoiled one among them. They had had to bedsit him all the way from the new city to this place. Maybe she was seeing something.

"Where is it coming from?" he asked.

Heather turned towards him immediately. He abided by her gaze and focused on Mira. The fire crackled, but the flames were getting weaker. It would soon be off, and they would only have their other senses to trust. The sense of sight was overrated anyway.

"There," the girl said and pointed.

She was pointing into the air. At the same time, the realization dawned on Carl that he could only feel the earth, not the air. If something was cooking from the top, then Mira could be saying the truth. She was in sync with the air after all.

Heather glowed a bright red. It meant danger was close. The three of them that were awake quickly sprang to their feet, poised for battle.

"Can you describe it?" Heather asked. There was that fear and excitement intermingled in her voice. It was one of the things that Carl had admired about her the first time they met. She did not hide her fear, and she did not hide her excitement or meet her fears either. She was always prepared, always ready to battle. It was sad that she would not understand whatever he had to say anymore. How could he tell her that the earth was crying or that it was talking to the moon at night? He did not even know what to do with this information. How could she know what to do with hers when the power she had could cause harm to the earth. She was like an enemy to the earth.

"Feathers, beaks, claws," Mira said hurriedly.

Almost immediately, a shadow darker than the night swooped down on them. Heather saw it quickly and rolled on the ground to avoid sharp claws digging into her body. As she rolled, fire flew from her hand towards the feather. But it missed slightly, barely grazing the creature's wings. The grass where it fell upon caught fire while the creature soared back high into the sky. That was the first attempt. The second would be closer.

Carl was panting now. The creature was big. It seemed every damn thing in this place had grown in size. But he could not place the bird. It looked like a hawk, a giant hawk, but he had seen two pairs of eyes. It was the eyes that he saw that had made him stand rooted to the spot. The eyes were full of intelligence, malevolent intelligence.

"Where did it go?" Heather asked.

In the ground, Levi still slept, not wakened by the commotion around him.

"There," Mira pointed.

Carl was suddenly apprehensive. The creature had come from the north. He was sure it would come from the south the next time it swooped down—that was where the girl was pointing. Levi was there, a little distance away from them. The creature would swoop him up before they would realize it was not even coming for them.

In quick strides, he ran over, past Heather and Mira. He was just in time to come face to face with the creature. It was already swooping down, claws outstretched to grab Levi from the ground. When it saw Carl, it changed its flight, and went after Carl instead.

Carl swung with his heavy, rock fist and missed at the same time the creature grabbing him by the neck. His body shield came on late, when he had already been cut in the neck. He screamed as the creature took him high up into the air. Arms flailing, legs kicking in the air, he was hopeless against a giant hawk.

Mira

The man was airborne in no time.

Heather was on the ground, firing fireballs after fireballs at the creature. It was useless. The creature could see the balls from a mile off and was dodging them easily.

"Do something!" Heather screamed.

But Mira was at a loss on what to do. Seeing the man captured, grabbed by his neck, and flown up into the sky had struck dread into her body. The dread had a paralyzing effect. It pinned her to a spot and disoriented her senses.

"Mira! Do something! We can't let him die!"

Heather's screams reminded her of Roland. She had been too weak to do anything to protect Roland. Not anymore. She had some ability and she was not using it. She looked up into the sky. It was dark. There was nothing to see. The bird had disappeared, carrying Carl with it.

Mira knelt down and shut her eyes. The first thing she had to do was to feel the wind and understand its mood. Controlling an angry wind would have a disastrous effect.

Satisfied that the wind was not enraged, she sent it off after Carl and the monstrous-looking bird. She was not yet as strong as she was supposed to be, so the toiling was taking a lot from her body, but she stuck with it.

She felt them in the wind: the bird and its prey. She felt the air around them, then she sent the world.

The bird struggled against the wind, but the wind kept pushing it back. Still, with her eyes shut, Mira locked the bird in a vacuum formed by a body of swirling wind. The bird flapped its wing angrily. Mira shut her eyes tightly. She waved her hand and got up from the ground.

"I found them," Mira said, proudly.

"Where?" Heather asked.

"They are coming back now."

True to her words, they heard ruffling among the leaves of a nearby tree before something slammed into the ground with huge force. The bird was up almost immediately, but it was locked inside the windy cage that Mira had made for it. On the ground, some distance from the bed, Carl lay, groaning.

Mira wanted to run over to him and check how he was, but she could not. She had to keep the bird at bay. It had a beak that could swallow someone twice her size whole and without difficulty. She continued swirling the wind around the bird, causing it to be disoriented as it sought for a way out of the airlock.

Suddenly, the bird stopped moving and turned towards Mira, as if it knew where the power to lock it up in this place was coming from. Mira felt shocked. There were two pairs of eyes looking at her with hatred. She could see her death in the bird's eyes and knew that if the bird made it out of its prison, it would tear her to shreds with its wicked-looking claws.

The bird started waving its wings, pushing the wind away. It was taking a lot of strength to keep the whirlwind running around the bird. The bird was trying to get free, and Mira knew she could not hang on for too long.

Heather

She hoped Carl was not dead.

Nobody had died since after The Event. Not even the mini squabbles among people of different elements had produced a dead person. But then it had only been one year since The Event and the discovery of the different psychic powers. No one knew what would happen if another died. No one knew to what extent they could be pushed before they died.

She ran towards the fallen Carl, ignoring her brightly glowing body and the bird that Mira had locked in a whirlwind, and knelt down beside Carl.

"Are you okay?" she asked, feeling for his pulse. It was weak. He had lost some blood and there was an ugly gash across his neck. His voice was feeble when he spoke and she could not hear him.

Before her eyes, she saw his neck slowly closing up. When she felt his pulse again, it was getting stronger.

"Come on, Carl," she said. "Wake up."

"Behind you," Carl said. This time she heard him.

When she twirled around, she saw Mira getting pushed by the wind and trying hard not to fall over herself. The bird was flapping its wings harder now, pushing all the wind towards Mira.

Intelligent creatures.

There was something fundamentally evil about the creatures they had been encountering. They seemed to have psychic powers of their own, and they used them. Since they embarked on the journey, it had gotten difficult every step of the way.

She flung her balls of fire at the bird, but they were swept away by the wind. One of the fireballs hit Mira instead when the bird redirected it. Mira lost her footing and was thrown over. Immediately she lost her balance, the bird hurried towards her.

Heather stretched her hand instead of the fireballs and started to heat up the bird from the inside. But she realized it was going to be too late. The bird was too close to Mira.

Someone rushed past, Heather. It was like a blur. When Heather turned to the bird, she was in time to see the impact of a heavy blow on the creature's beak. The bird swooned and staggered backward and away from Mira. Carl was in front, ready to strike again. But the bird recovered quickly and tried to peck Carl apart. Carl put up his hand in defense. It turned into a rock and the bird's beck hit it, making an unsatisfying sound. Carl struck out, hitting the bird on the neck. The bird went over, tumbling on and on.

Heather focused now, and in no time, the bird was roasting from the inside. It got to its feet, staggered forward as if it wanted to attack Carl, but stopped on the way. Smoke was coming out from every opening in the bird. It screeched out in pain, stumbling about the place.

"That is a cry for help!" Mira shouted.

"I don't understand," Heather replied.

"They are coming," Mira said. "This is just a scout."

Almost immediately, they heard the sound of a million wings clapping through the air.

"Fuck me," Heather cursed.

Taking down one of the birds had forced three of them into action. How were they supposed to fight thousands of these birds? A cloud of birds covered the sky, making it darker as the giant birds swooped towards them, eager to tear them into different shreds.

It is a pity, being killed by hawks.

CHAPTER 32

Levi

It seemed like a dream.

He could hear shouts and the sounds of footsteps all over the place. It seemed so real. At a point, he felt he was about to be attacked, but Mira saved him. Mira, it seemed the girl had an eye out for him. Well, he had his eyes on her too, and it did not matter if she had nearly gotten married. The world was hanging on a balance anyway, trying to heal. It would make sense if they got together.

Then he heard wings, the sounds of wings clapping against the wind. He sprang up from the ground and found that it was not a dream. His three companions were poised for a fight, looking towards a cloud that had bloated out the moon completely.

"What is happening?" He cried.

There was no response. The body language of each person was tenseness. His eyes went to the giant, feathery bird lying by the side of the fire, then he looked back into the sky again. It was them that he understood what was happening apparently the birds were coming to take vengeance.

"We need to work together," he shouted, running into the semi-circle they had formed.

"Prepare to fight," Heather yelled back.

The sounds of the wings were getting closer. Levi shut his eyes and searched for the nearest water body. He found it. It was not far away from where they had settled for the night. He gritted his teeth as he had not done this before. It would be the most strenuous thing he had ever tried, and if he pulled it off, he knew he would never be the same afterward.

The sound of the water dropping on the ground came to the ears of the fighter's moments after he had pulled enough water from the stream. Heather looked confused, seeing Levi's strained face. But the latter paid her no mind.

In no time, the water was swirling over their heads, looking like a black diamond in the reflection of the light coming from their dying campfire. On and on it swirled till it was moving fast enough to form some kind of shield about them.

"Carl, stones!" Levi screamed.

At first, Carl looked as confused as to their leader, then he understood.

Heather

The boy was just waking up, disoriented.

That explained everything that was happening. If not, how did he think he was going to stop a flock of giant birds from getting to them by swirling water over their heads?

"Carl, stones!" the boy screamed.

Stones? She understood now. The boy was onto something. It was not just water that was going to protect them from the carnivorous birds, it was water filled with huge chunks of stones and swirling very fast.

It was not their best idea, but it was something. Heather hoped it would protect them against the onslaught of angry birds that were headed their way.

Carl's stones had just made it up to the water swirling over their head when the first onslaught slammed into the shield. The shield held. Heather could catch glimpses of the birds slamming their head into the rocks and falling back. Carl had pulled the huge rocks into the water. Heather wondered what would happen if Levi lost his resolve to keep swirling the water. The shield presented as much danger to them as it presented protection. The stones could as well fall on their heads.

There were just too many birds. Although most of them were being repelled by the heavy chunks of rocks and the swirling water, those at the back kept pushing forward. Some of the birds were flung to the side and left disoriented.

"Ahhhh," Levi cried. Veins were popping out from the sides of his forehead.

Their fire was dying.

"Mira," Heather called.

Mira was cowering under the shield, watching it with doubtful eyes.

"Mira," Heather called again. This time, she turned towards Heather.

"I will need your wind. Levi is getting tired."

Mira nodded.

"You can let go now," Heather said as Mira started another shield away from the one they were under. The four of them dashed into it. The wind was swirling around them now while the first shield had the water and the rocks hitting the ground. The birds, realizing that their prey had changed their flight directions and headed towards the moving whirlwind.

This had better work.

Heather knew that Mira did not have the mental strength to keep the wind against hundreds of giant birds. She snapped her fingers and the flames appeared. As the wind went round and round, she threw her flames against the wind, so they had flames being swirled around by a whirlwind.

The shield was complete, fire and wind covering the scouts while they watched the birds fly around them. It seemed the birds did not like the fire because they did not slam into the wind of fire the way they did with the water of stones.

Heather wondered how long they had to keep this up to the birds would give up and return from wherever they came from. A look at Mira showed she was not straining themselves. She decided it was possible they could keep this up throughout the night until the birds were no longer with them.

**

Mira

The next morning came with clarity in the sky. There was no sign of any of the carnivorous birds. Beside their fire, they saw that the body of the scouting bird had been eaten. There was nothing left except the bones.

"They eat their own," Carl said, stating the obvious.

"Hawks do not eat their own or something dead. They are not vultures," Levi said.

"Well, those are not hawks. They are something else. Something we have never seen," Heather said.

Mira agreed with her. The world had become the stuff nightmares were made of, and none of them was ready to face that.

"Well, we have to keep moving," Heather said. "Our mission does not end here."

Mira admired her, admired the way she pushed off a near-death experience like it was nothing. She was still feeling the pain of her heart beating and trying to push out of her chest.

They parked up, scattering the remaining ashes from the fire they had made last night. They had to be careful and hide their tracks in any way they could. Some animals could hunt them. After facing off the giant hawks, there was not one person among them that still wanted to face stranger creatures.

"When do we begin the journey home?" Mira asked.

"When we have found enough survivors," Heather said.

She seemed to be the only one who had faith in their mission. Mira would have said Carl also had great faith in their mission, but she could never tell what was on the man's mind. His face was always a mass of depressing clouds that let nothing out.

"Do you really think we can find someone in all these ruins?" Levi asked. The boy thought the same way Mira did. They both would rather be in the cities, partying and living out the rest of their lives in what little comforts they could find. But as was the case with youthful exuberance, they got caught up with the spirit of adventure. Now, they were already tired of it.

They trudged on, with Mira floating on air. For trekking long distances, her ability was convenient, and she used it all the time. If not for any other thing, just for the look of irritation that Heather tried so hard to hide. As for Carl, he did not care. He could walk a mile and he would feel nothing. Levi was too busy gaping at old, dilapidated buildings to feel jealous about her ability. So it always came back to Heather and her.

They came upon a building that seemed to have survived the blast miraculously. It was a small bungalow, but the doorpost and window sills had weed growing all over it. It did not look like any of the scouts had come upon the place. There was no way they were supposed to anyway. The areas assigned to each group were completely different from themselves.

"Let's check this out," Heather said.

Levi

He did not think they should check the house out.

Who knew what was lurking behind the door? Maybe it was something that could bypass Heather's glow, her warning sign. She seemed to have complete trust in her body, something that had always been foreign to Levi, even now.

He slowed down so that Heather and Carl went before him. At the door, he turned to Mira. There was the same look of disapproval on her face. They should not be stopping by this kind of house even though that was exactly what their job needed. They were tired of being scouts anyway. He wondered if she felt the same way he felt about her. Maybe stopping by this house was not that much of a bad idea, especially if they were going to spend the night here.

"We could stop here for today," Mira said, stating Levi's mind. She breezed past him and went after the other two.

He followed her. She said it again, and Heather pretended not to hear her.

"Would it be a bad idea?" Levi asked, lending a voice to his attraction.

"Let us go through the house first," Heather replied.

They did. The house was dusty. It might have survived the blast, but there did not seem to be one single survivor in the house. They went through the house, discovering foodstuff that had expired a long time ago. For Levi, they brought a pathetic, mind-stinging nostalgia. He remembered his time with Ashley, what they had drunk in her house, the cookies they had eaten. Then he went to the fridge.

There were bottles of wine, which were left unattended. Quickly, he found a bag and filled them with the bottles of wine. Nobody said that a sojourner does not deserve the taste of wine.

The TV in the room suddenly came to life. Levi was the only one that saw it. It showed static, then went off again. Levi was stunned. Nothing worked outside of the southern territories, which had only surviving humans. He thought he heard something outside. He rushed to the window and stared outside.

He was just in time to see it. A drone!

The fuck!

The last time anyone saw a drone, the world was still sane, and people were still making use of cell phones.

"A drone!" he screamed.

The others ran to the window. There it was, a drone flying away like it had come to spy on them. They watched it, spellbound. In the former world, the drone represented law and order. It was the drones that helped wipe out terrorists and extremist groups. The drones could get anyone anywhere, but they had suddenly disappeared. After their disappearance, The Event happened, almost as if they knew it was going to happen.

"Well, I'd be damned," Carl said. "I never knew I was going to see any of those things ever again."

It was the longest Carl had spoken, and it was easy to understand. Nobody knew that the drones were still alive. The others were struck dumb themselves.

"I have to call this in," Heather said after the moment passed.

Levi shrugged. It would be a miracle if she could get anybody on the crude instrument she had been given.

Carl

Something called to him outside. He could feel it vibrating on the ground.

He walked towards the door like one in a spell while the others watched him. They would not understand. How would they understand that he was in a fellowship with the earth? That the earth spoke to him from time to time.

When he got outside the house, he went down on all fours and felt the ground with his hands. He could feel what he was going for just lying around on the ground, abandoned. It was not there before, if not he would not have just noticed it now.

"Where is he going?" Carl heard the young male ask Heather.

"Follow him," Heather replied and went after Carl.

Maybe she understands.

What if he told her about the sadness that had gripped the earth, this sadness about a loss that he could place his finger on? It was there. It was raw, and it kept him up most nights.

He stood up and walked towards the thrushes. He guessed that it must have been placed there by the drone.

He found himself at a clearing after a minute of walking. On the ground, he found a small black case, no less than 5 inches lying on the ground. He pushed himself towards it, once again realizing a reason for trusting his new body.

"What is that?" Heather asked when he picked it up.

"I don't know, a record of some sort," he replied before he could hold back. He was getting too free around her again. This would not end well. Nothing ended well on earth. How badly it ends depends on how badly one wants to make it.

He handed the little, strange-looking material over to Heather. Heather took it from him and examined it slowly.

"There are buttons on it," she said.

"Press one," Mira said. She and Levi were just catching up with Carl.

"We don't know what the buttons could mean," Heather said. "We should hand it in."

"Maybe you should press the button," Carl said.

It was the first time he had insisted on something being done. Heather pressed one of the buttons.

Nothing happened.

"Nothing," she said.

"Try again," Carl said.

Heather pressed another button. A hologram sprang out of the box. It was so sudden that Heather dropped the case on the ground, startled.

The man the hologram showed was none other than Barry Stivers, the man that invented the end of the world.

He stood, looking at them. Then he blinked.

Is it on? He said to somebody in the same room with him.

Yes, a voice replied. It belonged to Andre. *I would be damned!* Heather. Then Andre actually walked behind the man to the other side before he disappeared from view.

If you are getting this, the doctor said, *it means that the evil humanoids are trying to take over the world, or some other terrible stuff has happened after The Event. Things are so volatile that I cannot even predict what it is. But whatever it is, I am sure it has brought the world to its knees.*

The four scouts drew closer, watching the man they had only seen on the TV, or read about in newspapers.

Heather, Carl, Levi, Mira. You were chosen for the good you did on earth while you were alive.

"While we were alive?" Heather repeated.

Do not be confused. You are the same persons, the same mind, the same emotions, and I could bear to let you die without er... recreating you.

"What the fuck is he talking about?" Mira asked.

Andre has you. He is the drone. Or rather he controls all the drones. No one knows this, not even the top officials in the government. I would love to see you. Something is coming, a war.

"What in the world is he saying?" Levi shouted.

Humanity is gone. You are the next humans, the good humanoids. Some of the evil humanoids survived alongside you, and they would everything in their power to wipe you off. Carl, follow the trail the drone leaves for you. You have to be prepared for what is coming.

The tape ended and the hologram disappeared. Carl flexed his fists. He was confused, yet at the back of his mind, the pieces were coming together with one after the other. He had heard of the muon energy that could be used to power humanoids. Could that be why they survived the blast? Why the blast brought out their abilities rather than kill them?

There were so many questions going on in his mind, and when he turned towards the others, he found the same questions in their eyes. When did they stop being humans and become humanoids? There was only one person who could answer that. They had to find him.

"We have to find him," Carl said.

Heather

"No," Heather said. "I don't believe any of this. I'm human. I'm not a fucking robot!"

Her voice rang hollow. Her mind mocked her. How could she be a human who glowed when danger was near? A human who had the power to make a fire? That sort of thing only happened in movies.

Fuck.

Levi and Mira were examining their bodies strangely. Maybe she should have insisted on taking the box back to the settlement. There, it could be easily destroyed before the mad man confused them.

"We have to," Carl said. "What do we have to lose? If he's wrong, we would have found another survivor and the drones."

"This is a joke," Heather said. "This has to be a joke."

"Maybe it is not," Mira said. "I have often wondered how I can do the things I do. This Gary guy..."

"Barry," Heather corrected.

"Barry, whatever his name is, he can let us know why."

"This is not right," Heather insisted. "It is not right."

"Come on," Carl said, leading the way.

Heather watched the other two trudge after him. She had no choice but to join them. Within her, the battle raged, the battle where she struggled with the fact that everything about her had been a lie.